OUTLAWS HERE, THERE, EVERYWHERE

A TERRENCE CORCORAN WESTERN

JOHNNY GUNN

WOLFPACK
PUBLISHING
— EST 2013 —

WOLFPACK
PUBLISHING
— EST 2013 —

Published in the United States by Wolfpack Publishing, Las Vegas

Wolfpack Publishing
5130 S. Fort Apache Road 215-380
Las Vegas, NV 89148

wolfpackpublishing.com

Paperback ISBN 978-1-64734-584-6
eBook ISBN 978-1-64734-575-4

OUTLAWS HERE, THERE, EVERYWHERE

CHAPTER ONE

Camp was in a glade filled with cottonwood, aspen, grass, sage, and blazing bunches of rabbitbrush. It was above eight thousand feet and it was late October. Trout were seen to dance in the meandering brook, and the campers had to break ice to make coffee in the morning. There was good wood for the fire and good grass for the horses and mules. A picture-perfect hunting camp.

The men standing in the bright sunshine felt it but didn't say it. Fall in the high country of northern Nevada was as wondrous as the colors of the sky and what grew in the surrounding rugged mountainsides. Trees responded to the failing light in grand style. Aspens offered their yellows as did the cottonwoods but it was the rabbitbrush, with wild splashes of brilliant yellows, that held the eye.

And the sky. It was so blue it almost hurt to look at it. It was an exciting yet fulfilling time of the year and those who lived it, knew it was also hard work. Fulfilling because the campers will have several weeks of elk, hard work, though, manhandling several hundred pounds of fine venison.

"Gonna be a chore gettin' this monster back to town, Cleve. Biggest elk I've ever shot, I think." Eureka Deputy Sheriff Corcoran, Terrence Corcoran, was standing next to a large bull elk in the Diamond Mountains north of the little mining and ranching community. "Gonna help feed a lot of families, I think." This giving the meat from an elk was a tradition that Corcoran had begun several years before and, for some families, it was the only meat they would see that winter.

"We'll quarter him, Terrence. That's why we brought the pack animals." Cleveland Cirrus Colgate, stood next to Corcoran admiring the animal. "You're an interesting man, Corcoran. Outlaws, even those on the fringe, fear you desperately, and others show nothing but love. I'm proud to call you my friend." The elk was hanging from a cottonwood tree along the banks of a cold mountain stream. "Liver and onions tonight, my friend, and then it's back to civilization in the morning."

"That's the worst part of a little adventure like this," Corcoran said. "Could live like this real easy, Cleve. No outlaws shootin' at me, clean water, fresh air, and mountains reaching for the top of the sky. When you get back, day after tomorrow or so, tell Ed I ain't comin' back."

"Sheriff Connors would send out a search party," Cleve laughed. "I agree, though." Cleve Colgate was nearing fifty and was the town's blacksmith, knife maker, and horse doctor all rolled into one. "Hope we have a raging winter, keep folks locked at home so I can sit by the fire with a tumbler full of whiskey."

"The whole winter?"

"Damn tootin', Terrence," Cleve laughed. "How about you?"

"Winter seems to bring the worst out in those that get bored easy. I'll be bustin' drunk and disorderly heads at the Bonanza Hotel, whuppin' on fools who think it's all right to whup on their women folk, and chasin' varmints trying to take what don't belong to them."

"Too much work, Corcoran."

"Maybe I'll just find a rocker and sit by the fire with you, then. Drink whiskey and tell tall tales." He chuckled and poured some coffee. "Nope, sure as there's air to breath someone would start a fight, steal something, or just raise hell."

Terrence Corcoran had reddish hair that hung in long waves. He was born on a ship four days out from Ireland and came west as a teenager, worked on ranches, railroads, and found his true calling with a badge several years ago. Women have found him attractive, men have stepped aside, and criminals have run in fear.

He had his side of the elk mostly skinned out, saw that Cleve was almost finished as well when he heard three rifle reports, fairly close by. "Sounds like somebody else is gonna be eatin' liver and onions," Cleve stepped back to take a look around. He cocked his head to one side. "Sounded rather close, old man."

"Sounds like someone howling for help, Cleve. Let's go." Corcoran slipped his big knife back in its leather, grabbed his rifle, and started out across the small meadow toward a high ridge to the north, Cleve right alongside.

They made their way through a couple of hundred yards of heavy timber and tumbles of rock, hearing someone calling loudly for help. "Over that way, Cleve. In the bushes there. See him?" They made their way through tangled brush to a man spread out across a sagebrush, bleeding. "Let's get you out of the bushes, mister. Better get a fire started, Cleve. We're gonna need hot water to clean this mess up." Corcoran eased the injured man out of the bushes and laid him out in some grass.

"This is a bullet wound," Corcoran exclaimed when he opened the man's jacket and shirt. "What's happened here? This wasn't an accident," Corcoran said. He couldn't see a weapon near the man and knew there were three shots fired.

The man was whimpering in pain, his eyes wide in fright, but didn't answer. Corcoran was looking at a man in his thirties, slight of build, three or four-day beard, and long unkempt hair. The one thing he didn't see was that of a man on a hunting trip or one who engaged in long mountain hikes. *He doesn't belong in these mountains so why is he layin' here, gun-shot?*

"What's your name and you better tell me what happened. My name is Corcoran, Terrence Corcoran and I'm a deputy sheriff in this county. Understand?"

"Yes." The man coughed, groaned in pain. "Name don't matter none. Man that shot me is Walt Neighbors. Took my gear and poke too."

"Why would he do that, Mr. no name? Better tell me and be quick about it. You ain't gonna live through this little mess you've started. You're gut shot and we're two or three days from the nearest doctor. Why did Neighbors shoot you?" Corcoran looked over at Cleve who had a good fire going and gave him a wink. "Never seen a gut-shot man live very long, how about you Cleve?"

Cleve looked down at the wound and saw that it was a simple slice of skin that was bleeding profusely. The bullet just grazed the man. "Worst I've seen in some time. You got kin we should notify? Never make it back to town, Terrence. Nope. Never make it." He turned to stoke the fire and hide his grin.

"Well, there you be, Mr. no name. Better lay it out, Pard." Corcoran took the wet rag Cleave handed him and wiped blood from the wound, shaking his head in sorrow. "Hate to see something like this. Why did Neighbors shoot you?" The man kept trying to rise up on an elbow to take a look and Corcoran kept shoving him back down.

"Name's Sam Weatherby. Got a sister in Denver. Name's Wilma. Neighbors and I have been riding together for a couple of weeks. He went crazy this morning, shot me and took everything."

"That's it? He went crazy and shot you? Don't make much sense to me. Maybe there's some more you don't want to tell? Eh?" Corcoran stood up and looked at Cleve, then back to Sam Weatherby. "Why were the two of you up this high in the mountains?"

"We were hunting," Weatherby said. He was groaning with pain, almost whimpering.

"You ain't the best liar, Mr. Weatherby, but I guess we got to help you out, here. I'll expect you to help with camp on the way back to Eureka. Knock the fire down, Cleve, while I get our guest on his feet. Come on, Weatherby, on your feet." He jerked the man up hearing squawks of pain. "Don't hurt that bad, boy. It's just a scratch."

Weatherby's attitude changed when he found out he wasn't going to die and his surely personality came into the open. "You're a liar," he yelled at Corcoran.

"And I think you're hiding something from me. You two weren't up here hunting, you were hiding. What were you hiding from? You and Neighbors got into a beef. Why? Maybe something about the split from the last job?"

Weatherby clammed up and Corcoran pushed him into a walk back to their camp. "See if you can find where he and Neighbors might have been camped, Cleve, while I take our new found friend back."

Weatherby was holding his side, whimpering with every step as they made their way back down to the stream and camp. Cleve joined them right away.

"Ain't much of a camp, Terrence. Looks like they got there last night. Found this." He handed a sheet of paper to Corcoran. "Looks like a map of Eureka with the bank highlighted."

"Well, well. A couple of bank robbers, eh? How about that."

"That's not mine," Sam said.

"Of course it ain't. Gonna hold you for more questions when we get to Eureka. Sit." Corcoran tied him to a cottonwood and finished skinning the elk. He peppered the man with questions the rest of the day and into the evening but got no answers. "Well, we got a long ride back to town so I'll just keep right on asking," Corcoran said. He took a long pull at his flask, savoring the bite of good whiskey. "Shame you can't have some."

CHAPTER TWO

"Something I need to ask, Terrence," Cleve said. "We heard three gunshots and they were rifle shots, not pistol shots. This old boy ain't got even one gun with him. You think there might be someone else running around up here with a gunshot wound? There wasn't anything but a bedroll and fire pit up there."

"I've been wondering about that myself. I'd bet Weatherby was running from Neighbors, but Neighbors tracked him down and shot him. They were probably outlaw partners and Weatherby ran off with whatever they had. Thinking he was dead, Neighbors packed up Weatherby's camp, got back their loot, and lit out. Must have Weatherby's guns and horse with him, too." Corcoran shook his head, looked over at his prisoner.

"Neighbors came for his share of the loot, eh? And you were looking to hit the Eureka bank next? Don't worry too much about it, Sam Weatherby, we'll get it all figured out." Corcoran shook his head and had to chuckle. "Hell of a mess, eh? Neither one of them was much of a shot. Walt Neighbors," he mumbled. "Name don't register."

"You gonna make that poor wounded outlaw walk all the way back to Eureka?"

"Naw," Corcoran chuckled. "We can tie him onto one of the packs when we load up."

"What have we got here, Corcoran?" Eureka County Sheriff Ed Connors was leaning back in his old swivel chair, feet on the desk, coffee in hand when Corcoran walked in with Sam Weatherby. "Oh, and by the way, welcome back. Have any luck?"

"Got an elk and a bank robber." He chuckled and pushed Weatherby. "Found him up in the mountains, Ed. Calls himself Sam Weatherby. Says he was shot by his partner Walt Neighbors. Sure as I'm having elk steak tonight he's an outlaw."

"Don't know why you know that but it is true. Got this wire two days ago from Elko." Corcoran read the wire that said two masked men, believed to be Walt Neighbors and Sam Weatherby had robbed the Hazelton Dry Goods of several hundred dollars. To be considered armed and dangerous. "Looks like you might be in for some reward money, Terrence. Now, my trusted deputy, if you escort this gentleman into a cell, he will be able to introduce you to Walt Neighbors, currently in cell number two."

"Well, ain't that something? Just show up, did he?"

"Came in the bank while I was in there, pulled a gun on me and I knocked him silly with the butt of my shotgun. Why is the one you're holding bleeding?"

"Neighbors creased him with a shot and left him for dead. Elko sheriff is gonna like this." Corcoran led Weatherby into the jail area and put him in cell number one. "Guess I don't have to make introductions, eh? Have a good time discussing life's little twists and turns. Supper at six."

Avery Johnson was the sheriff in White Pine County and was sitting in his office in the county seat of Hamilton when Deputy Jake Russell rushed in with a wire from the resident deputy in Ward, a mining town in a valley east of the Egan Range. "Damn," Johnson said. "Make me up a pack, Jake. I gotta get down to Ward. Looks like Sinclair is gonna die. It's the Henry Storm gang again."

Henry Storm had been robbing stages, hitting mining company payrolls, and making himself unwelcome in other ways, too. Killing the resident deputy though, was a step up in his ladder of success. "I'm going to appoint Tomaso Bono as resident down there."

"As long as you don't appoint me, that would be fine. Tomaso is Italian like Henry Storm, Sheriff. Think that might be a problem?" Jake Russell said. "I've been to Ward once and that's enough. You going alone?"

"No, Bono's a good lawman, tough as nails. Jake, I want you to come along." The sheriff chuckled seeing the man's face fall. "Storm needs to know what it means to shoot a White Pine County Deputy. We'll rip that gang to pieces. I won't stand for anyone shooting one my deputies. Pack enough on that mule for a two day ride, Jake. We'll leave when you're done."

Avery Johnson believed every crime needed to be atoned for with as much force as was available. Getting drunk and disorderly was as big a crime as shooting your neighbor or robbing a bank. Bare knuckles, busted heads, or broken bones would change an outlaw's look on life, was his attitude. "Storm has four men riding with him most of the time, so be prepared for some heavy action. Ain't gonna put up with this."

Johnson was pacing around the office, pounding his fists on anything available and cussing loud. Johnson loved to make a show. He let his hand fondle the handle of his sidearm, actually grasped it once or twice, and finally settled into a chair near the fire. Russell had seen Johnson upset many times and knew that men would die before this ride was over. "We'll need those big shotguns and lots of ammunition, Sheriff. You want me to wire Bono?"

"No, I'll do that. Get to packing. I'll meet you back here in an hour, ready to ride. Ain't nobody gets away with shooting one of my deputies."

Tomaso Bono was hailed by the telegraph operator as he walked across the street from the doctor's office. "Whatcha need, Fingers?"

"Wire for you from the Sheriff." Fingers O'Callaghan picked up the nickname from being so fast on the telegraph key. "Sheriff seems to think Sinclair is gonna die? Was he shot that bad?"

"He is dead, Fingers, and you know it. You sent my wire to the sheriff. What kind of game is this, now?" Bono took the wire and read it. "Looks like I'm the resident deputy, Fingers. Johnson's coming down for a visit. Wouldn't want to be Henry Storm right now. Johnson's sure to shoot him on sight."

Bono stood about five feet and nine inches, weighed a hefty one-seventy-five, and took part in all the mining games during town festivities. He was champion at single jack rock drilling, held town records for mucking, and could lift twice his weight any time a lovely lady dared him to. He was dark skinned with hair so black it seemed to be blue and his steel-gray eyes could pick out a single lass in any large group.

"Don't be spreading the word on Johnson coming down, Fingers. Don't want Henry Storm to up and leave these parts. He's needed killing for a long time now."

The town of Ward was three or four streets running east and west and as many north and south. One of the north south streets, called Main Street was also part of the long road from Pioche in the south to Wells, north in Elko County. The Ward National Bank was on the corner of Main and Third Street and kitty corner to the east was Ward's Grand Hotel, which featured a fine restaurant, saloon, and gambling hall. The three-story Grand Hotel was the centerpiece of Ward's social life.

Stephen Poindexter had come to Ward when silver and gold were discovered and opened his Ward

National Bank and one year later had the Grand Hotel built. Poindexter came into his money from Papa Poindexter when the old gentleman kicked off many years ago. He's married to Mary-Anne who was born in County Cork, Ireland, and is twenty-three years younger than Stephen.

Mary-Anne is tall, statuesque even, with long red hair she lets hang in curls and waves. Her bright green eyes sparkle when she's amused and seem on fire when she's not. She fully enjoys being married to Ward's leading citizen but rumors suggest she also enjoys the company of younger men. Some say they have seen her in the company of Tomaso Bono.

She walked across Main Street and into the bank, knowing so many miners and other men had watched. "Take me to lunch, Stephen. Do you like my new dress?"

"Delightful, darling," Stephen murmured. "Oysters and champagne? Or shall we just have what the special is?" He took her hand and they walked back across the street to the Grand Hotel. Henry Storm watched her make both crossings from his table at the Silver Springs Saloon, across Third Street from the Grand Hotel. Storm felt as safe sitting in the saloon as would have at his mountain hide out. After all, because of his gun, there wasn't any law in Ward.

CHAPTER THREE

Shorty Whipple rode up to the front of the Silver Springs Saloon and waved at Henry Storm through the window. He walked in and sat down across from the gang leader. "Old Sinclair died this morning, Henry, and Fingers says the sheriff is coming to town. Thought you might want to know."

"I gotta get better at my shootin', Shorty. Sinclair lived two days after I shot him." He slapped the table hard and laughed loudly. "I'll practice on the sheriff when he gets here." He and Shorty laughed some more while Shorty poured the whiskey. "He bringing Jake Russell with him? Man's a crack shot with that Henry he carries."

Henry Storm didn't give a hoot that half the patrons in the saloon and gambling den were listening in on his conversation. He was almost talking to them when he said, "Ain't no law in Ward. Resident deputy's dead. Let's drink it up and have a party." The Silver Springs Hotel was where he stayed when he left his mountain hideout and came to town. The owner, Iron Jaw Ransom, and those who worked there protected the dangerous outlaw, let him know when the law was around, when strange men were about, strangers like Wells Fargo detectives.

Ransom picked up his moniker years ago when he served time in Carson City. He dared people to knock him out and if they couldn't, it was his turn to throw a punch. The iron jaw never failed him. He had few rules in his saloon, believing the men would spend more if they weren't hampered by someone telling them they shouldn't fight, spit, or shoot.

Henry sucked on a cold cigar, drank his whiskey, and talked loud and long. "Jake Russell is one proud man of that Henry. Might just take it off his body after I kill the fool. Might just shoot him again with his own rifle."

"Russell's coming and Bono is the new resident deputy. Sheriff will be here day after tomorrow according to Fingers. Think we should high-tail it out of here?" Shorty Whipple didn't like all the looks they were getting. Storm thrived on them.

"Hell no," Henry said. "What we'll do is set up a

little welcoming party for them. Gotta come in from the north and how many places have we already used to hit the stages coming in?" Whipple cringed at what Henry was saying. "A nice culvert to cross, a narrow pass, a stand of trees, and we'll toast White Pine County's fine new sheriff." Henry Storm leaned back in his chair, nodded to those close, and drank some more whiskey.

Empty glass in hand, Storm stood up. "Let's find the boys and go build a trap. Ain't been fired up by a job in a long time, Shorty."

The Henry Storm gang was nested in a deep, broad canyon south of the Ward townsite that featured a small springs and lots of trees to filter campfire smoke. A small line shack, used by ranchers, had been taken over by the gang. A rustled calf was being skinned by Ornery Jake Johnson when Pete Cameron spotted two men riding in and sounded the alarm. Louie Hernandez strolled out from a stand of cottonwoods, rifle in hand.

"Glad it's you, boss. Caught me with my pants down, you did. Got word this morning from that jerk at the bank that a new shipment of gold coins is coming in next week. Small wagon and big escort, he said."

"That's good news, Louie, but I got better news.

Let's sit around the stove. Find a bottle, will you?"
Storm spat some tobacco juice into the dirt and continued chewing on what was left of the cold cigar.

The five men gathered around to hear what
the boss had to say and were as excited as Henry
when they learned they would get in a fight with
that new, sadistic sheriff. "When he was in Lander
County he beat people with his shotgun butt for
spittin' in the street, Henry." Ornery Jake spent a
month in the Lander County slammer and knew
Johnson personally.

"We'll ride out north in the morning and set our
trap in that ragged ridgeline about seven miles or so
out. They gotta ride through those tight passes and
we'll be waitin'." He looked around. "Any man picks
off that sheriff before I get a shot in will die. Understand?" He got chuckles and nods from the group.
"Avery Johnson is mine and mine alone."

It was a brilliant fall morning that found Tomaso
Bono walking the streets with his new badge in
place. At the Grand Hotel, he learned most of the
town already knew. "Fingers can't keep that trap of
his shut," he growled. "Shove a cold beer my way,
Dean. What else did that fool say?"

Dean Miller came to town to work in the mines

only to find many of the mines were pulling back, letting people go, not hiring. Poindexter learned he had been a deputy in Pioche and hired him in a bar-man/security capacity. The large and quick Miller found it a good fit even if it wasn't the good money he would have made in the mine.

"Said the sheriff's coming down from Hamilton to clean out the Storm gang. That true? It would make things nicer around here." He drew a beer and shoved it down the bar. "Old man Poindexter has made it clear that he don't want any of the men that ride with Storm to come in here. Storm either. You're leaving the mine to be a lawman? Poindexter should feel good about that."

"Smart man." Bono chuckled and saw Poindexter walk toward the dining room. "The man I came to see, Dean. Catch you later." He downed the beer, his breakfast of choice, and followed the banker into the dining area.

"Good morning, Mr. Poindexter, hope I'm not interrupting anything but I have something important for you."

"Not at all, Bono. Please, sit down. Coffee?"

"Thank you. Resident deputy Sinclair passed on, I'm afraid. Wounds were just too much for him. Sheriff Johnson has named me resident deputy. I understand you have a gold shipment coming in. Are you taking all necessary precautions?"

"Is nothing sacred in this town? That's supposed to be highly secret, Bono. I got the wire yesterday and it's already all over town?"

"Fingers O'Callaghan doesn't believe much in the word secret, I'm afraid," Tomaso said. He couldn't hold in the smile, thinking he would have to remind the telegraph operator of his obligations. "Because of Sinclair's death, the sheriff and a deputy are coming down to take on the Henry Storm gang. I'm afraid all this might be happening at the same time."

"For your information, and I'm sure you understand this must be just for you, the wagon with three guards will be arriving sometime late tomorrow. Would that coincide with the sheriff's arrival?"

"It's possible. I'll keep myself visible and available, Mr. Poindexter. Thank you for the coffee." Bono and Mary-Anne Poindexter usually went out of their way not to look at each other but Tomaso had to touch his new badge and give her a big smile. It was returned.

Bono left the hotel smiling and walked down Main Street thinking about what might be coming his way. A ruthless gang probably knows that a large shipment of gold coins would be arriving and that would be a big target, guards or not.

"He said three guards," Bono murmured. "The Storm gang is at least five strong and every one of them is a killer. And the sheriff might be riding in at about the same time. Sure glad I took this nice cushy job." He smiled at his reflection in the window of Sheridan's Gun Shop, took a swipe at the badge and continued walking.

The Ward city complex was on the northwest corner of First Street and Main and included the courthouse and jail. The rock structures looked sturdy but there were always complaints about windows and doors not being secure. Bono walked into his new office and found jailer Skeets McDougall busy sweeping up. "Mornin' Skeets, meet your new boss."

"Heard about that last night, Tomaso. Welcome to our little world. It was a quiet night, cells hold one recovering drunk and one rowdy buckaroo. Yours truly booked 'em in. The drunk was found in the middle of Main Street and a couple of the boys dragged him in and the buckaroo was brought to me by the security boys at the Grand. Didn't figure you would need to know."

Skeets was an older man, gimpy in one leg and unsure of himself on the other but a willing worker who rarely had too much joy juice to make his shift.

"Good job, Skeets. Did Fingers tell you anything else?" The grin and chuckles were obvious.

"O'Callaghan is going to lose that job one day because of his mouth." Skeets laughed as he put the broom away. "Yes, he did tell me that Sheriff Johnson is on his way and that the bank will have its vault full of gold soon, too. With Henry Storm feeling all gritty killing Sinclair, it might get rowdy around here, Tomaso."

Skeets sat down next to the stove. "I'd like to have Fingers's job. It pays well and I'm getting too old to be fightin' these damn drunks every night."

"You know how to operate those keys? I've actually stood with my mouth open watching Fingers. I know I couldn't."

"Sending's easy, Tomaso. It's receiving that's hard. Gotta catch each letter as it comes through and some of those boys are faster than Fingers. That's saying something. Learned it in the army about the same time I got my legs all shot up. Coffee's boiling and if you look in the second drawer of that desk, you'll find a fine flask nicely filled. Just part of my job, boss."

Bono laughed, pulled the flask, and added some whiskey to their cups. Those who had been in the old mining camp for any time were aware that Skeets had a good handle on current affairs. If you needed to know something or someone, he was the man to talk to. "Who in town would be a good man to depend on if things get rough around here, Skeets?"

"Any of Poindexter's men but, in particular, I would have a little talk with Dean Miller, the barman at the Grand. He's worn a badge when he was in Pioche and that's one mean town." He took a breath. "Any of the security boys at White's mine."

"I didn't know that about Miller," Bono muttered. *Nice to know that. Miller's a straight shooter, ain't much afraid of anything. Have to have a talk with that boy.* He drained his tin cup and headed out the door. "Turn those two out when they're sober, Skeets. I'll be back."

CHAPTER FOUR

"We're making good time, Sheriff. Head through that pass up there and we should be able to see Ward. Could use some good whiskey and a big steak."

"Looks like we're about to have company, Russell. A wagon and three out-riders coming our way in a hurry. Might mean a bank or mine delivery. Let's hold up and join them for the ride into town. Make sure they can see our badges if it is a bank delivery. Those boys shoot first."

They were stopped in the middle of the wide roadway, their coats open and shiny badges gleaming in the bright autumn sun. The wagon with four up and its three out-riders pulled up in a cloud of dust when the sheriff raised his hand to hold them up.

"I'm Sheriff Johnson. Want a little added escort into Ward?"

"I've never turned an offer like that down. I'm Dirkson escorting the gold shipment to the Ward bank. Let's keep 'em moving Charley."

Charley Mooney flicked the wheelers and they moved off at a smart trot toward the first of three almost connected passes that wended through a series of sharp up-thrust ridges. The passes were the only break in the steep rise in the desert floor and were narrow enough that Mooney would have to slow the teams down to make the tight turns.

"What brings you and your deputy down from Hamilton, Sheriff? Hope we're not riding into trouble." Dirkson and the Sheriff were gently loping fifty yards or so in front of the money wagon.

"Henry Storm's gang shot and killed my resident deputy in Ward. Coming to town to put an end to the bastard. He needs a good beating before we hang him. Had any trouble along the way?"

"Quiet and peaceful, Sheriff. The way I like it. This Henry Storm fella, seems he's been hitting banks and stage runs all around the county. That bank of Poindexter's is one nice target for a man like Storm. We're nearing that first pass, better drop back closer to the wagon."

"I've never been more sure of anything in my life, Henry." Louie Hernandez stepped off his horse and handed the reins to Shorty Whipple. "I was watching the trail from those high rocks and saw Sheriff Johnson and that Deputy Jake Russell join up with the wagon carrying the gold coins to the bank. There are three guards with the wagon."

"I swear I was born at the end of the rainbow, boys. We get to kill Sheriff Johnson and steal Poindexter's gold all at the same time. Let's get forted up in these rocks and shoot to kill, boys. That gold's mighty heavy so let's not bust up those good horses. We're gonna need 'em." It was Storm's practice to stop the stagecoaches by killing the lead horses.

There was little wind on a warm fall afternoon as the small caravan entered the defile not knowing there were five rifles aimed at them. Johnson and Dirkson were leading with Dirkson's two men on one side of the treasure wagon and Deputy Russell on the other.

Storm's men were spread out on just one side of the pass and Storm wanted first shot. "One of you takes my shot is gonna get shot," he snarled. He leveled his rifle, let the bead fall on Sheriff Johnson and slowly squeezed the trigger. Johnson turned in the saddle just as Storm fired and the bullet sliced across his back and shoulder, throwing him from his horse.

Rifle fire crackled like thunder in the close quarters of the pass and men fell from horses and wagon, some returning fire, some not moving after hitting the ground. Johnson knew he was hurt bad but snaked his way behind an outcrop and looked for a target. Russell lay dead, Charley Mooney was desperately trying to get the horses under control despite bleeding heavily from an upper chest and shoulder wound.

Mooney was thrown off the wagon but was able to hold onto the reins of the crazed four-up. Dirkson saw two of his men fall to the ground and joined Johnson behind the rocks. "How many, Sheriff?"

"Storm usually has four men riding with him. They're in the rocks to the right. Shadows are on their side."

"Only one of my men left, so it's gonna be a tough fight. Give me some cover. I'm going off to the right and see if I can get around the wagon. Might be able to see better."

Johnson had his rifle in hand when he was thrown from the horse and held on to it when he hit the dirt. He put five quick shots into the rocks and let four more follow from his Colt. The songs of ricocheting bullets and loud blasts from Johnson's guns kept Storm and company tucked behind the rocks. Dirkson was fast and moved across the narrow road and around the wagon. He dove behind a sturdy sage almost landing on Sean O'Malley. "You shot?"

"No, Dirk. Looks like Mooney's got the horses under control but they'll knock him off quick if we don't make some kind of move. Who's doing all the shootin'?"

"Sheriff. Let's move toward that big rock over there and see if we can get some shots in. Only place within fifty miles to set up an ambush but we might yet save that gold." They crawled out from their lair and moved quickly along the rock wall toward where Storm and his men were hiding.

"Got two of 'em on my left," Sean said. He had the rifle up and got a round off fast. "One down."

Dirkson wasn't fast enough to catch that second man but kept crawling and spotted Ornery Jake starting to take a bead on O'Malley. He pulled his rifle up and got off a quick round, knocking Jake back ten feet. A second round finished the bandit.

"We've got the odds in our favor now, Sean, boy. Let's move nice and slow." How many times had he and O'Malley been in a position like this? They had been a team protecting valuable property being transported across open desert or high mountains for several years. It was almost as if one knew what the other would do in situations like this. "There's only three of 'em left, Sean. Let's get 'em."

Despite his wounds, Charley Mooney had the teams under control and was behind the front wheel of the heavy wagon. As Sheriff Johnson had done, he emptied his rifle into the rocks and Johnson, reloaded, emptied his once again.

That was enough for Henry Storm. "Let's get the hell out of here, boys. We can take that gold once it's at the bank. There's enough lead flying around out here to take out the Seventh Cavalry." Only Storm and two others raced for their mounts.

Dirkson led O'Malley toward the high rocks of the pass. "Why isn't the sheriff in this fight?" Sean O'Malley was reloading.

"Got a bad wound. Listen," Dirkson said. "Horses. Moving fast. They're running off, Sean. We did it." Dirkson was on his feet running through the last twenty yards of the narrow pass to see Henry Storm and two men racing off toward Ward. He fired a shot just because he could, knowing they were way out of range.

"I'll chase you down, Henry Storm. I'll get you." He howled it out, turned and walked back into the rocky pass. "Best we tend to the wounded, Sean.

Doubt if they'll come back but don't like sitting out like this."

The ride into Ward was slow with several horses carrying bodies. "Bring the wagon to the bank, Charley and we'll move everything from there. Lost some good men in that fight."

"Yes we did," Charley Mooney said. "Saved the gold, though. That's what'll be remembered."

Tomaso Bono was north of the Grand Hotel and saw the caravan ride past. Bodies tied on the backs of horses, wounded men swaying precariously in the saddles, and Bono hurried down the block to catch up. "I'm White Pine County Deputy Bono," he yelled up at Dirkson. "What's happened here?"

"Attacked, Bono. Your sheriff is badly wounded and Deputy Russell is dead. Henry Storm hit us in the pass north of town."

Bono grabbed a man gawking and sent him scurrying for the doctor. He motioned for two others to come with him and they ran to where the wagon pulled up in front of the impressive bank building. Bono, Dirkson, and O'Malley helped get Johnson out of the wagon and eased Charley down from his blood-soaked seat. "Doc'll be here soon, boys," Dirkson said. "Better let Poindexter know we're here."

"I watched you coming in, Dirk." Poindexter walked out of the heavy double doors and over to the back of the wagon. "Must have been a mess out there. Good job, Dirk. Good job."

Bono kneeled down next to Sheriff Johnson who, because of his wound, was on his stomach in the dirt. Bono had his shirt ripped open, holding in a gasp. The bullet tore a trail across Johnson's back and shoulders laying a deep path of ragged flesh and broken bones. "How bad is it, Bono?"

"You ain't going nowhere for some time, Sheriff. Bones should be here soon." He handed a canteen to the sheriff. "Dead ones are Ornery Jake and Pete Cameron, so it was the Storm gang that attacked you."

"Get some help, Tomaso. In my name, get some help. There's nobody in Hamilton can help. They need to stay there and it's just you and Skeets down here. Put the word out." Johnson was starting to slur his words from loss of blood when Doctor McFadden arrived.

Bones McFadden was a retired army doctor and moving wounded men was nothing new for him. "Get this man flat on his stomach and on a door right now. He needs to be hauled to my office in ten minutes or less. Anyone else injured?"

Sean O'Malley helped get Charley Mooney to the doctor. "Get him over to my office right away. Why wasn't that wound tied off? What's the matter with you men? You want these people to die? Now, move it."

Bono chuckled, remembering how many doctors he had heard yelling instruction in the thick of battle. "Don't miss those Indian wars," he murmured as he made his way across the street to the Grand Hotel. "First man I need is Dean Miller but I'll need more than just him. Skeets is good at the jail but that's all." He took a chair at a table and motioned for Miller to join him. "Get someone to take over the bar, Dean. We got lots to talk about."

"I saw the wagon and horses come through. What happened?"

"Henry Storm happened. Sheriff's bad wounded, Deputy Russell's dead, and that leaves me alone. Mr. Miller, I understand you wore a badge in Pioche. That true?"

"Did," Miller said. A slow grin slipped across his face, his eyes lit up some, and he waited for the invitation.

"You'd be a lousy poker player, Deputy Miller," Bono said. "Run down to the office and have Skeets swear you in and get a badge on you. I gotta come up with at least another name and get some wires sent out." He had to laugh at how fast Miller made it out the door and turned his attention to coming up with at least one more name.

Before coming to Ward, Bono remembered, he worked the big mines in Eureka County. *Terrence Corcoran could drink more beer in an hour than I could in a day and still walk tall. Best damn lawman I ever knew. Probably laugh in my face but I'm gonna ask for his help.*

Wires were sent to Hamilton telling of the attack and one special wire was sent to Eureka. Fingers O'Callaghan was going to enjoy telling Henry Storm who was coming to kill him.

CHAPTER FIVE

"Got a wire for you, Corcoran." Skipper yelled out from his little office next to the Bonanza Club. "Important."

"Thanks." Corcoran walked into the Bonanza for his mid-day meal and flagon or two of cold beer. "What's on the free lunch board today? Hunger pangs are all fired up."

"Beef, elk, boiled tongue, sliced lamb and some cheeses, Terrence. Dive in, my friend." Jimmy Henderson was among the first to come to the Eureka mining camp and the Bonanza Club was his first venture. It started as a walled tent and has grown to two stories with a fine saloon, honest gambling, a restaurant, and hotel.

"This old town has grown from those first days, eh, Jimmy? Now you offer free lunch. Understand that's available in Denver and New York. Pretty fancy my friend. You have warm rooms for rent and serve your own brewed beer. I'm mighty comfortable in this town of ours."

"You need a woman, Corcoran. A wife and ten kids running around."

"Maybe in my next life," Corcoran laughed. He had to fight off remembering Shaggy Hair. *I'll never find another woman like her. I wonder where I would be if she had lived?* He blinked, shook his head, and took a long drink of cold beer.

"I get along just fine with the lovely lasses we have here. They all love me and I love all of them." It was true, Henderson thought. Every woman in town loved Terrence Corcoran and he did everything in his power to encourage that love.

Corcoran filled a plate, grabbed his beer, and settled in at a table near the windows to read the wire. "Remember Tomaso Bono, Jimmy? That big Italian who could whup just about anyone in town?" Henderson nodded.

"He's the resident deputy over in Ward. Got a big fight going with that bastard Henry Storm. Storm's been raiding all the small towns around White Pine County."

"Sure glad you and Ed chased him out of here.

Ward, eh? Heard the mines are starting to run low out there."

"Got a few more good years in 'em," Corcoran said. "Looks like I might be making a run to Ward if Ed will let me go. White Pine Sheriff, Avery Johnson got himself all shot-up by Storm's gang. Never did get along with that man but Tomaso? He and I get along fine."

"Sure, I remember Bono from the drilling and weight lifting contests." The sheriff was reading the telegram one more time. "Sounds to me like he's got some real trouble brewing down there. You've got time coming, Terrence. It'll be winter soon and that's usually a quiet time around here. Want to take anyone with you? Storm's a nasty varmint to go up against."

"Thanks, Ed. No, I'll go alone. Probably leave at first light. Got a good-sized mountain range to cross gettin' there. Just me and Dude and a good mule to carry a camp. Probably take three days at least. I can't think of any way better to prepare for a fight with a nasty outlaw than spending three days alone in the high mountains.

"Just me and trees, rocks, and cold fresh air. Shoot a sage hen or a couple of quail, have some boiling coffee."

It was a fair journey but certainly not three days. Corcoran would make it in a day and a half if he was chasing someone but, in the fall, all that fresh air, so many things to see and think about, three days might not be quite enough.

"Knock it off, Corcoran. You'll have me riding right along with you if you keep that up." Ed Connors had to chuckle thinking about a nice three days in the mountains. "If I remember right, you and Sheriff Johnson got into it once. You all right working with him?"

"Don't much care for the way he treats people. Everyone's guilty and every crime demands the harshest penalty is his way. I'll be spending most of my time with Bono so it'll be fine. Johnson's pretty much out of the picture." *I hope he's out of the picture. I don't like that man and he don't much care for me.* He had a scowl on his face when he left the office. *Wonder how Bono came to be carrying a badge? Minin' sure pays a lot more than being a lawman.*

Corcoran sent a wire to Ward and spent the night packing for the long jaunt. "Henry Storm," he muttered as he mounted Dude. He trailed the old mule and made his way east watching the skies slowly lighten.

"What is it about men like Storm? Killing is a way of life, taking things that don't belong to them is so natural. I've put a lot of them in the ground and even more behind bars and they just keep coming." His first encounter with the outlaw didn't go well but it was the second one he enjoyed remembering.

That first meeting was when the Storm gang robbed the stage that ran between Eureka and Palisade to the north. Storm had the gang leave out in four different directions and Corcoran picked the wrong one to follow. Louie Hernandez evaded capture by mingling with an immigrant group and Corcoran lost his trail.

When Storm came back through the county, Corcoran led the posse that chased him down after he robbed the Eureka Bank. "Put your skinny behind in the Carson City Prison, didn't I, Storm? How did you get out so soon?" He wanted to remember that question when he got to Ward. "Only been a year or two," Corcoran muttered. With a Horst and mule as listeners, Corcoran had some lively conversations all day.

"Three days on the trail, sage hen for supper two nights in a row, and there's Ward, sitting in the middle of that wide open plain down there. I'll be there in time for supper with Deputy Bono." The trail from the west became First Street and Corcoran turned north on Main Street, found the Ward Corrals and Blacksmith.

"You're packing yourself a load of trail dirt, Mister. Welcome to Ward."

"Glad to be here," Corcoran said. "Take care of my animals and give me directions to the sheriff's office, if you'd be so kind." Corcoran stepped down and handed the leads to the smitty. "Name's Corcoran, Terrence Corcoran and I'm looking for Tomaso Bono."

"Heard you were coming. I'm Buford Waring and I'm sure I saw Bono head for the Grand Hotel just a short time ago. Right down the street there," he said, pointing the way. "that's the sheriff's office right over there." His arms were going in two different directions and Corcoran had to chuckle while interpreting the moves.

Corcoran helped unload the mule and unsaddle Dude. "I'll come back for my personals after I meet with Bono, Mr. Waring. Right now, a cold beer is most important."

Ward was an orderly town but carried a tainted reputation during its short life. Outlaws holed up, murders were committed, and the town's leaders weren't always flagrantly legal in their dealings with the city's monetary resources. Corcoran walked the two blocks to the Grand, nodded to the few people he passed, looked in shop windows, and wondered how long it would be before Henry Storm found out that he was in town.

"There you are." Bono's deep voice bounced off all the walls in the Grand Hotel's Golden Spur Saloon. He walked over to Corcoran's side and the resident deputy grabbed Corcoran's hand in a mighty grasp.

"Haven't lost any of that strength, I see," Corcoran said. He feigned an injured hand. "Anything happen before I got here? Henry Storm is one despicable and dangerous man."

"Calm before the storm, Terrence. Let's take our beer into the restaurant and talk about this particular Storm over a big steak."

The restaurant featured large tables with white linen and comfortable chairs but what caught Corcoran's eye was the tall lady with the red hair sitting with an elderly gentleman. He offered a large smile and enjoyed the smile that was returned. *I certainly hope that lovely lass is his daughter. Beautiful eyes and everything else, too.*

"I see you've spotted our leading couple, Terrence. I'm afraid she's off limits. The gentleman is Stephen

Poindexter and he's sitting with the charming Mrs. She's Mary-Anne Poindexter, late of County Cork. Poindexter owns the bank, this hotel, and holds stock in most of the mines, too. It was his gold that Storm was after."

"Probably still is," Corcoran said. "It's always a shame when I find out such a lovely lady is married." He noticed that Mrs. Poindexter spent considerable time giving Bono favorable smiles as well. *Maybe that's why he said she was off limits?* He wanted to chuckle as they took a table some ways from the banker but Corcoran sat so he could keep a good eye on the lady. "From Cork, you say? Well, then. We have something in common, eh?"

"Shall we talk outlaws, Terrence?"

"By all means, Tomaso." *I'd best be careful. The lovely creature has already let it be known that her head can be turned by the lure of gold and the almighty dollar. Married women have always been safe from monsters like me. Damn shame, though.*

"Tell me about the criminal element in Ward, Tomaso. Does our fine Henry Storm have friends around that can hide him, feed him information, protect him? Which is the rowdiest saloon or area of town? Need to know the dirt of this place you call home."

The Grand Hotel sat at the northeast corner of Main and Third. Directly across Third was the Silver Springs Saloon and according to Tomaso, that was where most of the mining camp of Ward's problems hung out. "Henry Storm has eyes and ears in the place, even has his own little private drinking parlor, walled off, but with a window that looks out over Main Street."

"Cozy," Corcoran said. "He can just come and go in this town? He's a wanted man and he has a private drinking room?"

"Previous resident deputy wasn't up to your standards, Corcoran. Looking for trouble, the Silver Springs Saloon is your answer." Tomaso Bono laughed. "Might even be your style."

"Might have to have a beer or two over that way. Is this where I'm staying? Mighty fine hotel but expensive."

"County has a contract with Poindexter. You have a room for three weeks. Think we can wipe Henry Storm out in three weeks?"

"Three seconds when I see him, Tomaso. I'll get my gear put away and check out this evil town you call home. See you in the morning."

"Don't want company?" Bono asked.

"No. Nobody knows who I am. I'll just be

another drifter working my way somewhere and might just find out something or other." He knew better, knew because of the man at the corrals that he was expected but, in reality, Corcoran was simply a loner by nature.

CHAPTER SIX

It took just a short time to get his kit tucked away in the hotel and Corcoran walked the short two blocks to the corrals. "Find Bono, did you?" Buford Waring asked. "Ward's a small town, so you shouldn't have had any problem."

"No problem, Mr. Waring. Just looking in on Dude. Got him some grain, I see. Don't be spoiling him, now," Corcoran joshed. "Where would I find some good brandy, local gossip, and a friendly game of cards?" Getting two opinions, one from Bono, the law, the other from a business owner.

"We have two options, Corcoran, the Grand Hotel or the Silver Springs Saloon. The Grand is more likely to have cleaner drinking glasses."

"Ha. Nice way of saying that. You should be a politician, not a blacksmith."

"Oh, but I am, I am. I sit on the Ward town council, sir. That's why I'm so glad to have you in town, to rout out that Henry Storm gang. They're not good for business."

"Thank you. I won't let you down." Corcoran walked out of the large stables and headed for the Silver Springs Saloon and hopefully some answers. He wrapped his buffalo robe coat tighter as a cold wind swept down Main Street, blowing dirt, leaves, and other debris in various levels of whirlwinds.

He could hear piano music coming from the Silver Springs, as he got closer, and voices raised in anger, too. "Well, good," he muttered. "I'll get here in time for a good fight." It was just two men arguing, he found as he came through heavy swinging doors. They were sitting at one of the poker tables yelling at each other. "How about a cold beer to go with the entertainment," he said when the barman approached.

"You must be Corcoran, the tough guy Bono brought in to clean up our little piece of heaven."

"Just how would you know that?" Corcoran wasn't really surprised. He'd lived in small towns most of his life and if there's something that's almost gospel, if you want to know what's going on in a small town, ask the barman at the local saloon.

"Whole town's been looking for you since you wired Bono that you'd be coming."

I did wire Tomaso that I'd be here in a few days but he's not the kind of person to spread that about. And that leaves the telegraph operator. Wonder what else gets known because of him, like gold shipments, payrolls, money exchanging? Glad I came in here.

"Need to get my supper settled. Got some decent brandy tucked away back there?" Corcoran took in the sights of the saloon and found he was comfortable being there. He watched a heavy-set man try to manhandle one of the lovely dancehall girls. "That's enough, mister. Pick on somebody your own size." He turned to the slight girl. "Step away from him, Miss. He won't ever hurt you again."

The gorilla charged Corcoran, almost growling, and Corcoran spun with the attack, driving the man's head into one of the ten by ten mine shaft posts holding up the bar. More than one drink was spilled when the oak bar shuddered. Corcoran stood the man up, saw bleary eyes staring back at him and let him fall to the floor.

Corcoran nodded to the barman to refill his brandy and took it to a table. "What's your name, Miss? You should get tough with these fools who won't show you proper respect." He motioned for her to sit with him.

"Mindy," she murmured. "Mindy Shepherd." She looked at this huge man who just kept Ed Brown from causing her serious injury. Every working girl in Ward could talk about bruises, broken bones, or black eyes from Bad Man Ed Brown as he likes to call himself.

"You've just made yourself an enemy. That's Ed Brown on the floor."

"Ed Brown, eh? Well, Mindy Shepherd, Ed Brown will never hurt you again." He took a sip of his brandy and gave Mindy a long look. *Just a wisp of a girl, really. Needs to eat more regular, but she does have a nice smile and bright eyes.* "Mindy, I'm Deputy Sheriff Corcoran." He smiled. "Terrence Corcoran. You let me know if Mr. Brown tries to give you any trouble. You're a lovely lady and it's been a pleasure meeting you. Good night."

Corcoran drained his glass, slipped into his buffalo robe coat and walked out of the Silver Springs Saloon. Many eyes followed him out, and many conversations continued, most dealing with the new deputy sheriff arrival in town.

An older, heavy man walked up to the barman. "That the new man Bono sent for?"

"It is, Mr. Ransom. Took out Ed Brown inside

of five seconds. Think Henry Storm can stand up to him?"

"If he uses his guns," Ransom laughed. "Let me know next time he comes in. Like to talk with that gentleman."

"He rode in late, Henry. Has a room on the second floor of the Grand. He and Bono spent a couple of hours together. Even caused a ruckus at the Silver Springs." Louie Hernandez had been in Ward waiting for Corcoran and got the word back quickly.

"He's just as big as I remember," Hernandez said. "I gave twenty to Fingers to keep us informed if things change. You still planning on hitting the bank?"

"I want to, Louie, but I want to bust up the stock exchange first. According to Fingers, they keep several thousands of dollars in that safe. It's only locked at night, so this will be a daytime hit. You, me and Shorty can take it easy. Ride like hell west and then turn south past the old charcoal ovens. They'll never find us in that wild country. We'll give it a week or so and then hit the bank when they get their next payroll shipment."

They sat around a hot stove that night laying plans for the Ward Stock Exchange. The camp was a permanent mountain cowboy line camp built for the buckaroos who spent long summers in the high country tending cattle. Storm took possession and so far no one has complained. There were camp cots, a table and chairs, and most importantly, a wood stove for the cold nights and mornings.

They were deep in a canyon that reached miles into the towering peaks of the Egan Range. High mountain springs fed a stream that ran down out of the canyon, grass was plentiful, and the sides of the canyon were covered in heavy timber.

The Ward Stock Exchange building was a two-story affair with a seamstress salon and millinery shop upstairs. The building was on the corner of Fourth Street and Main, a block south of the bank and opened at ten each morning.

"You and I will go in, Louie, and you hold the horses and watch for trouble, Shorty. Don't be afraid of shootin' anybody that pokes their nose out. We'll run hard west, then south. Let's get there at five minutes before they open." He had a nasty smile as he took a swig from a bottle and handed it off. "If we're lucky, that damned Irisher, Corcoran, will show up. Or, maybe Sheriff Johnson, all crippled up, will pop out of the doctor's office."

Laughter echoed through the cabin, filtered

through the trees, and rolled down the hills southwest of Ward as the men finished the bottle. There was plenty of whiskey talk about killing lawmen, led by Henry Storm. "Corcoran put me in the Carson prison but he ain't never gonna get that chance again."

"Has that deputy got word from anyone else coming to help him?" Shorty Whipple had seen Corcoran in action and knew he was better with his guns than any of them. "Fingers said he sent wires to others."

"They all turned him down," Hernandez laughed. "Poor old Bono is left with a cripple for a jailer and a womanizer for his back up."

"Sounds funny, Louie, but that womanizer put me and Shorty in prison. Don't take Corcoran lightly. As much as I want him, if he crosses your sights, shoot."

CHAPTER SEVEN

Heavy black clouds filled the early morning skies over the White River Valley and a cold wind blew down from the mountains. "Ain't gonna be fall much longer, Terrence. Already feels like winter." Bono and Corcoran were in the sheriff's office, sitting close to the fire drinking coffee. "Did you make it to the Silver Springs last night?"

They watched two men, each with a pack mule loaded with mule deer carcasses ride by. "Those boys will eat well this winter," Corcoran said. "Yup, I was there and they knew who I was, that I was expected, and almost quoted our wires back and forth."

"Fingers O'Callaghan," Bono snarled. "Local telegraph office. Damn fool."

"Tell me about this banker, Poindexter. He knows money, obviously, and has a fine eye for beauty.

Would he be a help if Henry Storm hits his bank or just get in the way?"

"He's got a temper but also a good mind. He wouldn't get in the way but he would demand a strong response from us. He seems fair in most of his dealings with those that owe him money and can be generous with those who find themselves in financial straits." Bono sat back in his chair, still looking out the window.

"I think he gets involved in mining interests. Invests in mining, I know that. All in all, I think he's a good guy."

They watched Dean Miller cross the street and head for the office. "That's my new deputy coming in," Bono said. Miller hustled in the door and headed straight for the stove and coffee. "Dean, I want you to meet Terrence Corcoran, in from Eureka County to help us."

"Corcoran, eh? Heard about you when I worked in Pioche. Good to meet you." They shook hands, sizing each other up. "Expected somebody ten feet tall the way they talked," He laughed and poured some coffee. "Sheriff Knotts said you saved his life."

"Knotts So Good. That's what we called him and he'd get all riled but one hell of a fighter when he got his blood up. He took on three men, two with knives and one with a broken bottle, as I remember it, and I shot the one with the bottle. He took the other two out swinging his empty rifle. Pioche needs a man like that."

"He's about to retire, I think. Gang hit the bank last year and Knotts took a round in the knee. Gonna be crippled for the rest of his life. Damn fool banker is leading the call for him to retire."

"What brought you up here, Miller?"

"Thought I'd get one of those high paying jobs in one of the mines, but that didn't happen. Worked as barman and security for Poindexter at the Grand until last week. Talk around town is that this Henry Storm gang is gonna hit the bank soon. That why you're here?"

"Yup," is all Corcoran said. "You believe in a show of force, Tomaso?"

"I've seen it work." He chuckled and opened the case that held shotguns and rifles, handing a shotgun to Dean and taking one for himself. "Guess you'll be carrying your rifle, Terrence?"

Corcoran nodded and the three gathered up their heavy coats for the two-block walk to the bank. "We'll walk in the street, not on the boardwalk. Side by side, not in line. Makes for a fine show."

"It wouldn't have the same effect but I wish we

were taking the horses," Bono said. "It's cold out there."

"We want to be seen," Corcoran said. "We want people in town talking about the change in the sheriff's office. Tough bastards with big guns looking to clean out Henry Storm. We need to build our reputation, boys."

It was a cold wind that was driving the clouds, heavy with winter's first punch as Henry Storm led his little gang as they rode out of their canyon lair toward Ward. They turned north out of the canyon and wanted to enter town on Fifth Street. They would be one block south of the Ward Stock Exchange building. Across Main Street from the exchange was the Wells Fargo complex and east of that a few businesses and a line-up of bawdy houses.

The three outlaws, horses at a nice slow walk turned north on Main Street and made their way toward the exchange. "Ain't no one out in this weather," Shorty Whipple said.

"Anyone stick their noses out when we're inside, shoot 'em, Shorty. No witnesses, nobody to get all big and brave on us." Henry's teeth were sunk in a cold cigar as he took long looks up and down the empty street.

As they rode up to the exchange building, Darrel Shapiro unlocked the doors, stepped out, and darted back in quickly, getting out of the icy wind. "Just in time, boss," Louie Hernandez said. Across the street, Alphonso Paoli swept the boardwalk in front of the Wells Fargo office.

"Looks like some buckaroos down by the hotel but that's all," Shorty said. "I'll keep an eye on 'em."

Henry and Louie stepped down from their horses, shotguns hidden in the folds of their long winter coats. Shorty stayed in the saddle, took their reins, and kept looking up and down the street. Henry led the way into the exchange office, saw Shapiro behind the cage and Wallace Greene at his manager's desk. The open vault was behind Greene. No one else was visible in the large and spacious office.

"Good morning, gentlemen," Henry Storm said. He pulled the shotgun out and aimed it at Greene while Louie got the drop on Shapiro. "Need to make a little withdrawal, sir. If you'd be kind enough to fill these sacks with all the cash in that safe behind you, I'd be mighty appreciative." He gestured with the shotgun and Wallace Greene jumped to his feet, which caused Louie to take his eyes off Shapiro.

The clerk reached for a shotgun under the counter but wasn't fast enough. Louie caught the movement, whirled and let loose both short barrels of the heavy scattergun. The cage exploded as did Shapiro and, while Louie reloaded, Henry made a beeline for the vault. He smashed Greene across the head with his shotgun as he passed by.

"Let's get these sacks filled, Louie, and get the hell out of here. That blast is sure to bring trouble."

"Had to, Henry. Had a gun in his hand." They were filling sacks when they heard Shorty screaming at them.

"Hurry, they're coming," Shorty Whipple yelled. He saw Paoli come out of the Wells Fargo building, gun in hand and took two quick shots at him. "Hurry damn it," he howled again. He saw Paoli dive back through the door but also saw those three buckaroos down by the hotel start running toward all the noise.

Paoli eased the door open and fired his Colt at the outlaw across the street, kicking up dust well off to the side. Shorty fired back and heard Paoli yell out in pain. He put another shot through the door just to be sure.

"Damn it, boys, we've got company coming hard."

Louie and Henry raced out of the exchange with heavy sacks full of money, jumped on their horses as a fusillade of shots whistled through the cold morning air. "Let's go," Storm yelled, racing south.

"Gunshot," Corcoran yelled. The three were about to turn off the street and into the Grand Hotel when the first shot was heard.

"Stock Exchange or Wells Fargo," Bono yelled. "Let's go." The three were in full stride in half a second, racing through the bitter wind toward the shot when more gunshots rang out.

"Man on a horse, holding two horses, shooting toward the Wells Fargo building," Bono yelled.

Corcoran pulled his rifle up and took a long shot at Shorty but missed. The three watched two men race from the exchange building, mount, and ride hard south. "Damn," Corcoran said. People were coming out of the Grand Hotel and the Silver Springs Saloon along with those few with residences right in town.

"Go get our horses, Miller, while Corcoran and I find out the damages. Those men carried feed sacks so I'd bet the exchange vault is empty. You see what damage was done at Wells and Company, Terrence."

Miller turned in mid-stride and raced back for horses while Bono ran to the exchange and Terrence pulled up at the Wells building. He found Paoli with two gunshot wounds, bleeding some, but not in danger of dying. "We'll get you some help. Recognize who shot you?"

"Shorty Whipple," Paoli groaned. "Bastard."

Corcoran ran across the street to the exchange. "Wells agent said it was Shorty Whipple who shot him. My, God," Corcoran exclaimed, looking at the remains of Shapiro. He saw the bleeding Greene struggling to get up with Bono holding him down.

"Took several thousand, but it's the killing of Shapiro that will end that gang," Bono said. "They've gone too far this time."

A crowd was starting to gather despite the cold and Corcoran sent someone for the doctor. When Miller went for the horses, he sent Skeets McDougall back to help with crowd control. "Could use another hand or two," he muttered getting the horses saddled at the blacksmith's.

Henry Storm led the three south out of town and then turned west toward the mountains and their hideout in the small canyon. They circled around the west side of the charcoal ovens and into the rolling foothill country. "We better move through some rocky spots before going right for the camp," he said. "it won't take 'em long to start the chase and we got a storm coming down on us."

They rode hard for more than half an hour before

finally easing up on the horses. "Better if we get as high in those mountains as we can," Louie Hernandez said. "It's sure to snow tonight and we'll lose whoever might be trying to track us."

They walked the horses and then moved west into the high mountains another hour later. They left the main trail that cut through the range and went cross country. By the time they were nearing the eight thousand foot level, they were riding in snow flurries.

"Got a bonus coming for that quick thinking, Louie," Henry said. "Let's get a little higher and then turn south and drop out of the snow and find a good place to camp. We'll get back to our own camp tomorrow."

"We can ride slow and easy in the snow, Henry. Our prints will be gone in half an hour and we ride right on into our canyon. No one could possibly follow and we won't have to make a camp."

"Yeah," Storm said. "That makes sense. I just don't like knowing someone is trailing me. Just don't like it."

CHAPTER EIGHT

"They're riding for the high country, Bono. They get into the snow, they're gone." Corcoran chomped on his cigar and looked at the heavy clouds moving down the mountainside. "Snow'll be a foot deep up there in no time. I'd be wrong to think they have a camp way up there somewhere."

Bono, Corcoran, and Miller left Skeets to take care of the crime scene and raced south, knowing they were well behind the killers. They spotted dust miles out across the flat valley. "They just left the main road," Corcoran said. "they're heading for the high country and deep snow." The smattering of dust was miles out, blown about by the storm. It was hard, cold riding and Corcoran knew it would get much colder the higher they climbed. "Their hide-out can't be in that high country.

They're racing for the snow, knowing their trail will be covered in short order."

"Storm and his men are seen around Ward often enough to make me think they're set up fairly close." Bono said. "Before the attack on the gold shipment, the entire sheriff's office was the dead deputy and Skeets. Nobody tried to follow any of the gang out of town. Ain't gonna like giving this report to the sheriff when we get back."

The snow was coming at them as a wall and, within half a mile, visibility was reduced to ten yards or less. Snow covered rocks, tracks, and the trail Henry Storm was leaving and Bono finally called the pursuit off. "Let's head back boys. These mountains top off well above ten thousand feet and Storm's gang could turn north or south anywhere along the way and we'd never know it."

"Is there somewhere in town that they particularly hang out? The Silver Springs Saloon, one of the bawdy houses? Somebody in Ward must have some knowledge of where their hide-out is, where they live. That was a damn brazen attack this morning. I'm wondering if it was a warm up for an attack on the bank." Corcoran was thinking as he spoke. "Storm is certainly aware of the gold currently in the bank's vault."

"He'd need more than three men and horses to run off with a load like that," Miller said. "Wagons and teams along with many guns. Won't get any information but those who hang around Storm are usually drinking at the Silver Springs Saloon."

The long slow ride back to Ward gave each of the men time to think and to plan. Corcoran knew that if Storm was able to put together a larger gang and come up with a wagon and team, Bono would have to have more than what he has right now. "The three of us ain't enough to fight off a large attack on that bank."

"After I get all the information from Skeets and write it up, I'll have a talk with the sheriff. He's in bad shape. Infection, broken bones, and enough stitching across his back to hold a horse together."

"I don't like the man, Tomaso, but I'd like to be with you when you deliver it."

"I'd like that, too. He's gonna be one angry man."

"He was born angry, Mr. Bono. Did he give you any reason for not sending deputies down from Hamilton? He should have a nest of 'em up there."

"All he said was no. No reason given. Have no idea." Bono said.

Stephen Poindexter was at his desk, an hour before opening, discussing financial matters with his chief clerk. "Gunshots? Sounds close, Hank." The bank opened at ten o'clock sharp every morning and Poindexter noted it was only nine. He raced to the window and saw Deputy Bono and two men running south. "Look, Hank, that's that Whipple fellow doing the shooting. He's a member of Henry Storm's gang."

They stood all but mesmerized and watched the rest of the action play out. Poindexter became fully aware of just how vulnerable his bank was. *I've got to make plans for such an attack. The Stock Exchange opens at nine and that's when they hit. The cold wind is probably the only reason no one was out and about but even so, the attack was well thought out.*

Poindexter had a three-man team for security at the Grand Hotel but that was reduced now to two with Miller leaving. He had an armed guard in the bank's public area and there was a night guard in the building every night. "Hank, I want you to hire another guard for the bank and one to fill Miller's position at the hotel."

"I don't know if that will be enough," he muttered. "I'll talk with Sheriff Johnson and demand he bring more deputies to Ward. This Henry Storm must be stopped."

It was a short walk from the bank to the Grand and Poindexter took the stairs to the second floor where Avery Johnson was recuperating. *The timing is terrible. I can't let this Henry Storm get in the way of what Clive Kleindorfer and I have working. Too much money involved. Too much to lose.* The nurse let him in. "I heard the shooting, Stephen. What was it all about? I sent someone to fetch Deputy Bono but he hasn't come back."

Poindexter thought it strange that after all this time the sheriff was still flat on his stomach. He sat down next to the sheriff's bed. "Not healing, Avery? It's been two weeks, at least."

"Infected is what Bones tells me. Rips loose every time I move. What the hell was going on out there?"

"Henry Storm is what. He and two men hit the Ward Stock Exchange. Killed the clerk, I was told, and Greene's head is smashed. Shot up the Wells Fargo offices, too. You better get some people down here, Avery. My vault's full of gold, Sheriff. That's one big target. I've supported you all along but this attack this morning gives me second thoughts about your abilities."

"Bono said he called in a deputy from Eureka County and I gave him permission to hire a second deputy for the town. That's three deputies plus a jailer, Stephen. I can't call anyone from Hamilton, they're needed there. Would you let me deputize a couple of your security people?"

"No, Avery, I won't. They're needed at the Grand and the bank. I would like to see a lot more action than I'm seeing," Poindexter said.

"They're moving the entire county offices, everything, from Hamilton to Ely, Poindexter. I simply can't bring people down here. Protection of the county's assets takes precedent, I'm afraid," Sheriff Johnson said.

Poindexter stood, shook his head, nodded to the nurse, and left the room, not happy with his little talk with the sheriff. *I want a lot more than what I'm getting. Might need to start looking for a more aggressive sheriff. Someone who won't be asking me too many questions but who will attack the likes of Henry Storm.*

Tomaso Bono had his report in hand and he and Terrence Corcoran made their way down Main Street to the Grand and a meeting with the sheriff. *One dead, two seriously injured, and several thousand dollars gone. Johnson ain't gonna like this.* Corcoran hadn't seen Johnson for a couple of years but knew his terrible temper.

"That's Poindexter leaving the hotel, Terrence. Bet he just left the sheriff and we're gonna catch hell.

Sure you still want to come along?"

"Oh, yes." Corcoran chuckled, remembering the last time Avery Johnson tried to read the riot act to him. "I arrested a bank robber just inside the old Lander County line, yes, inside Johnson's territory, and Johnson went into a high lope over it. Riled, he was. I pulled the cuff key and started to let the man go, said something about he's all yours. Johnson changed his tune but cussed me for a full minute. Had a good laugh many times remembering that."

Bono laughed right out and tried to hold more in as they walked down the second-floor corridor. He knocked and the nurse took them to the sheriff. "Feeling better, Sheriff?"

"Poindexter gave me his side of the story. What's yours? That you Corcoran? What are you doing here?" Johnson tried to squirm around to see the men and groaned in pain.

"Lookin' to catch some banditos, Sheriff. You are more than short handed down here."

Johnson muttered something and scowled at Bono. "Well?"

Bono outlined what happened, who was dead and who was hurt. "Got several thousand from the vault. They ran west into a snow storm before we could catch 'em. Corcoran seems to think this was a run-up to hitting the bank."

"So does Poindexter." Johnson scowled at Corcoran. "Storm ain't smart enough to do that. The bank's holding gold coins and they would need a wagon and more men than he has."

"If he does, Sheriff, Tomaso is just as short-handed. Henry Storm can call in help, I hope you can." Corcoran stood next to the bed seeing a fresh blood-stain on the sheet covering Johnson. "You aren't in any condition for a fight, Avery, and you won't be for a long time. Tomaso needs help."

"You send out wires?" Johnson snapped the question out.

"To Elko, Eureka, and Lander. Only Corcoran could come. I'd like to deputize a couple of the security people at White's mine. Oliveira and Rosso are good men."

"Do it and send more wires. Henry Storm's days are numbered, Bono. With the attack on the gold shipment and now the exchange, the bodies are piling up." He tried again to get up on his side and almost cried out in pain. "Damn it. Bastard. Storm is gonna pay for this. What would you do, Corcoran?"

"Get more people first, but I would also do what I could to find out where Storm's hideout is and attack him. Seems your previous resident deputy didn't have that thought. Last thing Storm would think of. Too arrogant to think someone would attack him. Why don't you have deputies from Hamilton down here? You've got a big crew up there."

"Humph," Johnson said. He looked at Bono. "Get more people." Corcoran could not think of a single reason for the man not sending his men down to Ward.

"Why, Johnson?" Corcoran snapped.

"This is White Pine County, Corcoran. You're a guest. You better remember that." Johnson eased back down on his stomach. "So you know, the county seat is about to be in the new town of Ely. My men are protecting the county records and assets during the move. There are no men available."

Bono and Corcoran eased their way out and down the corridor. "How would you find out where the hideout is? I like that idea," Bono said.

"You said members of the gang come to town from time to time. They hang out at the Silver Springs? They probably have a few friends and given a little incentive, friends like to talk about friends."

"Incentive?" Bono looked around. "What, money? Sheriff would shoot me."

"Whiskey, my friend. Whiskey."

"I like that idea, too, Corcoran. Most of the rougher crowd hangs out at the Silver Springs Saloon. We can keep an eye on that. I'm riding out to the mine and see if I can spring those two men."

"Think I'll have a cold beer at the Silver Springs Saloon." Corcoran pulled the badge off his coat and shoved it in his pocket. "Don't know why I just did that. I pretty much introduced myself the other night" He laughed. An ironic chuckle, actually. "Today I'm good old mean sumbitch me."

CHAPTER NINE

"Mornin'," Corcoran said to the barman. "Winter's comin' on." He shook himself out of his heavy coat, flopping it across the bar. "How about a cold beer?" The Silver Springs Saloon was a two-story affair with drinking and gambling on the first floor, a set of offices and working girl's rooms on the second. Decor was rough board walls, oil lamps, and a piano. The barman brought the beer and Corcoran noticed not a word had been said.

He took the beer to a table so he could watch what little crowd there was in the place. *Interesting. I expected a little more.* There were a few men who appeared to be miners in from the graveyard shift, a couple of die-hard poker players who had been up all night, and one painted woman hovering near the miners. No one was near the piano. He looked all around, couldn't find the skinny little Mindy Shepherd or the bad man, Ed Brown.

Ain't nobody give me a second look as I can tell, including the bug behind the bar. Doesn't look like I'm going to learn anything sitting here, either. Good beer, though. Corcoran drained the glass and walked out the heavy doors. He watched Mary-Anne Poindexter leave the bank and walk toward one of the shops along Main Street. "Would like to know more about her," he mumbled. Instead of following, he turned south toward the Wells Fargo complex.

"No," he muttered. Corcoran turned back into the Silver Springs Saloon. "Barman called me by name once and ignores me now. Interesting. Got in a fight with a local bad man and nothing is said?" He decided to drink at the bar, make conversation. "Thought I could get away with just one." He chuckled, dropping a half eagle on the bar. "Good beer. Came in to make sure little Cindy Shepherd is all right. She around this morning?"

"Haven't seen her," the barman said. He stood with his back to Corcoran, wiping a glass with a towel.

"Let her know I asked about her when she comes in." Again, the barman didn't say anything, just brought the brew and walked down the bar. Corcoran gave it another few minutes and gave up, walked out the door and down to the Wells Fargo office. *Somebody's either in there that I'm not supposed to know about or is expected. Think I'll keep my eye on the place. I wonder if Cindy would do for an extra set of eyes?*

The Wells Fargo clerk barely looked up when Corcoran entered. "How's Paoli doing?"

"He'll live," the clerk said, without looking up. "Help you with something?" He closed the ledger book he was looking at. "Oh. You're the deputy who helped yesterday. I'm station manager, Jeb Whalen. That was a mess. You men need to do more to stop that gang. Two times in the last month we've had robberies."

"Workin' on it," Corcoran said. "People I talked to instantly recognized Shorty Whipple, the man who shot your clerk. Is he that well known? Where does he hang out?"

"He comes into town from time to time. Deputy Sinclair didn't do much about it. Don't know about Bono and never seen you before. Seems like this Sheriff Johnson don't much care."

"Where would I might likely see one of the Henry Storm gang members? A lot of people seem to know them." Corcoran was getting frustrated with Whalen's attitude but, on the other hand, understood it. "Never met Deputy Sinclair. I'm a deputy from Eureka County in to help Tomaso Bono. I've known him for a long time. With a little help from those that live and work here, we can stop this gang."

"About time, too. You'd have to ask somebody else where they hang out, as you put it. I wouldn't know."

"Tell Mr. Paoli I asked about him." Corcoran turned and walked out the door. "They demand service but they won't help. No wonder Storm can run wild in this country. Killing Deputy Sinclair was a big mistake." Corcoran was muttering as he walked into the Ward Stock Exchange where he asked the same questions of the clerk there. He had to snicker thinking about the sheriff. *Johnson's lost two good men, is shot up himself, and won't send any of his people down here to help. That man's lost his edge.*

"Me and the missus don't get out much," the clerk said. "I wouldn't know what to tell you. I'm going to miss Mr. Shapiro. He was a good man. They don't know if Mr. Greene is going to live after that blow to his head. I sure hope you catch those men. This is becoming a dangerous town."

"Thank you," Corcoran said. *Better attitude but no help. I better find Bono.*

Henry Storm, Shorty Whipple, and Louie Hernandez were sitting around the table in their cabin, a large fire warming things up. There was some snow on the ground but most of the storm, at their elevation, came in the form of rain and cold. "We gotta have some help to take that bank, Louie. A lot of that gold has already been turned over to the mines for their payroll but there's a lot left. More than a couple of horses could carry." Henry passed a bottle to the heavy Mexican gunman.

"Next payday at White's mine is three days from now. The mine always sends a wagon and two messengers to bring the money up. The week after that, the mine will send their gold to the mint. Big ingots, hard to handle, hard to get rid of. While we wait for some help, we could hit that payroll wagon."

Louie Hernandez and Shorty Whipple had a list of friends, five all together, that they could send wires to. "We get this list to Fingers, hit the payroll wagon, and count our money while we wait." He laughed and grabbed the bottle from Shorty.

Henry was laughing just as loud and slapped his thigh, too. "Good, good," he said. "Can you slip into Ward and get that list to Fingers?"

"Sure," Shorty said. "He's usually at the Silver Springs Saloon for his morning pick-me-up. I'll

ride in tonight. Give me a chance to see Wanda,"
he chuckled. "She keeps a room upstairs at the
Silver Springs."

The storm moved off the mountain and through
the valley quickly, leaving a mantle of snow above
seven thousand feet and cold rain in the valley. The
day began cloudy but, by mid-afternoon, the sun was
shining brightly. The outlaw camp was seven miles
from Ward, tucked in a deep canyon that flared
some at its closed end. Springs fed a small stream of
icy water and even smoke from their stove couldn't
be seen outside the canyon.

Shorty waited for sunset to make the short ride
to town and came in from the east side after circling
well to the south. He worked his way through wet
sage to where Third Street petered out and stayed
in the shadows as much as possible. He rode up to
the back of the Silver Springs Saloon and slipped in
through the storage room.

Wanda Peppard spotted her man immediately
and whisked him upstairs to her room. "Whole
town's looking for you, Shorty. You shouldn't be
here. That new deputy, they call him Corcoran, has
been in twice. Beat the hell out of Ed Brown." They
had their arms around each other, kissing and hug-
ging, grinding some, both getting bothered quickly.

"Corcoran? Man needs killing. Listen, I need some help with a project." He was fighting to get his boots off watching Wanda slip out of her dancehall girl's dress. "Fingers been in tonight?"

"He's downstairs now, battling the tiger." They let the conversation go and enjoyed their passion.

"You've got your mind on something other than me," Wanda sniffled.

"Maybe," he said. "I need to get a note to Fingers and then we can only think of each other. Can you run it down to him?" He handed the folded paper to her, she slipped into her dress, muttering some, and scurried out the door.

"That was quick," Shorty said when she came back almost immediately.

"He's gone. Cindy said he lost his money and left."

"I'll find him in the morning. Come here, beautiful."

Shorty Whipple snuck out the back door of the Silver Springs hoping to get to the telegraph office without being seen. It was just coming sunrise and no one was out and about to see him. Fingers had a small storeroom in the back of the telegraph office where he slept and Shorty had to knock on the back door several times before the wispy little telegrapher opened the door.

"You shouldn't be here," Fingers said. "My god, man, the whole town's looking for you and Henry. Get in before someone sees you."

"Boss wants you to send some wires out, Fingers. We need some men." He handed the sheet over. "Heard you lost all your money last night. Bucking the tiger ain't your game, Fingers. Henry sent this double eagle for your help. Stick to five-card, Fingers." Shorty chuckled and stepped out the door. Fingers read the note and the five names listed, smiled, and sat down at his key table.

Looks to me like old Henry Storm is about to hit Poindexter's bank next. That's some mighty fine information to have. He saw that it was just seven as he started tapping out the first wire. *Storm offers these twenty-dollar gold pieces like they were diamonds. Selfish bastard. I could sure use a lot more of them.*

Fingers O'Callaghan made his way to the Grand Hotel dining room after sending out the wires. He didn't open the telegraph office until ten and some mornings, instead of a whiskey and beer breakfast, had toast and coffee at the Grand. Usually, not quite this early.

"Morning, Fingers. You're up early." Tomaso Bono and Corcoran were at a table filled with biscuits and gravy, pork chops, and pots of coffee.

"Join us, please." Bono gave a nod to Corcoran and a quick smile.

Fingers knew he couldn't say no to the offer, felt the shivers running up and down his back, and took a seat. "Just coffee, thank you," he said. *This is the one called Corcoran. Even Henry Storm is afraid of him. What do they want from me?*

"Your company has some strict rules about the handling of private information, Fingers, but the government also has some strict rules, and these have nothing to do with losing your job. They have to do with losing your freedom. The penalties include long terms in federal prisons." The scowl from the huge man was enough to make Fingers want to run clear out of town.

Fingers wanted that whole cup of coffee but was afraid to pick the cup up. The shakes would not look good right now. "You're becoming a known associate of Henry Storm, Fingers, and that ain't the best place to be. You talked with Storm or any of his men lately?"

Fingers was looking around the room, almost frantically, and Corcoran was sure he was about to make a run for it. "I don't think we've met," Corcoran said. "I'm Deputy Sheriff Corcoran, Terrence Corcoran. Are you being forced to pass information to the outlaws? Are you being intimidated? Threatened?"

Bono liked the way Corcoran turned his threat into an opportunity for the little man. "If Henry Storm or any of his men are threatening you, maybe Corcoran and I can help. It would be illegal for them to intimidate you."

"I don't know Storm or any of his men," Fingers lied. "I don't know what you're talking about." Corcoran saw a lot of fright and planned on making it worse. He looked at Fingers, smiled, and took a long drink of coffee, never taking his eyes off the little man.

"The Henry Storm gang hit a gold shipment recently, Fingers. The only people who were supposed to know about that shipment were the White Pine County Sheriff and Stephen Poindexter. Poindexter got his information from a wire sent by the federal bank in Reno. How did Henry Storm come to know all about it?"

Corcoran smiled at the greasy little bastard and Bono picked up the conversation. "We can help if you're being forced to give out this kind of information," Bono said. "But if you're being paid to give it out, we will hurt you. Give it some thought, Fingers. We'll be in contact."

"Are you sure you want to be seen sitting with us?" Corcoran held his smile and chuckle until Fingers all but ran from the restaurant. "That might just pay off, Bono. Just might."

They know. Fingers O'Callaghan was visibly shaking in fear as he hurried back to his office. His mind wasn't slow, just frightened. *I wonder if they would pay for what I know? Storm would kill me in a second if he found out, but what if what I offer makes them give me protection?* He spent the rest of the day arguing the two sides.

Corcoran turned his eyes to the café entrance, mostly to watch Fingers leave, but also to watch a most attractive lady enter. "My, my," he almost whispered.

"Careful, my friend. Be very careful." Bono wasn't laughing. "She's flirty, will lead someone along and then laugh when she pulls the pin."

"My kind of woman," Corcoran said. "Is she waiting for someone or just trolling?"

"Poindexter will be here shortly and yes, she's also trolling. That kind of woman. She loves to play with men. It's just a game with her. Let's get our mind back on business."

Bono's actions, though, spoke a different language. He gave Mary-Anne a big smile as she approached and it was returned. Corcoran watched the little game be played out and wondered, which one is playing. *Or is it possible that neither one is playing this cat and mouse game? Is she teasing him or do they have something going? Mr. Bono has a way with women and she obviously has a way with men. Might be fun to just watch.*

"I talked with Oliveira and Rosso and they are now deputized." Bono said. "They both drink at the Silver Springs so we'll have eyes on the place. Seems that Shorty Whipple was in town last night. Spent the night with one of the working girls."

"Why didn't they arrest him? You seemed to think these men were good. Should have pulled down on him at first sight. Any idea why he was in town?"

"My fault, I think. They were under the impression I just wanted eyes open for the gang. They know better now. Lost opportunity. As far as why was that killer in town? Who knows? He spent the night with one of whores."

"I was in the saloon, too. Not impressed. They called me by name, Tomaso, the first time and ignored me the second. Talked to clerks at the Wells Fargo office and the Stock Exchange about the gang. No information available. People here are afraid of the gang, feel they are in danger because of Henry Storm, but seem to think they don't need to help, either."

Corcoran shook his head. "Men died when that wagon was hit, Shapiro was blown to hell at the Ward Stock Exchange robbery, and there's not a bit of help offered. I wonder what's next?"

"White's mine will be transporting their payroll from the bank day after tomorrow. Eight thousand dollars in gold coins, Terrence. I'll bet all my thousands of dollars in future income that Henry Storm will hit them and I'm not certain we can stop him."

"Might answer why Shorty was in town. Getting information."

Corcoran watched Stephen Poindexter come in and join his wife. *His feelings for her can be read from twenty feet away but I don't see the same from her. She likes the money, the prestige, the position in the community, and puts up with him to have it all. Bono's right. That is one dangerous woman.*

"How does that transfer work, Tomaso?" Corcoran was talking to Bono but watching Mary-Anne Poindexter. She was watching him and sent the slightest smile his way. He generously returned it.

"Women chase you down, Terrence, but you might not want to be caught this time," Bono chuckled. "The mine will send a wagon with two security people as outriders to pick up the payroll and that's about it. Straight in, straight out. There are several points along the road where an ambush could take place."

"Those that ambush usually have the upper hand," Corcoran said. "Kill off the guards, kill one or more of the horses, and it's all over. Only two guards and the driver? Easy pickin's, my friend."

Poindexter and his wife got up together and walked to the table. "May we interrupt, Mr. Bono?"

Tomaso and Corcoran got to their feet and welcomed the pair. "Of course. Please, sit down," Bono said. Corcoran pulled a chair for Mary-Anne and offered a wide smile as she sat down. "Something on your mind?" Bono sat across from the banker and Corcoran sat across the wife.

"Henry Storm is on my mind. That attack on the Stock Exchange was well planned and I'm holding the next payroll for the mine. I had a short talk with Sheriff Johnson and he's going to be laid up for some time. Is that payroll in jeopardy?"

"We were just discussing that," Bono said. He looked around the room to make sure no one could hear their conversation. "Storm is in no position to rob your bank, sir. There's only three of them, now, but the shipment is vulnerable once it's on the road to the mine. There are numerous places along that road to ambush the wagon and drivers. You look like you have something on your mind."

"I do," Poindexter said. "I talked to White about it and he scoffed, told me I was seeing trouble when there wasn't any. I suggested that instead of taking the gold to the mine, have the men come to the bank to collect their pay."

"That would end the threat," Corcoran said. "Why would White not give some thought to such an idea? That's a good idea as far as I'm concerned."

"I thought so," Poindexter said, "but it's his money and he's about as bull headed as any man I've ever met. I have two security men at the bank now, Bono. You still think Storm will not hit the bank?"

"He'll go after your bank when he has the men to do it, sir. If we see some strangers come to town we might want to fort up." He smiled saying it. "I think you and me need to take another ride out to the mine, Corcoran. Talk some sense into that crusty old buzzard."

Poindexter stood and offered his hand to Bono. Corcoran helped Mary-Anne up, took her hand gently in his and smiled. "It's been a pleasure," he said. She nodded and smiled, squeezed his hand, and turned to her husband.

"It sounds like these two men have things under control, Stephen. Shall we?" She reached out and took

Tomaso Bono's hand, held it tight, and finally let it go. Bono couldn't hold in his smile, saying goodbye.

Corcoran took great pleasure watching them walk from the dining room. "He should be as worried about her as he is about his precious gold, Tomaso. Tell me about the mine owner."

"White struck it big time, created our little town, and believes he is invulnerable. Has never been through a real threat to his person, his mine, or the money he's made. His security people are tough but never tested."

"We'll remind him that the stock exchange had never been hit before, either." *I wonder what it will take to make these people believe there's a problem? Henry Storm has had it easy up to this point.*

"Actually, it's a short ride to the mine but there are two distinct places that we should look at. A steep hill with sharp turns and heavy rock walls that would be a fine opportunity for an attack and a deep ravine that has never been bridged for whatever reason. It's surrounded by rock pinnacles and a heavy stand of trees."

"You called it a ravine?" Corcoran asked. "Running water, more like a stream bed than a culvert?"

"Exactly. Steep sides on the ravine. That would be my spot to attack." Bono said.

CHAPTER ELEVEN

White's mine offices were on a knoll overlooking the vast valley with the Egan Range off to the west, towering into massive late fall clouds. "Nice layout," Corcoran said. "On the ride you picked out a few places where an ambush cold be set up easily. The one crossing the stream would be my choice. Tough place for the animals and the teamster and his guards would be busy with them."

"Yup," is all Bono said. "Tough place to defend, too. The rock pillars is where the outlaws would hid, and that leaves open range for us to hide in." They rode through a gate that hadn't been closed or locked for years. "Man thinks he's invulnerable. See any guns aimed at us?"

"Nary a one, Tomaso. At the Eureka mine, and they've known me for years, I still have to show my badge to get in. This is folly." The two lawmen rode right up to the office building and tied their horses off without a soul attempting to stop them.

"Morning." Bono said to the clerk behind a small office fence, sitting at a large desk. "Here to see Mr. White."

"He's right in there, Tomaso. Go right in. Tell him I'm bringing coffee. That your new deputy. He's about as big as you are."

"Thanks Gypo." Bono nodded to Corcoran and headed down a long hallway to White's private office. "Gypo only works underground when they're in high grade ore. A little high-grading and, thus, his name. He takes it as a compliment," Bono laughed as they walked down the hallway.

"Morning, Mr. White. Can we take a little of your time? This is my new deputy, Terrence Corcoran, from the Eureka County Sheriff's office. Got a problem brewing with the Henry Storm gang."

"Come in, Tomaso. I've heard good things about you, Corcoran. Welcome to Ward. Sit down. I was about to have a taste of brandy. Join me?"

Smiles around and the two men nodded. Corcoran found himself instantly liking the gentleman. Neither Bono nor Corcoran mentioned that coffee might be coming their way. White was a bruiser of a man, almost five feet and ten inches tall but weighing in excess of two hundred pounds. There were no indications of fat anywhere. The man's hands were large, the knuckles showed considerable wear, and Corcoran almost chuckled looking at White's rather crooked nose.

No wonder Bono says the man thinks he's invulnerable. Probably been in fights all his life and never has known defeat. He's going to be hard to convince that a gang of three can take out his payroll wagon. Probably want to ride guard himself.

"You here to convince me to have my miners pick up their pay at the bank?" He had a jovial look on his face. Corcoran also saw an open invitation to argument.

"That we are, sir," Bono said. "This Henry Storm gang has probably already passed the planning stages for an ambush on the road to the mine. We've been over this before, Mr. White. That payroll wagon could be ambushed by idiots. You've said so yourself, as I recall."

"When you worked for me, Tomaso, I did. And, it is a dangerous prospect but, if I do as you suggest, I'm showing weakness. I won't do that. I'll fight Zeus himself before I'll show weakness to an outlaw."

Corcoran wondered if the man was afraid of anything. *He's afraid of showing weakness, but I wonder if he has a weakness. This isn't just bravado, though. He's tough as the hammer he uses to break up hard rock. Thor. Sitting right in front of me. At the same time, he's putting people who work for him in danger just so he doesn't show weakness. I gotta know more about this man.*

White produced three brandy snifters and a bottle from his rather tidy desk and poured generously. "To the demise of Henry Storm and his pitiful little gang." White drank heartily and refilled the glasses. "Now, let's talk about safely bringing that payroll to my men. I will have my driver and two security men as outriders. Do you plan on riding with my men?"

"No sir," Corcoran said, "we weren't. Bono, Dean Miller, and I will be working to bust up the ambush before it gets started. If you were an outlaw, Mr. White, where would you attack the payroll?"

"Interesting question," White said. He sat back, thinking, looking at the two, looking out the window, and finally said. "There's a small creek that runs all year with high banks that make it difficult to cross. And it has to be crossed. Road would have to detour ten miles or more to evade that crossing. I've wanted to build a bridge over that creek for years but the banks are too unstable." He turned and looked west out large windows.

"There's a stand, no, actual pillars of rock nearby. That's a perfect location for an ambush." White sat back in his chair and took a sip of brandy.

"My thoughts, exactly," Corcoran said. "The most difficult place to ambush the ambushers, as well. That's where Storm will hit. So, sir, how would you defend?"

"You've a quick mind, Corcoran. I like that. You're putting me in a position where I will say to you, maybe the best solution is to have the miners go to the bank for their pay." He had a broad smile, his eyes seeming to dance, and his deep laugh filled the room. "Well, just damn you, sir, I won't do it. How do you plan to defend my payroll wagon?" His cagy smile and bright eyes challenged Corcoran straight out and his laughter again filled the office. "Better have another drink while you think of an answer."

I love this man. It's his money, payroll for his work-ers, but it's our responsibility to get it from the bank to the mine. This is no time for me to be wrong, either, because he would pounce on that. Corcoran took the offered glass of brandy, nodded and offered a toast, and thought about that road. Rough country, deep trenches for the stream, granite palisades and pillars in awkward places, and three men with rifles and shotguns looking to kill and rob.

"Well, sir," Corcoran said. He had a smile on his face and sipped his brandy. "I'd spend tonight in a cold camp near that crossing. Near enough that my rifle would be well in range of the creek, and hope I picked the right ambush spot. The outlaws would want to be there well before the wagon and its guards and I'd have the upper hand instead of them."

"So, you see, Tomaso, There is no reason not to bring the payroll to the miners instead of them having to go to the bank." A self-satisfied smile, deep laughter, and another generous pouring of brandy all but ended the conversation, if not the meeting.

"Nice going, Terrence," Bono laughed. "Glad I brought you along. All right, then, Mr. White. Corcoran, Miller, and I will be camped near the creek crossing. Do me one favor, though. Do not tell anyone, and I mean anyone, about this plan. There are just too many people who know far too much about what's going on."

"You're thinking of the gold shipment that was attacked." Bono nodded and White continued. "Word that I heard was the telegraph operator works for Henry Storm. He pays the man for everything that's passed to him. No, don't worry about that. I'll say nothing but let's hope my guards don't shoot you."

"We're gonna be settin' up our camp almost in the dark, Bono," Corcoran said as they rode from the mine. I'm going to stay right here and find us a good ambush spot while there's plenty of light. You head back to town and bring Dean Miller and a camp set-up back. I'll watch for you."

"That'll work, Corcoran. Do you think Henry Storm would bring his gang out late tonight or wait for morning?"

"Damn," Corcoran said. "Don't want to think about him showing up tonight but it is something we'll have to have in mind. That's rolling ground, so I'll find somewhere to camp where we can't be seen from the road but somewhere come morning we can watch the crossing. Hurry back, Bono."

Bono shook his hand and rode off toward Ward. *This is what I have been looking for all my life. Working hard in the mines is good for the body but doesn't help the mind much. Listening to White and Corcoran jousting with each other, playing chess, I think, was a hell of a thing. Henry Storm, you bastard, you don't stand a chance.*

Bono's ride back to Ward was filled with thoughts of tomorrow's clash with the outlaw gang coupled with watching towering clouds build over the Egan

Range. Late fall in eastern Nevada can mean warm summer temperatures or bone-chilling winter storms. Sometimes both in a twenty-four-hour period. The wind was already starting to kick up as he rode down Third Street and turned north for the offices. Dust wasn't flying, it was still mud, but many of the autumn leaves that danced in the wind were still attached to their branches.

Mr. White's a brilliant man, I think. He turned that whole conversation making Corcoran have to prove that with our help the shipment would be more than safe. Now we're gonna be fighting outlaws and the weather.

"Food for tonight and the morning, cold, remember, and bedrolls," Bono said to Skeets McDougall when he got back to town. "And not a word to anyone. Where's Dean Miller?"

"Poindexter called for him. They were to meet at the Grand."

"Have everything ready in less than an hour, Skeets." Bono made the quick walk to the Grand Hotel and found Dean Miller and Poindexter at a table in the restaurant.

"How'd the meeting go?" Poindexter had a half smile on his face, anticipating a negative response.

The look on Bono's face told him they would be making the shipment.

"White will have his wagon and guards at your bank at the prescribed hour. I hate to interrupt this meeting, Mr. Poindexter, but I need Mr. Miller at the office. We may have some information on Storm's hideout." He lied but it appeared that Poindexter didn't catch it.

They left quickly and Miller asked if what Bono said was right. "Not even close, Dean. We're riding out for White's mine right away. The shipment is on, Corcoran and White believe it will be ambushed, and we're setting up our own ambush. Get your cold weather gear and be at the office in fifteen minutes. Not a word to anyone."

"Where's Corcoran?"

"We'll meet him. Hurry."

CHAPTER ELEVEN

"When they drop off that rise they'll have to cross the creek and that's a steep and muddy bank on the other side. We can ride out from the trees, shoot everyone, and keep the wagon." Louie Hernandez was laughing as he detailed the planned hit. "We'll need the wagon when we hit the bank."

"The way the wind's blowing we'll be stealing the gold in a pretty good storm." Shorty Whipple threw a couple of logs in their already hot stove. "They usually pick up the gold at the bank about seven so they can be at the mine to pay their men before noon. We need to be at that creek crossing well before ten o'clock."

Henry Storm poured some whiskey in his tin cup and paced around the cabin. The wind was cold and snapped the canvas window coverings. "I'm not worried about taking on those mine guards, even in a wild storm. What have you heard about this Corcoran? Is he really here? Bastard is the one who put us in prison, Shorty."

"He's here. Word I got, he even got in a fight with Sam Brown in the Silver Springs Saloon. Beat him up good. Bono deputized him and Dean Miller, the security at the Grand. They been seen walking around town with their rifles and shotguns. Think they'll ride with the shipment, Henry?"

"Won't know 'till we see 'em." Henry Storm laughed and passed the bottle around. "Hope Corcoran shows up. Man needs killin' in the worst way. Let's get some sleep."

They woke to a cold wind whipping a mix of rain and snow. Piñon pine branches sang some high notes, wet tumbleweeds raced across the flats, and the lowest clouds were being hustled down off the jagged Egan Range. "It's gonna be a mess at the creek crossing, Henry. Gonna be a mess just us getting there." Louie Hernandez nursed a fire from the few embers left from the night before. "We can't just ride out to that creek. We have to get there cross country. This storm is cold but there's not enough snow to hide our trail or not enough rain to wash it out."

"Damn. You're right, though. Don't want to be seen riding out." Henry paced, kicked a chair, and finally poured more coffee. "I want that money. I want Corcoran dead. Damn." He was fighting off the impulse to call off the hit on the payroll shipment. "Did Fingers get those wires sent off? Are we going to have visitors in the next few days? Damn."

"I gave him the names and a double eagle, Henry. There's no reason to think he didn't. They won't answer, of course, so we won't know until one or more show up. What are you thinking?" Shorty Whipple saw fear in his boss's eyes and that brought a pang of fear into his.

"Thinking of giving this up this morning and waiting for our help to show up and taking the bank? That's what I'm thinking."

"I can't think of any good reason to call off today," Hernandez said. He looked over at Whipple and knew he wouldn't be getting any help from him. "Wind, rain, and snow have always been on our side. I know you aren't worried about Corcoran." He threw that little jab in to get Storm's head back in the game.

"Damn right I ain't," Henry snarled. "You saying something?" His right hand was holding a tin cup of coffee but Hernandez knew Storm could drop the cup and still be faster than he, and more accurate. Shorty moved back a bit from the fire and made sure his hand was far away from the iron on his hip.

"No, Henry. Not sayin' nothin'." He stepped up and grabbed the coffee pot. "Just thinkin' out loud. There ain't any reason not to make this hit. Lots of gold and silver coins on that wagon. The mud, wind, and cold are friends of ours."

Henry Storm wasn't a thinking man, didn't, as he said, waste time worrying about things. "I'm fine, Hernandez. I think more anxious than anything. That gold belongs to us." He took a long swig from a tin flask and tucked it back in his coat.

"All right then, let's head out. Louie, you know this country best, lead us to that mud hole without getting on a road or being seen by anyone on a road." Did he still have doubts? His questions were mostly answered, but, still. Henry Storm wasn't a thinker, didn't spend a lot of time planning, and when he made up his mind, it wouldn't be changed. "Don't kill the horses. As Louie said, we'll need that wagon to haul the rest of the gold we get from the bank."

Corcoran was first up and nudged Miller and Bono up. "It's a cold storm moving in, boys. I'm going to take a quick look around. Didn't hear anything during the night so I don't think Henry Storm has moved in yet."

Their camp was more than two hundred yards from the rock outcrop near the little creek, in a swale that was deep enough to hide the tall rocks. It was those pillars of stone from where Corcoran anticipated the outlaws would strike. They didn't light a fire the night before or in the morning. Even if fire light couldn't be seen, the smell of the smoke would give them away.

Corcoran eased himself to the crest of the rise and crawled under a sage to get a good look. "Not there," he mumbled and got to his feet. "Don't want to get too close. If the bandits show up and find fresh boot prints, they'd hightail it." He was mumbling as he worked his way close to where an ambush would be set up.

The wind was howling down from the northwest, carrying sheets of rain and shards of ice, not snow. Corcoran moved close to the rock pinnacles using what sparse growth of piñon and cedar that was available. He was hunkered down in brush when he saw the mine wagon and two guards come down the road.

They'll be at the bank soon and if I was Henry Storm I'd want to be right here very soon. Corcoran watched the horses ford the stream, saw just how slippery the mud was, and knew the robbery would have been successful if he and his boys weren't there.

The storm was just wet enough that the banks on both sides of the creek were muddy and slick, and the teamster had a big fight getting the wagon down, across, and up the other side. Both guards had to take part in the crossing. "By the time they get back from the bank it's gonna be a whole lot worse," Corcoran muttered.

Back at camp, he told Bono and Miller about what he saw. "When do you think Henry and company will show up?" Dean Miller was wrapped in a bearskin coat fighting off the cold and wind. "We don't dare start a fire."

"I'm gonna play like Mr. White would, Corcoran," Bono chuckled. "If you were robbing this shipment when would you arrive?"

"Sounds like you learned something, Tomaso. I would want to be here within the hour, get my men set up, light a fire, and wait."

"Fire?" Bono looked surprised.

"Gotcha. No fire, Tomaso," he laughed. "So, knowing that, what should we do, Mr. Resident Deputy?"

"They are wanted killers and outlaws, Corcoran. When they arrive, we attack. No warning. No quarter."

"Excellent," Corcoran said. They had their horses tied off in a stand of pine trees and Corcoran moved toward them. "One or more of those outlaws will run, Bono. Criminals are cowards. They only fight when trapped. We need to have our horses ready to run, too. Dean, move back to where I crawled out earlier and keep watch. Let's saddle the horses, Mr. Bono."

Miller eased his way up and out of the swale and slipped under a big bush. The storm was getting more intense and vision was less than poor. Heavy rain, blown by strong winds clouded his vision and Miller moved out from under the brush toward a stand of cedar thirty yards closer to the high rocks.

"Damn," he muttered, back pedaling quickly. He slipped over the brink of the swale and ran to the horses. "They're already here." He said as he ran up to Bono. "They were just getting off their horses when I spotted them. They're to the right of the highest rock."

"Let's move on 'em," Bono said. They were on their horses and moving out toward the pinnacles. "Dead or alive," Bono said. "It don't matter. They are wanted killers."

"Not too fast now," Corcoran said. "We want to

be as close as possible before they see us. This storm is the best thing to happen. It may hamper our vision but it really messes up theirs. There they are." He put the spurs to Dude and the others followed.

"What are you looking at?" Shorty Whipple was standing next to his horse staring off into the storm, the reins firmly in his hand. Henry Storm was looking for a bush to tie his horse to as well.

"Thought I saw something moving over there. Damn rain and snow. Can't tell for sure."

"Need to get set up," Henry snarled. "Ain't the time to be seein' things. Let's keep our horses close, though. Bono don't think like a lawman but Corcoran wrote the book. What's that crossing look like, Louie."

Hernandez chuckled and said there was good water running in the creek and plenty of mud to go around. "They'll have a grand time getting that heavy wagon up this side, Henry."

"Good. Remember, no witnesses. Kill everyone, don't be shooting the horses. We'll just ride off with the wagon."

"Did you see that?" Shorty was pointing into the heavy shadows of rain and snow. "Sure as hell that was a man on a horse."

Before anyone could respond Corcoran led Bono and Miller down off a slope, howling at the tops of their lungs, guns ablaze. Henry Storm froze for less than half a second, was on his horse, and at a full gallop across the creek and up the other side. Louie Hernandez wasn't ten feet behind him but Shorty Whipple had already tied off his horse.

He pulled his sidearm as he flung himself into the mud and tried to find a target. The three riders were still forty yards or so off and he fired a couple of rounds. "Two are running," Corcoran yelled out. "Take out the one staying, Miller. Come on Tomaso, let's ride." They splashed across the creek and climbed up the other side despite the mud just as quickly as Henry and Louie had.

Miller jumped from his horse, knew where the returning fire was coming from and began working his way toward Shorty. The howling storm was fully on Miller's side as he worked through heavy brush and scattered rocks. *That ice and rain is pounding the back of my head. It must be right in that fool's eyes.*

Miller was prone, under a sage, and saw Shorty moving through the heavy mist toward his horse. "Not this time," Dean Miller muttered. He took a long aim with his rifle and drove a 45-70 through the middle of Shorty Whipple who thrashed about in the mud and finally died.

"You won't be robbing and killing no more, Shorty." It was a fight getting Whipple's wet and muddy body laid out across the saddle. Icy rain pelted Miller as he tied the body tight. "Damn storm. You ain't helping things right now," Miller almost shouted. He gathered up his horse and ponied Whipple's across the creek and up the muddy slope on the road to Ward. "Gonna like walking this boy through the middle of town but really, I wish I was chasing Storm. I like this Corcoran."

Miller met up with the payroll wagon less than half an hour later as they made their way to the mine. "You boys will have a safe, wet, and cold ride in. This here's Shorty Whipple. Tell Mr. White that Bono and Corcoran are chasing Henry Storm and Louie Hernandez."

Fists were pumped and kind words were said as the wagon full of gold moved off in the cold and wet. "Good for you, Mr. Miller. We'll let the boss know what happened."

Cold rain and wind cut the meeting short. "Ain't seen nobody chasing nobody," one of the guards said. "Hope they get those fools. Bye, now," and they hurried off.

I'll drop this outlaw off with Skeets and let him get

with the undertaker. He'll have to do the paperwork. Dean Miller couldn't help but chuckle. *Then I'll try to find Corcoran and Bono.*

He rode down the middle of Main Street and one poor soul making his way out of the Grand Hotel hollered out. "Who you got there, Miller?"

"Shorty Whipple from the Henry Storm gang. Won't be killing people now. Spread the word. The Henry Storm gang is busted up."

"Poindexter's inside. I'll tell him. Might be good for a drink or two." Miller laughed watching the man stumble back into the hotel.

CHAPTER TWELVE

"They're heading for the mountains again," Bono yelled. "Their horses and ours aren't gonna run that far and this fast. Mud's deep, wind is strong and cold, and we're running straight into the teeth of this storm."

"It's a nice day for a long ride, Tomaso." Corcoran slowed Dude to a comfortable walk. "We've got a good trail to follow, let's slow down and follow it. They're outlaws, means they don't think straight. Might even lead us right into their hog wallow."

Bono had to laugh. "Not staying on a road or marked trail sure does make it easy to follow the bastards. Ward is off several miles to our right, those nasty Egan Mountains are straight in front of us, and between here and there is a lot of broken up country. Where would you hide in this weather?"

"There's a couple of big ranches out this way and I'd surely stay away from them. I'd head for my camp. Shame we don't know where that is."

They were riding into the rolling hills and deep ravines and canyons that lead into the mountains. Every fold of the mountain is filled with a creek and thick woods, other smaller creeks are fed by springs that run year round, and the riding wasn't pleasurable like if they were on a well-used trail. "I haven't seen them since they lit out, Mr. Bono, but looking at the trail they're leaving for us, I'd say they are still running their horses as fast as they'll go."

"They'll run 'em into the ground if they keep it up."

"Where did they come from?" Louie Hernandez was laid out across the neck of his horse, urging the animal for more speed. Henry was slightly in front as they pounded through open but not flat country. "Never heard or saw anything until all hell erupted."

"Don't think Shorty made it," Henry said. "We gotta run these animals all the way to our camp, Louie. I ain't leaving anything for the vultures. We can fight 'em off from camp. That's why we built it that way."

"We won't make it Henry. My horse is give out and yours don't look good. Gotta slow it down or we'll be walking soon. We gotta find a place to fort up." Louie Hernandez was a far better horseman than Storm and knew he was right.

"You're probably right and I know it, Louie, but you gotta know Corcoran is coming hard behind us. Let's ride for the camp but if we find a good bunch of rocks to fort up in, we'll take it."

They were about five miles or so from camp but their horses were still gasping for breath when Hernandez spotted a stand of cottonwood trees amongst scattered rocks the size of cabins. "Looks like a nice place to make a stand, Henry. All the comforts of home."

They found good grass, an overhang to get them out of the wind and rain and, despite limited vision because of the storm, they could watch their back trail. "Let's try to get a fire started. Take care of the horses, Henry and I'll find some wood. If we can get warm and dried off some before Corcoran gets here, it'll make for an easier fight." The wiry man laughed as he handed reins to Storm.

"This isn't a party, Hernandez. Knock it off." Henry took the two horses behind a large rock and tied them to a cottonwood. There was good grass but no shelter from the storm. "This will keep them close," he muttered.

Hernandez was muttering, kicking wet branches and rocks out of the way, finding some almost dry wood. "That man gets angry at life itself, I think. Tequila, woman, and a laugh in the face of life is my way. I think I'll just shoot him." He had an arm full of wood when Henry came back.

Henry was still upset with Hernandez for taking their situation so lightly. "Corcoran can follow our tracks right up to us. If he even has a hint we're forted up, he'll work around to our blind side. You know that." Hernandez wouldn't take the bait.

"If one of us looks one way and the other the other way we ain't got a blind side." It was all he could do to not chuckle. Hernandez was working hard striking his flint starter and with the help of some black powder got a small flame going. He added more kindling, then larger pieces of wood, and had a smoky fire going in minutes. "It's wet and smoky but with this storm, who cares? Couldn't see it if they wanted to."

They sat with their backs to the fire, out of the storm, one looking east, the other west. The face of their lair pointed south. "Corcoran will be right on top of us before we see him," Henry Storm said. "Let's hope we see him first." He wanted to run, not stand and fight. He spat tobacco juice onto the fire and grumbled some.

"Did you unsaddle the horses? We might still need to make a fast run out of here." Hernandez was thinking if they wounded Corcoran they could still get away to their camp but would need to get away fast.

"No," Henry said. "I was already thinking about that. They're ready to run."

"They've slowed down to a walk, Bono. Our horses have had a good blow. Let's pick it up. We're coming into the steppes, the foothills. Maybe they're leading us to their camp after all."

"We're lucky that the snow is blowing as hard as it is. Otherwise, we'd never see their tracks. They aren't that far in front of us," Bono said.

The terrain was rolling fantails from the Egan Range, a few steep areas with razorback ridges, some almost meandering slopes filled with pine, cottonwood, aspen, and brush. The outlaw's trail moved around, over, and in some cases, through the obstacles, but always with what appeared to be a destination in mind.

As they moved higher the rain turned to soggy snow but it wasn't hiding the trail made by the fleeing outlaws. The horses splashed through the easily seen prints in the mud. "It'll get colder the higher we go and, if we don't catch up soon, we can kiss this chase goodbye," Bono said. "We've probably got about two hours, maybe three at the most, to catch them."

"We know we're not that far behind them, Tomaso. Can't be." They ran their horses for more than an hour at a solid trot through soggy snow that was beginning to stick when Tomaso Bono pulled up short.

"Smell that?"

"Oh, yes I do. There's only one reason to smell smoke out in the wilderness like this and it ain't from hunters." Corcoran knew which way the wind was blowing, knew which way the outlaws' trail led, and started riding off at an angle. "They ain't half a mile over that way, Mr. Bono. Let's give 'em a surprise." The clouds were right down at ground level as the two rode slowly through rain, snow, and fog.

As they moved through the deepening snow, their horses at a slow walk, they could see a stand of trees through the mist of the storm, and some large boulders strewn about. "Their nest, Tomaso. Somewhere in that little park is their nest. We can get closer without being seen but we will be walking through snow and mud soon. Time to be quiet."

Using the folds of the terrain, large rocks, and

trees, they made their way into the grove of cotton-woods. "I'm using the smoke as a guide," Corcoran all but whispered. "See that large overhang? Hard to see in the storm but it's right over there. Bet the fire is under that overhang along with our boys. Can't come straight in, though." They dismounted and tied their horses off.

"Let's split up," Bono said. "I can come in from over that way and you come around from over there. They gotta know we're coming after 'em."

"No, we stick together. They will expect us to follow their tracks in but let's move so we come in at a right angle. Sure as hell they're watching front and back, but not to the side. We need to keep about ten feet apart, stay low, and be quiet." Corcoran had captured more than one outlaw and Bono didn't argue with the man at all, just nodded.

Snow was already several inches deep when they came up on some large cottonwood trees. Busted branches spread about told Corcoran the trees had been through lots of storms like this one. They got in behind a big one and could see a fire burning under the rock overhang. "Looks to be about fifty yards," Corcoran said. "That's Henry on the left and Hernandez feeding the fire." Corcoran chuckled. "He's giving us good shooting light."

They stayed as low as possible and moved slowly toward the overhang. It was awkward because of ice under the snow and not being able to see rocks and branches. There were trees and large brush to get behind and they made it about half way before stopping. "Are you planning to call out to them or not?" Tomaso asked.

"No." Corcoran stood up slowly, pulling his rifle up. Bono followed suit but one foot went out from under him in the ice. The deputy kicked rocks around catching his balance and Hernandez spun around and spotted him immediately. He fired two quick shots and knocked Bono down with a bullet to his thigh. Blood poured from the split vein and Corcoran pulled him back behind a bush, not getting a shot off.

He ripped his neckerchief off and was tying it tight around the leg when they heard horses running hard. "Lost 'em, Corcoran. Damn me, I'm responsible, too."

"We'll get 'em. Just not today," Corcoran said. "I gotta get you back to town. That's a bad wound, Tomaso. Bad." He tied a small branch to the kerchief and wound it slowly, seeing the blood flow come to a halt. "Hang onto this and don't let go until I get back." He ran for their horses, slipping and almost falling several times.

I'm not going to lose this man. So close. Tomaso is going to be a fine lawman and I just hope he doesn't think himself out of it. Slipping in ice, mud, and snow is something that could happen to anyone.

The ride back to Ward was long and slow through deepening snow. Corcoran had to stop from time to time to release the pressure on the leg wound and then tighten the tourniquet again. Bono fought hard to stay conscious but as they moved into the mining camp he was slumped in the saddle, barely hanging on.

"Give me a hand here," Corcoran yelled at a couple of men. "Need to get Bono into the doc's. Hurry. He's hurt bad." They eased the deputy down from the saddle and hustled him inside. Bones McFadden must have seen them coming and had the door open and directed the men where to go.

"Gunshot to the leg, Doc. Bleeding bad," Corcoran said. "Got it tied tight."

McFadden nodded and chased everyone out. "He's mine now. Come back later, Corcoran. We need to talk about Sheriff Johnson."

The two outlaws rode hard for fifteen minutes and didn't pull up until they were close to the canyon that led to their hideout. "Never saw 'em until that one slipped in the ice," Hernandez said. "How did they know where we were? What do we do now, Henry?"

"We light a fire, drink whiskey, eat something, and talk, Louie. Are you sure it wasn't Corcoran you shot? He's not putting me in prison. Ain't goin' back, ever."

"It wasn't. It was that big Italian miner, Bono. Hope I killed him." They nursed a good fire and got a pot of coffee boiling, passing a bottle back and forth. "Snow won't let them follow us into the canyon, Henry, so we can relax a little bit. I still don't know how Corcoran knew we would be at that stream crossing. How did he know we were planning to hit the payroll wagon?"

"Don't matter none, Louie. Next time we meet he dies. It's that simple. We got to get word to the men coming in that we can't meet them in town. How the hell are we going to do that?"

"Hell, Henry, we don't even know who's coming. Only person we can half way trust in that town is Fingers O'Callaghan and I'm not that sure about him. Other than the three of us, he's the only person who might have known about our plans to rob the payroll wagon. Shorty might have said something when he was in town."

"Damn fool, Shorty. He's probably dead now. One of us has to get to town, Louie, and it ain't gonna be me. I want you to find Fingers and when our boys get here, you bring 'em out here."

"Just like that, eh? You lookin' to get rid of me and just ride off?" Hernandez was bigger than Henry Storm but Storm was a better shootist and the two stood in their cabin, warmed by the fire, playing out a difficult hand.

"Easy, Louie, I ain't planning on nothing but robbing that bank and killing Corcoran. We can't both go and I'm too well known. Somebody would shoot me on sight just for the reward. You can get to Fingers, I know you can. We got to be able to get those boys coming in to help us."

Louie took the bait. "You really think I can? Not gonna be easy, for sure. If I find out you've run off, Henry, I'll hunt you down like a dirty dog. I'll leave out first thing in the morning."

Snow fell all day and well into the night, leaving a foot-deep blanket at the hideout and well over six inches on the valley floor. Corcoran and Dean Miller walked from the office to the Grand Hotel down an empty and cold Main Street. "Don't look like a joyous celebration of winter, Mr. Miller."

"No, it don't." Miller snorted, kicked some snow, and had to chuckle. "What did the doc say when you dropped Bono off? He lost a lot of blood, that's for sure."

"He'll be fine. No broken bones but he'll need some time to get his strength back. When I went back Bones said that Johnson's wound ain't healing properly. Infection, maybe even gangrene setting in. We're not going to get any help from him. I'm not going to like what Johnson's going to say."

"The sheriff? Why would he be upset? The payroll is safe and Shorty Whipple is dead."

"Mark my words, Dean, he'll say I should have left Bono and chased after Henry Storm. You wait. That's exactly what he'll say."

"I've heard he can be an ass but leave your partner to bleed to death? I hope he doesn't say anything like that. Maybe I was wrong taking this badge."

"You weren't wrong, Mr. Miller, he is."

The hotel lobby was warm and Corcoran and Miller made a slow climb to the second floor and their meeting with Sheriff Avery Johnson. "Feeling better, Sheriff? Hell of a storm out there." Corcoran shook himself out of his buffalo robe coat and walked to the bed. "Got some good news and some bad."

"I heard that Shorty Whipple was shot dead. That's good. Put his body on display so the whole town can see what we do to outlaws in this county. Put it, naked, on a plank so people can see the death wound.

"Now, what's the bad news?"

"Ain't gonna do that, Sheriff. Ain't right to do that. We jumped the gang and chased Storm and Hernandez, got in a gunfight, but Tomaso was shot bad in the leg. Almost bled to death right there. I got him back to town and he's at the doc's now."

"Meanin' that you lost 'em. Damn, aren't there any decent lawmen left in this state?" Corcoran and Dean Miller stiffened up and Miller saw Corcoran's jaw muscles get so tight he knew there would be broken teeth.

One more comment like that and I'll put six holes in your head, Johnson. Corcoran's eyes were narrowed, his whole frame stiff as a steel rod. *Can't imagine a sheriff saying that to someone come to help. Might just head back to Eureka, but that would leave Bono and Miller alone. Damn, he is one fool.*

"Don't believe in desecrating bodies, Sheriff, even if they are wanted outlaws. I rode in from Eureka County to help catch this outlaw, not run a circus. Don't much care for your comment, either."

"You get that body on display, Corcoran. Miller, you kill Henry Storm and anyone who is with him."

"Ain't gonna happen, Sheriff, and you ain't in any condition to tell anyone what to do." Corcoran stood over Johnson, glaring down at the big man. "You're a helpless old man, Johnson, and we'll get this gang behind bars or dead but we won't desecrate a man's body doing it. Come on, Dean. We got work to do."

Corcoran hefted his heavy coat and walked toward the door, Dean Miller right behind. Johnson was sputtering, howling obscenities, even tried to throw his coffee cup at the two. "You stop right there."

Corcoran stopped and turned slowly to face the angry sheriff. "I came to Ward on a request for help, Sheriff. You're out of the picture, your resident deputy is wounded, and you've got a murderous gang raising more hell than you've seen. You got nothing to say that I want to hear. You asked for help and I rode in. I asked for help and you said no. You say the wrong thing and I ride off. You got that? Have a good day, Sheriff."

Corcoran slammed the door leaving and then smiled. *Maybe a bit childish there, Terrence, old boy.*

"What do we do now?" Dean Miller asked.

"First, we find Fingers O'Callaghan then Stephen Poindexter."

"Why Fingers?"

"White Pine County officials need to know their sheriff is out of commission as does the sheriff's office in Hamilton. Poindexter needs to know about Shorty and Bono. Right now, Dean, you're the only law in Ward. I'm a guest and Bono's wounded."

Dean Miller shook his head as they walked out onto the street. *Just a few days ago I was working a bar and now I'm the law in Ward? Those boys down in Pioche would get a kick out of this. Lordy, life is a grand show if you have time to watch it.*

They found Fingers at his office and Corcoran wrote out the messages that needed to be sent. "You given any more thought to our last conversation, Mr. O'Callaghan? Any information you'd like to pass on to us?"

"I don't have any information. I don't know that gang. I can't help you." Corcoran could see the nervous man almost sinking behind his counter. Louie Hernandez was standing behind the door that opened to Fingers' sleeping room. One mistake, Fingers thought, and everybody would die.

"Get these sent then, but don't let me find out anything different than what you just told me. I'm not a friendly person when I've been lied to."

Miller and Corcoran could both read fear in

Fingers as he took the notes. "If there are responses to these, get them to the sheriff's office right away. Let's go, Mr. Miller."

Fingers took the messages and started keying in the words as fast as he could go, praying that Hernandez wouldn't step through the door, praying that if he did, he would be the one to survive. He hadn't taken a breath for some time and didn't until he heard the outside door close.

"That old boy's scared of something, Corcoran." Dean Miller looked back toward the office. "He's being threatened."

"He is, Miller. By me and probably by Henry Storm, too. He's a weasel, Miller. A blood sucker who will work for whoever has the money or take it from both sides. It gets awkward when both sides are angry at him."

"Poindexter should be in the restaurant. I know I could use something hot in my belly. I was pretty high bringing Shorty's body into town yesterday but I wouldn't want to be the one to put him on display. That ain't right. That's something they do in them traveling shows."

"It ain't." Corcoran led them into the dining room, spotted the banker and his wife and walked up to the table.

"Morning, Corcoran, Miller. Join us, please. I understand you have some good news and some bad. Mr. White should be pleased."

"The payroll made it through with very little trouble. Can't say the same thing about us, though. We caught up with Storm and Hernandez but Tomaso Bono took a bullet to the leg and we came close to losing him. Did lose the outlaws."

Mary-Anne Poindexter almost jumped to her feet. "Oh, no," she cried out. "Mr. Bono," she stammered. "Is he going to live?" Mary-Anne's eyes were wide and she held her napkin in a tight fist. "He was shot? That's horrible." Her reaction startled Corcoran.

"The doctor thinks he'll be up and about soon, Mrs. Poindexter. He's a big strong man." Corcoran turned his attention to the banker but couldn't get her reaction out of his mind. *She's showing the kind of concern a woman would show for someone close to them. What am I seeing?*

"Storm is down to just he and Louie Hernandez so, for the time being, he won't be any kind of threat." Corcoran sat back, looking at the banker, thinking about Mary-Anne and Tomaso. "Storm has some kind of relationship with the telegraph operator, though, and could have sent out for help. Mr. Miller and I will keep a close eye on things."

"Good. Keep me informed. Well, my dear, shall we?" He got out of his chair, Corcoran held the chair for Mary-Anne and got a big smile for the effort, and the two left the café.

"Breakfast time," Corcoran laughed, sitting down. *I don't think I understand that woman at all. Was she flirting? Right in front of her husband? All the while having an affair with Bono? I'm not having any of it. Ain't my style.* "I'm going to ride back out to where we jumped the outlaws and see if there's anything to follow. Might even get lucky and stumble into their lair."

"I'd sure like to ride with you," Miller said.

"No, somebody has to stay in town and that will be you. You have a good handle on this old camp, know just about everyone. Watch for strangers who might also be outlaws, keep an eye on Fingers, and arrest anyone you want."

They were in the middle of their breakfast when Geno Oliveira and Marty Rosso from the White Mine came in. "Skeets said we'd find you here, Dean." Rosso was a big man while Oliveira was tall and skinny. "Mr. White said Tomaso wanted us to work with him as deputies."

"I'm Terrence Corcoran, gentlemen. Join us please. Resident Deputy Bono took a round in the leg yesterday while we were chasing Henry Storm, otherwise he would be here. We sure could use your help in rounding up this gang."

Corcoran spent the next several minutes outlining what had happened and what he hoped would happen. "Henry Storm is a killer, not very smart, but determined. He had a five man gang when he attacked the gold shipment, a three member gang when he looked to attack the mine payroll and, now, it's just he and Louie Hernandez."

Corcoran chuckled when both Rosso and Oliveira pumped their fists. "We think he uses Fingers O'Callaghan to get information and has probably sent wires looking for help. If he gets help, his first job will be Poindexter's bank. This will be far more dangerous than what you've been doing, so you need to tell me you're in."

"Mr. White laid it on the line for us, Corcoran. I'm in," Geno Oliveira said.

"Count me in. I ain't never shot nobody," Rosso said, "but it would be a pleasure if Henry Storm was the first."

"Good," Corcoran said. "Dean, why don't you and Geno spend the day together here in Ward. Walk around, have a beer at the Silver Springs Saloon, be seen and look for strangers. Marty, why don't you ride with me to see if we can ferret out where Storm's hideout is. You just might get your wish." He remembered what Bono had told him earlier.

"You two are White Pine County Deputies. If you see a criminal, arrest him. You are not observers."

"We got that, Corcoran. It was my mistake and it won't happen again." Geno Oliveira said. "It won't." Oliveira stood up and walked around the table for a moment. "What would be proper if we run into one of Storm's men?"

That's a fair question," Corcoran said. "I would draw my weapon and place them under arrest. Always be aware of your surroundings. Is there more than one? Do they have friends nearby? Are you backed up? Lot's to think of in this business. Sometimes it's best to walk out, get backup before you make your play."

"Sure as all hell, Corcoran, I won't make that mistake again." Geno Oliveira sat down and tried to smile.

CHAPTER THIRTEEN

"Got my message, I see," Elmer Kelly said. "Glad you could come. Seems ol' Henry Storm's got himself a hand full of trouble. Might be some good money in this." Kelly dressed as a town dandy but was deadly with a gun or knife. He was a gambler in every sense of the word, cards, dice, and mostly, scams aimed at those who weren't gamblers.

He made most of his money as a thief and bilker of rich old ladies. He was thin, balding, wore an expertly trimmed beard, which was just as blonde as the few hairs on his head. His blue eyes only sparkled when he was killing someone or taking something. Slick and fast with words, knives, and guns.

"Haven't seen that shark since he got out of Carson prison. I need a good money job, Kelly. Things have been tight. Too many badge carrying saints in this world." Jack Mason was nearing fifty, over-weight, and in need of a bath and haircut. "Where we heading and what are we riding into?"

"Henry's down in Ward, a snarly little mining camp with a big bank, he says. He's short of men and is offering equal shares."

"Didn't Ornery Jake Johnson ride with him? And Shorty Whipple?"

"Yup, they did. Dead now, he says. So is Pete Cameron."

"Maybe we might want to ponder on this, Elmer," Mason said. "Lost his whole gang and he says the bank is an easy job? Sounds like someone's pounding sand to me. Hernandez still with him?"

"Louie is his gang," Elmer Kelly laughed. "You and me can ride in and take that bank, shoot Henry Storm and Louie Hernandez, and ride on."

"I need a good paying job right now. How far is Ward? I know it's south but that's all I know."

"It'll take us two, maybe three days of hard riding. Supposed to find a telegraph operator named Fingers to lead us to Storm. I've got us a mule and provisions, Jack. A bank full of money in a little mining camp many miles from any big town means there ain't much chance of finding some trigger happy lawman or two either."

"All right, Elmer, I'm in. I've really been down. Ain't even got a rifle, had to sell my good one, and bullets, too. You stake me?"

"I'd stake you any time, Jack Mason. We'll leave out at first light." *Wonder what he did to get his self beat down this low? Man can find an ace in five card anytime he needs one, can outshoot most anybody I know. Must have met a pretty girl.* Kelly chuckled thinking about it. *I chase ugly old women with pots full of money, he chases young ones looking for his pot full of money. I like my style better.*

"Those two had a pretty good little ambush spot, Corcoran." Marty Rosso was looking at the remains of the fire the outlaws had under the rock overhang. "Good vision all the way around."

"Vision was hampered some by the snow and wind, but not enough," Corcoran said. "When Bono tripped, Hernandez spotted him immediately. Two shots and they raced for their horses. If we can find where they were tied, there might be enough sign left to give us an idea of where their hideout is."

They were making their way through at least a foot of fresh snow and could not find any kind of sign. Wind and new snow had obliterated everything. "If we can't find a boot print we'll never find horse prints. Wherever they ran, I know it's south of here and that's all I know. Second time Storm's gotten away because of the weather. How long you been around this country?"

"Been here three years, Corcoran. White's mine only has a couple of years left in it but I'm staying when he closes. Got a place couple hundred acres north of where we are that will be filled with fat cows when the mine closes. It's near the ovens."

"Ovens?" Corcoran had a crooked smile on his face. "Ovens? What kind of ovens?"

"Before we had access to coal for the ore reduction fires, the mine used charcoal. The big ovens where they made the charcoal are about five miles or so north of us. The whole mountainside is stripped of trees that they turned into charcoal. Hell of a thing to see."

"Maybe I'll see it someday. Right now, let's work our way south and see what we can find. If Henry sent out for help, they'll have to find their way to his hideout. Me and Bono think that Fingers will either lead them or give 'em directions. Either way, there will be prints of some kind."

"Bono's gonna be all right?"

"Doc says so. No broken bones just tore up meat. He's tough. He'll be in the office in a day or two but can't ride. He'll drive old Skeets nuts."

"This is a beautiful valley with the Schell Creek Range to our east and the Egan Range on our west, Corcoran. There are hundreds of large and small canyons one could make into a hideout. Hell, a fortress. Peaks are well over ten thousand feet and most of the canyons have running water year round."

"You ain't helping any," Corcoran said. "Makin' it sound like we ain't gonna find the man. Got any ideas? He's got to be close. Within ten or so miles of Ward. They were at that creek crossing early in the morning meaning they didn't have too far to ride for their ambush."

Corcoran was frustrated not knowing the country like he knew his home country in the Diamond Valley and Diamond Range. "I want to depend on your knowledge of these mountains, Marty. Where would you hide if someone wanted to kill you?"

"Right up there," he said. He was pointing at a long and deep canyon that seemed to disappear into the clouds. "That grand cleft in these mountains has half a dozen canyons leading up the deeper in you get. I could hide in there for years. Good grass, good water, plenty of firewood. Could even live off the wildlife if you had to. If he's in there, you'd have to trail him in to find him. Too many places to hide."

"Even with winter coming on?"

"Probably taken over a line shack. Good cattle country, this valley, and those mountains are summer range. Buckaroo line camps have bunks and stoves, Corcoran."

"In every range in Nevada, Rosso. No known roads or trails in and out?" Marty shook his head and Corcoran continued. "You're right, we'll have to hope we can trail someone in. Let's head back to town. Need a cold beer or something stronger to get my thoughts in order."

Dean Miller, Skeets McDougall, and Geno Oliveira were drinking coffee and playing five card when Corcoran and Marty Rosso walked in. "Got a wire for you, Corcoran. From the White Pine County Commission. They're hot."

"Just exactly what I need," Corcoran said. He took the note and poured some coffee. "Anybody got a flask?" After reading the note, Corcoran looked around the room, smiled slightly, and got up, reaching for his buffalo robe coat. "Sheriff needs me, boys. I'll be back."

"Interesting," Dean said. "I thought he was going to shoot the sheriff earlier today. Johnson is a hard-nosed sumbitch and so is Corcoran. Wish I knew what that note said."

It was a short walk to the Grand Hotel and Corcoran took his time getting there. *I guess when the banker wants something done, it gets done. Interesting that Poindexter never said anything to me about this. This note will be in the hands of Henry Storm before it reaches the sheriff.*

"I have a wire here from the White Pine County Commission, Sheriff. It was addressed to me but it is for you." Corcoran was interrupting the work of Doctor McFadden but knew the message was important. "That infection healing up, is it?"

"Just give me the wire, Corcoran," Avery Johnson snapped. He read it twice before he said anything. "Poindexter threatened me before, Corcoran. I'm the elected sheriff of White Pine County. I don't serve at the pleasure of the county commission." He handed the note back. "Read it out loud, see if it sounds different."

Corcoran glanced at Bones and got a slight smile from the man. "It's addressed to me and reads, 'With Sheriff Johnson unable to perform his duties because of his wounds, White Pine County would be pleased if you would take the position of sheriff.'" Corcoran paused and looked at Johnson. "Ain't right, Avery, and you know it. The note goes on with a message for you."

"That's what's strange, Corcoran. Poindexter knows the county commission can't remove the elected sheriff, knows you can't simply be appointed sheriff. If this is a power play, he just fell on his face. What's your call on it?" Corcoran noticed the change in attitude and almost smiled.

Corcoran sat down next to the bed. "You and I ain't had the best working relationship over the years. I don't much care for some of your methods, you probably feel the same about me and mine, but I don't think they can do this."

"No, they can't," Johnson snarled. "I'm the sheriff and will be until the next election. Maybe even after. You staying on?"

"Yup. Don't believe in leaving a job half done." Corcoran reached in the pocket of his coat and found a flask. "Join me, Sheriff? I'm sure that Henry Storm has sent for help. He ain't the kind of man to take kindly to losing his men. He would consider it a personal affront."

Corcoran passed the flask to Johnson and continued. "Mr. Bono will be good for office and around town but his leg won't let him ride a horse for a while. Mr. White has loaned us two of his security people and Dean Miller is working out fine."

Corcoran took a long breath, knew what he had to say and remembered how it was accepted the last time. "Maybe you can explain to me why you can't assign a couple of your deputies in Hamilton. You've said no but not why. I think I deserve to know why."

Corcoran reached for the flask but Bones McFadden grabbed it first. "There are three of us in the room, you know. As far as Tomaso Bono goes, that wound is on the inside of his thigh and he won't be able to sit a horse for some time to come. Other than that, he's fit to come back to work. Don't expect him to run fast." He passed the flask, all but empty now, back to Corcoran.

"What about me, Bones? When can I start moving around? This is driving me nuts." Johnson had been on his stomach for almost two weeks and Bones was sympathetic, to a degree.

"We're making good progress on the infection, Sheriff. If you keep breaking the wound open it will keep getting infected. If you stay laid out on your belly you'll heal up." McFadden found his coat and headed for the door. "We'll have another session later. Don't be moving around."

"Yeah, yeah, yeah," Johnson said. "Do you think Poindexter is behind that note? Bastard threatened to stop supporting me."

"That's what the note says. He hasn't said a word to me, though. Do you have any idea who Storm might have sent messages to? It would be nice to know who might be coming into town, who to look for."

"He's got contacts in Elko County, up in Boise, even in Virginia City. Just have eyes on the streets. Something Bono would be able to do."

"You haven't answered my question, Sheriff."

"The answer is in that wire, Corcoran. There's a faction that's been working hard to sully my reputation. I need those deputies to keep a lid on that."

"Politics? You're jeopardizing the bank's money, our lives, because of politics? Maybe I understand Poindexter's position, maybe I understand why he sent a wire to the county commission." Corcoran was usually good at holding his anger, but he was about to lose control and knew he had to get out of that room. "I'll do what I can to keep you posted, Sheriff. You going to answer that wire?"

"You bet I am. There's more, Corcoran. Commissioner Kleindorfer may be involved in a mining scam and I'm reasonably sure that he has some well-heeled help. Lots of money behind the scam. That's why they want me out of office."

"Why don't you pay a visit to our banker friend

and see if he will come clean about being behind the wire. If it wasn't he, it would have to be Clive Kleindorfer. He's been against everything I've tried to do since this county was formed."

"I know the name," Corcoran said. "Monied rancher. He sits on the commission? Man's as much outlaw as you can get and still walk free. Think he's just using Poindexter's name?" Corcoran asked.

"Wouldn't put it past him. Maybe even getting his help. Talk to the banker. Keep under your hat, though, about an investigation into mine claim fraud. The conspiracy runs deep and only the state's AG and my office know about it."

Corcoran left with more questions than answers. *A crooked rancher sits on the county commission and is looking to oust the sheriff while the sheriff is out of town doing county business. The sheriff is investigating a mining scam that might be the work of the commissioner. Maybe I was too fast. Maybe it isn't just politics. Kleindorfer's looking to make things easier for him and his band of outlaws. Why would Poindexter help him unless he's involved?*

CHAPTER FOURTEEN

Kelly and Mason were hunkered down under a rock overhang, nursing a fire to life as the sun blasted its way onto the scene. Looking down a long brush-filled slope they could make out the mining camp of Ward, out in the flat of the valley. On a cold fall morning, the town was covered in blue wood-fire smoke. "Make it about eight miles or so, Mason. Get some coffee and side meat in us and we can ride right on in."

"How do we find Henry? He surely ain't staying right in town. Wouldn't put it past him, though."

Strips of side meat were frying in their own fat, coffee was boiling, and biscuits were broken up to be softened in the grease or coffee. "Supposed to find a man called Fingers. He's the telegraph operator. Fella that sent the message to me. He'll know where to send us. Give us a chance to look over that bank while we hunt for him."

"Always thought banks were a three-man job. Two inside and one outside keeping the yokels quiet. Shoot a nosy storekeeper and the rest stay inside is what I say. Worked in Abilene, worked in Waco, didn't it? Well, didn't it?"

"You're right, Jack," Elmer Kelly said. "It sure did. It'll work in Ward, too. It's after we have the money and gold, that we kill Storm and Hernandez. That makes our split even better." Laughter, hot meat, hot coffee, and Kelly and Mason enjoyed their sunrise.

The ride down the long slope and into the rich valley was slow as they fought snow in places and mud in others. It was well past mid-morning when they rode into town. "That's a mighty fancy hotel with a mighty fancy name," Mason said. "The Grand Hotel? The one across the street, the Silver Springs is more to my liking."

"The rooms there are for the women, Jack. You rent the women, not the rooms." They both laughed at Kelly's comment. "Look at that. The bank is right across the street. I think we need a drink at the Silver Springs Saloon my friend. Check out the local scene."

"I am checking out the local scene, Kelly. Will you look at that? The last time I saw a woman that beautiful was in New Orleans, twenty years ago." Jack Mason watched Mary-Anne Poindexter walk out of the Grand Hotel. "My god, Kelly, that's what I call a woman." Kelly took a quick look and turned away.

"What's the matter with you? I could spend many nights with a lady like that."

"That's your problem, Mr. Mason. Neither one of us could afford a woman like that. That's not class, Jack, that's wealth."

Mason nodded. He never had wealth, always craved it, but it was beautiful, young, willing women that motivated the man. After every job he'd ever been on, he splurged at the local houses, pleasuring until the gold ran out.

"That's why I rob banks, Kelly. So I can afford a woman like that." Jack Mason watched Mary-Anne as she walked all the way to the corner. The desire would have been obvious to anyone looking into the outlaw's face.

"I wonder where the telegraph office is?" Elmer Kelly needed to change the subject before Mason did something really wrong.

"I guess the barman will know. I'd just as soon find a room, Kelly. Gettin' long in the tooth for camping in the snow and ice."

"We can get both answers inside, Jack." They tied

their horses and the mule and walked into the Silver Springs. There were a couple of ranch hands and a few miners at the bar. Most turned when they came in. Some serious card players were at the faro table, serious enough they never even looked up when Kelly and Mason walked in.

"Gents?" The barman said. He looked quickly down the bar to a skinny man sipping a beer. "What'll you have?"

"Need a couple of shots each of whiskey and a few questions answered," Elmer Kelly said. "Is there a telegraph office in town. Need to send a couple of wires. And, other than that fancy hotel across the street, where could we find rooms?"

The barman reached for a bottle and nodded to the man at the end of the bar. "We've got a room upstairs we let out from time to time. The other rooms are for the girls." He poured generous glasses full and moved down the bar.

"Didn't say anything about the telegraph office," Jack Mason said. He started to wave the barman back but saw the thin man from the end of the bar approaching.

"Help you gents with a wire? Name's Fingers O'Callaghan."

"As a matter of fact, you can," Kelly said.

"Finish your drinks and we'll walk over to the office. Looks like you boys have been on the trail for a spell. Whiskey will warm you up some."

Corcoran walked out of the Grand in time to watch Kelly and Mason ride by. *Timing, Terrence me lad. Everything's in the timing. Are those two prospectors? No, they are not. Mule is packed for a long ride not for scratching at rocks.* He watched them tie off and walk into the Silver Springs Saloon. Corcoran walked across the street and into the bank.

"Need something, Corcoran?" Poindexter called out from his office. "I'm a little busy."

"Just gonna stand here and watch the doors of the Silver Springs. A couple of drifters just rode in. You a bettin' man, Mr. Poindexter? I've got a double eagle says they will walk out and head for the telegraph office."

"Won't take that kind of bet, sir. Let me know what you see. Speaking of seeing, night barman at the Grand told me that Louie Hernandez was seen in town earlier this morning. You heard anything about that?"

"Nope. I'll check it out." He sucked in his breath and a smile crossed his rugged face. "Well now, we hit a royal flush. Fingers O'Callaghan is taking our drifters to the telegraph office. Bye for now." Corcoran was chuckling softly as he slipped out the doors and made for the sheriff's office.

It took just a few minutes to make the two-block walk. "Will they get directions and light out or will Fingers take them? Maybe that's why Hernandez is in town if he really is." Corcoran mumbled the whole two blocks and was still talking when he walked into the office.

"Dean, saddle your horse. Oliveira, get your horse and go down to the Silver Springs Saloon. There's a pair of horses and a pack mule out front. Follow whoever leaves out with them. You'll have company. Rosso, go to Bone's place and get Bono. You and Bono scour this town and find Louie Hernandez."

"What about me?" Skeets McDougall sat at the desk looking left out.

"Arrest anybody does something wrong," Corcoran laughed. "Keep the town safe, Skeets." Corcoran grabbed his rifle and headed out the door. "We ain't got a lot of time, gents, let's move."

The four men sprinted to the stables to saddle up and Corcoran told them about the drifters, Fingers, and Hernandez possibly being seen. "The break we've needed, I hope," he said. "What we want to do is follow, let them lead us to Henry Storm. Even if Hernandez is with them, let them lead us in to that hideout."

Oliviera lit out alone, down Main Street to watch the outlaw's horses and mule while Marty Rosso headed for Bone's office. Corcoran led Dean Miller out of the corrals and moved off Main and took Alpine Street south to Third Street. They could see the telegraph office half a block behind the Silver Springs Saloon but were not obvious to those on Main Street.

"It's been less than half an hour since Fingers left with those two," Corcoran said. "It should get interesting soon."

"Take the main road south about six miles, Kelly," Fingers said. He was holding a rough map that Henry Storm had drawn. "You'll come to a fork in the road, take the right side, and when you get to this stand of cottonwoods, ride toward the wide canyon. It will be wider than any others you can see. Just ride right straight in and either Henry or Hernandez will pick you up."

"Must be more than one stand of cottonwoods after the fork, Fingers. How would we know which one?" Kelly wasn't pleased with what he was hearing. "Why don't you just lead us? You said Henry can't come in to get us but you could lead us. Are we riding into some kind of trap?"

"There are five cottonwoods in that grove. It's the only grove on the road with five trees. You can't miss it. There's a deputy called Corcoran who's been keeping too close an eye on me, Kelly. He'd follow or shoot me if I tried to lead you out. Just ride out slow and easy and no one will pay any attention. Prospectors and drifters come through town all the time."

"You sure we won't be followed?"

"No reason for you to be," Fingers said. "When you leave here, slip in the back door of the Silver Springs Saloon, just walk right out the front doors, mount up, and ride off."

Elmer Kelly and Jack Mason left the telegraph office, went through the saloon, and untied their mounts and the mule. "Don't like this at all, Jack. We gotta keep a close eye on our backs riding out of here. We'll be riding through country we've never seen before looking for a stand of five, not six or seven, but five cottonwood trees. Any fool could follow us."

It was a slow ride out of town and Jack Mason spent a lot of the time trying to see if someone might be following. "Don't be so obvious," Kelly said. They were out of town and on the road south for more than fifteen minutes before Mason calmed down.

"How much money did Henry say we would be getting, Jack? I've got a tornado working in my gut right now, telling me this is a dead end for me. I don't think I should have come."

"All Henry said was the bank was rich and it would be equal shares. I've been keeping an eye out behind us and haven't seen a thing. Let's at least hear Storm out before we decide. I didn't feel comfortable with that greasy little Fingers fellow. He ain't right."

When they came to the fork in the road, the right side trail was far less traveled than the left and their horse prints stood out in the mud. "Ain't nobody been on this road since the storm, Kelly. A blind man could follow us."

"I agree. We'll ride to the five cottonwood trees and make a decision." He looked to the west, to the towering Egan Range and saw what he supposed would be the wide and deep canyon they were to ride to, many miles out. "Must be Henry's canyon," he said. He pointed it out to Mason. "Looks to have half a dozen canyons of its own and has to be ten miles or more deep."

Oliveira waited several minutes before riding out of Ward behind Kelly and Mason. He was never able to see them but with the road covered in mud and stale snow, he had no trouble picking out their trail. "Corcoran said I'd have company. Hope that means him and Dean Miller."

When he got to the fork in the road he had to smile seeing how the outlaw's prints stood out on the seldom-used roadway. A movement behind him made him turn and he spotted two riders coming along at a trot. "That's Corcoran and Miller for sure," he muttered.

"Anything going on?" Corcoran rode up alongside Oliveira. "They sure ain't trying to hide their trail."

"They seem to know where they're going but aren't in any hurry to get there." Geno said. "Haven't changed from a walk since leaving town. There ain't nothing out this way that I know of except a ranch or two. If they're heading for that big canyon we talked about, they gotta turn west soon. That's it over there." He pointed west.

"They haven't met up with anyone according to their prints so Fingers must have given 'em a map or good direction. Keep a sharp eye out, boys, we don't want to be seen."

They rode over a high fold in the rolling plain

and saw two horsemen under a stand of cotton-wood trees half a mile ahead of them. Corcoran turned around fast followed by the others. "Hope we weren't seen. Damn." He stepped down from Dude and handed the reins to Oliveira. "Gotta have a quick look-see."

He edged his way to the top of the knoll, staying well to the right of the trail and keeping as low as possible. At the crest of the rise, he was able to see the two men apparently in a discussion about something. "Looks like they're arguing about something," Corcoran yelled down to the others. He saw the two men mount back up and ride off cross country to the east.

"Well now. They're riding east, boys, not west. Let's see if we can find out why." He ran back down the hill and jumped in the saddle. "They'll connect with the main road to Pioche going that way. Don't make any sense at all. Let's ride back to the fork and turn south there."

"What's your plan?" Miller asked. "Can't arrest them. Ain't done nothing wrong that I can tell."

"Let's hightail it back to the fork and turn south at an easy walk. Say how-do if they ride up on us. If they don't, if they turn south instead of back to Ward, we'll follow along." Corcoran chuckled and led off at a strong trot, making it to the fork in quick time. "Just a nice little ride now boys."

Louie Hernandez rode slowly into Ward, staying off the major streets and tucked his horse in a stand of trees near a neighborhood well. "Second time in in two days. Sure as hell I'm gonna get seen. Three blocks to Fingers' office. Hope that weasel has some information for us. This will be my last job with Henry Storm. Too reckless, too many mistakes."

A cold wind blew down from the Egan range and whistled through the streets of the mining camp as Louie made it slowly from building to building. Few people were out and those who were didn't pay any attention to the large Mexican huddling under his heavy coat, much the same as they were doing. Hernandez found the door open to the telegraph office and stepped in.

Fingers was adding wood to the pot belly stove and Hernandez got as close as he dared. "Cold, Fingers. It was a cold ride in."

"Damn, Louie, you startled me. Did you just run into two men? Kelly and Mason? They just left."

"Didn't see nobody. Elmer Kelly and Jack Mason? They're here? Good news. Which way did they go?"

"Their horses are in front of the Silver Springs

Saloon. I gave them directions to the canyon. If you hurry you can catch them. They're on the south road, the one Henry wanted me to send them on, not the trail you use."

Hernandez hurried as best he could back to his horse and rode south. He was about to join the main road and spotted Corcoran, Miller, and Rosso riding out. "Ten seconds earlier and I'd be one dead bandito right now," Louie chuckled. He watched them ride out and knew they were following Kelly and Mason.

"Not hitting that bank any time soon, I'm afraid," Hernandez muttered. He waited a full ten minutes before riding out of the shadows and onto the roadway. He made his way to a single track trail he and Henry used to move back and forth to the canyon hideout before putting his horse in a hard run.

Corcoran and the others only had to ride another mile or so south and saw Kelly and Mason coming toward them, also at a walk. The two outlaws spotted the three riders and pulled up short. "Damn," Kelly said. "Well, we can't run, not with all our gear on the mule. Let's just say hello and keep going."

"I see badges, Kelly. Suppose that greasy little wire operator gave us up? I got no paper out on me, how about you?"

"None that I know about," Kelly said. "We'll hear 'em out and keep going. I'm heading for Elko. Join me?"

"As broke as I am, I guess I have to. What if they get pushy? I ain't going to jail, Kelly. I ain't."

"Stay loose, Jack. Let me do the talking. Just go along with whatever I say." He paused. "Or do."

The two groups came together and Corcoran spoke first. "Morning, boys. Doing a little sightseeing are you? It's a little cold for that, isn't it?"

"Prospecting some," Elmer Kelly said. "Don't look like good country, though. Might head back to Elko."

"Might be a good idea," Corcoran said. "Name's Corcoran, Deputy Sheriff Terrence Corcoran. What's yours?"

"I'm Kelly," Elmer said. "That's Mason. Well, we'll be movin' on."

"How about you tell me about your visit with Fingers O'Callaghan? Get your wire sent off or did you pick up some information?"

"Don't know what you're talking about," Mason snapped.

Corcoran's rifle swung out in a long arc and knocked Mason right out of the saddle. Kelly was fast but Geno Oliviero was anticipating some kind of move and had his Colt pointed at Kelly's nose before the outlaw cleared leather.

"Well now." Corcoran stepped down from his saddle and pulled Mason to his feet. "Don't much care for liars, Mr. Mason."

Mason's head was bleeding freely and he was having trouble focusing on the big lawman who had a strong grip on his arm. "Would you be Jack Mason? The same Jack Mason who tried to run a crooked faro table up in Winnemucca a couple of years ago? Again, what were you doing at Fingers' place?"

Dean Miller had Elmer Kelly off his horse and in cuffs after taking his sidearm and rifle. "This then would be Elmer Kelly. Run out of Pioche not too long ago. You boys looking to tie up with Henry Storm, are you?"

Neither man said a word and Corcoran cuffed Mason and got the outlaws back on their horses. "Won't talk to us, eh? And us being so friendly and all. Skeets McDougall will be glad to have your company and the circuit judge will be through sometime next week, I think. Or the week after. I lose track, sometimes." Corcoran was having fun, laughing, joshing the boys, as they rode back toward Ward. Neither man said a word.

CHAPTER FIFTEEN

"Where the hell have you been?" Henry Storm had a tin cup full of whiskey standing next to the wood stove. Just weeks ago he had a real gang, feared by many, and now it was just he and Hernandez. "You were supposed to come straight back."

"Couldn't. All hell's broke loose in town. Give me the bottle and I'll tell you all about it," Louie Hernandez said. He told about his meeting with Fingers and then seeing the posse ride out of town following Mason and Kelly. "I rode as fast as I dared, Henry, but Kelly could lead that posse straight here. We gotta get ready for that."

"No, Louie, we'll ride out to meet them. Are you sure it was Kelly and Mason? Sometimes, I don't trust Fingers."

"I never saw them, just what Fingers said. He

sent them south to the cottonwoods, so they'll be showing up here soon."

"Knock that fire down while I saddle up. We'll ride out to meet them and then take that posse straight on. Three of them, you said? Wipe out that Corcoran bastard and ride right into Ward and hit the bank." He laughed loud and long as he saddled up and the two rode out. "Kelly's a good man. Don't know too much about Mason."

"Mason's a card cheat, fair with a knife, but getting older," Louie said. "Kelly will make you think he's on your side but he ain't. He's only on his side. Only." They rode cross country for the next hour, looking in every direction for their compadres.

"We'll be at the cottonwoods soon, Henry. Ain't seen no kind of trail. Suppose they got into it with Corcoran? They would lose."

They rode up to the five trees and saw where Kelly and Mason turned toward the east. "They're runnin' out on us," Henry Storm said. "They give up."

"Let's follow and see for sure," Louie said. It was an easy trail through sage and other brush and they rode up on where the two groups met. "Trouble," Louie said. "Those boys are in jail, Henry. What do we do now?"

"Let 'em rot." Henry Storm held his anger as

best he could. "They run out on us and got caught. Serves 'em right."

"Might not have, Henry," Louie said. "What if they saw the posse and turned east rather than lead it to us. We need to break those boys out, hit the bank and get out of this country. Head east. Colorado maybe."

Louie Hernandez was not going to let all those pieces of gold sit in that bank any longer. Henry felt the same way and they drifted toward Ward, working on plans to break Kelly and Masson out of jail and rob the bank, too. "With four of us, we can take that bank for sure, Henry."

"Guests." Skeets was smiling as he jumped up from the chair he had near the wood stove. "Why, thank you, Terrence, Dean, and Marty. Somebody to talk to." He took the prisoners to the empty cells in the back. "Well, I got some stories to tell you boys. All right now, let's get them cuffs off." One at a time they backed up to the cell bars and put their hands through.

"You missed dinner. Supper's at six if Maisie remembers. Forgetful woman but a good cook if you like chicken stew."

Geno Oliveira and Tomaso Bono came in. "Whole

town's talking about you bringing in prisoners, Terrence," Bono said.

"Why don't you two gentlemen run down Fingers O'Callaghan and invite him in for a little talk. If Henry Storm was expecting these two, we might anticipate a visit, too. Storm is just stupid enough to try to break those two out."

"I saw Fingers at the Silver Springs Saloon when we walked by," Oliveira said.

"Poindexter told me earlier that someone may have seen Louie Hernandez in town, too," Corcoran said. "See if you can find out more on that."

"We asked around about that," Geno said. "A lovely little bar girl and hostess at the Silver Springs said to tell you hello, Corcoran. Mindy Shepherd said you helped her out of some trouble."

Corcoran chuckled, started to say something and thought better of it. *I better get back in that little bar. She was definitely worth standing up for. Might even know something about these crooks we're working to stop.*

The two deputies headed back out into a cold wind. "If Henry Storm tried to break those two gentlemen out of our comfortable little jail, how would he do it?" Corcoran poured some coffee and settled into the chair nearest the stove. "This building is made of rock."

"The building was built by one of White's mining crews and it is sturdy. Problem is in the windows and doors. The casements are the weak points." Marty Rosso opened the door and gave it a big shove and everyone saw the casement move. "Windows would pop right out if they were tied to a horse."

"Many people in town know that?" Corcoran tried to hold in a chuckle. "You put those two boys in the same cell, Skeets?"

"It's a standard joke around town that if someone was locked up for something serious, they could get out easy, and yes, they are together in cell number one. Want 'em separated?"

"I think it'd be best. Two men pushing on those weak casements, well, you get the picture. Go with him, Dean. Mason has a bad reputation for knives. We searched 'em good but you never know. Keep on your toes."

When they opened the door to the cell area they saw just empty cells. "They're gone," Dean Miller yelled out. "Whole damn window's gone."

Skeets headed for the cells but Corcoran and Rosso went out the front door and around to the back of the building to find the window casement and iron bars on the ground and prints in the mud leading to the stables, half a block away. The two large men were at a full run in half a second and were close to the open doors when Kelly and Mason rode out at a full gallop.

Corcoran was knocked down by Kelly's horse and Rosso had to jump out of the way of Mason's, falling in the mud. Corcoran tried to roll away from the jolt and was able to get his weapon out but didn't shoot because of people on the street.

"Horses," Corcoran yelled and the two raced inside for theirs. They had been anxious to get Mason and Kelly in jail and had tied their horses off instead of unsaddling them. That's how the outlaws were able to just jump in the saddle and run. Corcoran and Rosso were out the doors quickly and on the trail. "Heading south," Corcoran yelled back at Rosso, putting the spurs to Dude.

Kelly was a length in front of Mason as they cleared town, leaning out over his horse's neck, urging him on. They rode hard toward the fork and Kelly decided to take it, ride to the cottonwoods, and head for that canyon and maybe tie up with Henry Storm after all. They were unarmed, had no supplies other than what might be in their saddlebags, and had no other choice.

Two riders were coming north as they neared the

fork and Kelly spurred his horse hard making the turn to the right. Henry Storm recognized Kelly and he and Hernandez joined the chase, trying hard to get Kelly's attention. Kelly only saw more danger and forced his horse faster. It was Jack Mason who recognized Louie Hernandez and yelled at Kelly.

It took some time for all four horses to come down from the sprint they were running, and Kelly's eyes were wide with fright when he finally recognized Henry. "Thought you boys were in jail," Louie laughed.

"We gotta keep going," Kelly sputtered. "Broke out. They're coming."

"Follow us," Henry said. He turned and spurred his horse into a fast lope out across the wide valley and toward the Egan Range. "We'll leave a good trail to follow. Louie, give Kelly your sidearm and when we hit the big ravine up there, take a position and knock a couple of the posse off their horses with that fine rifle of yours. I'll give Mason my pistol and take the second ravine."

"Kelly, you and Mason just continue to ride hard for that big canyon right in front of us. We'll join you when we kill the posse." He laughed hard. "Then, boys, we rob a bank."

Oliveira and Bono watched Kelly and Mason ride out of town at a fast gallop as they walked out of the Silver Springs Saloon with Fingers O'Callaghan. "What the hell?" Bono said. It was just seconds later and Corcoran and Rosso hurtled by at breakneck speed.

"Get your horse and follow, Geno. I'll take Fingers in. Corcoran is gonna need some help, I think." Oliveira ran toward the stables and Bono, with a definite limp, urged Fingers toward the sheriff's office. "Give me the slightest reason and I'll shoot you dead, Fingers. Let's move."

"You got no call to arrest me. I ain't done nothin'. What's going on, anyway?"

"Move it or die, Fingers." All eyes were on Bono, weapon in hand, limping, escorting Fingers O'Callaghan to jail. It was a long walk on a cold day but Tomaso had a hard time keeping the grin off his ruddy face.

"Got some company for you, Skeets. How did Kelly and Mason get out?"

"We'll have to chain him to the bunk, Tomaso. Those two yahoos just pushed the window out. Nobody hurt yet, though. Looks like a job opening at the telegraph office. Might give up this badge and take that job."

CHAPTER SIXTEEN

Corcoran and Rosso hit the fork and had to stop and sort out the prints. "Those two met up with two others, Marty. They took off cross country, straight for the canyon. Can't be any other two than Storm and Hernandez. What are we looking at in this chase?" They were already in a lope and Marty Rosso told Corcoran how they would encounter two or three deep ravines and several bends and folds in the wide valley.

"It looks flat out there, Corcoran, but the ground rises and falls, rolls and bends, and there are gullies and ravines, often with running water,"

"Deep ravines? Ambush type trenches?" Corcoran asked and Rosso nodded. "Let's ride hard but keep well separated. If we are riding into an ambush, we'll make it hard for them."

Following the outlaws' trail was the easy part of the chase. Hurtling through heavy brush, mud, and shaded areas with ice and snow was not just difficult, it was dangerous. Corcoran was on Rosso's left when he felt a bullet tear through his buffalo robe coat. He dove from the saddle, hit the ground hard and laid still and quiet for just a few seconds, long enough for whoever did the shooting to think he was down and out.

Rosso saw Corcoran go down and jumped from his horse, rolling into a heavy stand of sage, rifle in hand. *Damn. No, Corcoran, no. Gettin' to like that man, too.* Marty saw a rifle barrel sticking up from the rim of the ravine and crawled toward it. *One dead outlaw hanging onto that rifle when I get there. You shot my new friend and I don't like that.*

He was about twenty yards from the edge of the deep arroyo when Hernandez poked his head up to take a quick look around. He had expected the second rider to race into the ravine. Rosso saw him and leveled the rifle, aimed, and squeezed the trigger, blowing mud, gravel, and ice into Hernandez' face.

The outlaw rolled down the side of the ravine, raced for his horse and rode like the wind a hundred yards down the gulch, up the other side, and west at a high gallop. Corcoran heard more than saw the action and made for Dude, yelling at Rosso to mount up.

"He's running, Marty. Let's go." Corcoran made the dash down, across and out of the arroyo and spotted Hernandez, already several hundred yards away, making for the canyon. Rosso fought to control his horse, mounted, and rode to join Corcoran. The ground was sloppy wet, the horses were tired, and Corcoran had to ease up some on the speed.

"Want to catch 'em, not kill ourselves," he chuckled. "Keep him in sight, Marty. You said there are several of those arroyos?"

"At least two more." *There's something for me to remember. Don't set yourself up for that second killing shot.* Rosso spotted movement off to the side." There's somebody coming up behind us, Terrence. Back at least half a mile. You shot?"

"Let's keep the chase up, Marty. Whoever it is will come after we kill the bastard that put a hole in my coat. Too close but didn't hit me. Just my coat." Corcoran spread the two of them out again as they rode hard. The distance between them and Hernandez was staying about the same.

"He just hit the next gulch," Rosso yelled out. "Not coming out the other side. Better find some good cover." He pointed at a small grove of cedar and rode for it. Bullets splashed the mud near his feet as he dove for cover.

That wasn't the rider I was chasing who just shot at me. Couldn't possibly have gotten off his horse and raced to the rim that fast. Rosso watched Corcoran move into some rocks twenty yards or so to his left. "There's a second man down there." He yelled it out as a shot whistled through the overhanging cedar branches.

Corcoran took that opportunity to race forward to a piñon and dive into the mud. He saw a rifle barrel, aimed and shot. The bullet smashed into the barrel and his shot was answered from a gun several yards to the right. The bullet hit the tree and Corcoran fired back, splashing mud.

He caught Rosso moving from his rocks and fired three shots toward where he thought the outlaws were, keeping their heads down. Rosso slipped into a dip in the ground and fired three shots too, giving Corcoran an opportunity to move forward several yards. "Looks like we got company coming," Rosso yelled.

Corcoran saw Geno Oliveira dismount and move quickly through the brush toward his position. He turned and fired several times as did Rosso, allowing Oliveira to come at a run. "Glad to have you with us," Corcoran said. "Got two men with rifles trying to do us in, old man."

"Saw everyone racing out of town and always like a good party. Tomaso has Fingers at the jail. Who you got down there?"

"Could be Henry Storm, could be Elmer Kelly. Don't know for sure." Corcoran had his rifle reloaded again. "I'll put some shots at 'em and you move up to that brush over there. Then you shoot some and I'll move up. They ain't fired at us for several minutes now. Don't know if someone's hurt or not."

"Horses," Rosso yelled out. They could hear two horses racing down the gully and ran hard for theirs. They spotted the two riders as they raced out of the ravine and into the desert well before they reached their mounts.

"Almost like they had this planned," Corcoran grumbled, getting into the saddle. The three rode down and out of the arroyo toward where they could pick up the trail. "They're making good time boys and we're gonna run out of daylight before long. Let's stay on their trail as long as possible. Won't survive a night out in this cold without bedrolls and a good fire, neither of which we would have. At least we'll know where they are."

"Ride this hard, this far, and turn back? Don't

much care for that," Rosso said. There was a lot of anger in his voice and Corcoran saw Geno Oliveira agree with Marty.

"No, I don't either, Marty. We'll ride until we have to turn back or die. If they take us somewhere that we can safely spend the night, or if we catch and kill the bastards, that would suit me just fine, but we got to plan for the other side of the question, too. What's your thoughts, Geno?"

"Ain't much for turning back, but without a fire, if we was settin' up to be attacked, I also ain't much for dyin'," he said. "You been doing this kind of thing a long time, Corcoran. I'll go with whatever you think is best."

"Me, too," Rosso said. They were moving at a comfortable lope through heavy brush, climbing into the rolling foothills of the Egan Range. The wide mouth of the outlaw's canyon was several miles in front of them. "They get in there, they could pick us off easy, Corcoran. Don't think we could ride hard enough to catch 'em before dark, either."

"Let's stay on their trail as long as we dare. We left out following four horses, Marty. We're only following two right now. Where did the other two go?"

"Probably straight for the canyon. Almost, like you said earlier, Corcoran, what we're seeing is like a plan. First, a man in each of the gulches. Then, men near the canyon's entrance. We're riding into another ambush, my friend."

"We need to change the odds and the three of us can't do that." Corcoran pulled them up to a stop, looking around where they were. "We got to cut it off and come back another day. What would we come up with if we tried to form a hunting party posse, Geno? Would the town respond?"

"Some might," Oliveira said. He looked over at Marty Rosso who nodded. "Some might wish they were riding with Henry Storm. Maybe a man or two from White's mine, but not many. Give up a day's pay to put yourself in a rifle's sight? Not many."

"Just us, then," Corcoran said. "Let's head back to town, boys. Have something hot to eat and do some planning. We're following Henry Storm's plans right now. I want to follow my plans. With Kelly and Mason, Storm has four men and his first thought is going to be Poindexter's bank. We don't know if others might be riding in, either. We can't chase him into that canyon but we can keep him from robbing that bank."

Henry and Louie found Mason and Kelly half a mile in the canyon and the four rode to the outlaw's lair just as the sun dipped behind the high mountains. "Won't be coming in the dark, boys. We're safe." Henry was laughing. "Thought you'd gave up on us, Kelly." The laughter and smiles disappeared, replaced by frowns and a challenge.

Elmer Kelly didn't flinch, didn't try to lie, too much, just stared into Henry's angry eyes for a couple of seconds. Kelly was a good gambler, unlike his partner, Mason, and played the only hand open to him. Some truth, some not. "Gave it thought, Henry. Headed back to town to get that Fingers fella to lead us out. His directions didn't make any sense."

Henry Storm saw the lie but let it go. He had two more guns and the bank was close. Could he trust these men during the robbery? The danger would be afterwards when they had the money. Would they turn on him? He knew they would, was sure he could take Kelly, but Mason was a knife man. And, what about Louie Hernandez? Where would he stand?

"You're here now, Kelly. We'll hit that bank in the morning. Let's make up those plans right now. Louie, get a good fire going, I want everyone to know exactly what to do." They sat around the stove, almost red hot, passing a bottle around, and Henry Storm outlined what he considered a fool-proof hit for the morning.

CHAPTER SEVENTEEN

It was a cold ride back to Ward and Corcoran had everyone settled in chairs around the pot belly stove when they got back. "That bank will be hit tomorrow morning, boys, sure as I'm sitting here. Storm has four guns now and we don't know if there are others here in town. I'll alert Poindexter when we break up here."

Corcoran laid out a rough map of Ward and pointed out what he was talking about as he described what he expected in the morning. "The bank sits on the southwest corner of Main and Third with the entrance on Main Street. That's directly across Main from the Silver Springs Saloon, a known outlaw hangout and a danger for us. Everyone in there knows all of us by sight so using that saloon is out of the question."

"The roof ain't," Skeets McDougall said. "A man with a rifle has a good command of Main Street."

"He would," Corcoran said. "Got someone in minds, Skeets?" Skeets laughed and pointed a finger into his own chest. "Good," Corcoran chuckled. "How are you going to get up there without everyone in the saloon knowing it? You'd have the same command of the street from the roof of the Grand Hotel."

Skeets thought about it for a moment before agreeing. "They wouldn't run north if I was up there," he said.

"I'd be a much happier deputy sheriff if we stopped them before they robbed the bank, gentlemen." Corcoran said. "The rest of us need to be on the ground, near our horses, when they ride in. Just like at the stream crossing, we have to remember these are wanted men. We have no reason to give them a quarter of an inch. See 'em, shoot 'em."

Corcoran poured some coffee, well laced with good whiskey, and paced around the office. "These men are wanted killers. Remember what happened at the Ward Stock Exchange. Remember why the sheriff isn't riding with us. It would be best if they faced trial but that is no reason to give them quarter."

His pacing continued and he took the time to look each man square in the face as he talked. "Mr.

Miller, you take up residence at the Wells Fargo building. You'll have a good view of the bank and Main Street." Dean Miller nodded and smiled too. That was to his liking. He might get the first shot in.

"Think the station manager, Jeff Whalen, will let me in? He's said a couple of nasty things after Storm hit the Stock Exchange."

"You don't need to be inside," Corcoran said. "The people of this community demand law enforcement but won't support our efforts. Happens too often, I'm afraid." Corcoran poured a little more whiskey and looked around the room filled with brand new deputies.

"Mr. Rosso," Corcoran continued. "You be with Miller. The station manager might not want you there. Be there." Everyone chuckled, knowing those two big men wouldn't put up with nonsense from Jack Whalen.

"Mr. Oliveira," Corcoran barked, having fun now, getting all his men up, prepared, ready for war with the outlaws. "I want you, mounted, at the corner of Third and Alpine, right behind the bank. There is a good possibility that Henry Storm might lead them in from the west on Alpine instead of from the south."

"Where you gonna be, Corcoran?" Marty Rosso

asked.

"I'm gonna be inside with Mr. Poindexter's money." He laughed and thumped the desk. "That man opens his bank at ten sharp every morning. If Henry Storm was using the Ward Stock Exchange as a run up for the bank hit, he'll come hard for those doors as soon as they're unlocked. I'll be inside with two bank guards, surrounded by you men outside. Any questions, ideas? If not, I'm going to find Poindexter and alert him."

"Where do you want me, Corcoran?" Tomaso Bono was sitting near the fire rubbing his injured leg.

"Right here at the jail, Tomaso. You can't run or ride but if those fools run north on us, you'll have your turkey shoot. That should just about cover the town, boys."

Tomaso didn't say anything but had his thoughts in order. *He's right, I can't run hardly at all, but I know I can ride. I know it.*

Corcoran's plan was to find Poindexter but he walked right past the Grand and turned into the Silver Springs Saloon. On a cold fall night, the place was busy, cigar smoke hung heavy in the heated barroom filled with miners, ranchers, and gamblers. He spotted Mindy Shepherd near one of the faro tables and she walked over.

"I wondered if you'd come back." She had make-up spread across a bruise on her cheek, but her eyes were bright and shining. "You look cold."

"Been outside for a while," Corcoran said. "Got time to sit and talk for a few minutes? Most of the pain gone?"

"Mostly," she said. "Probably get yelled at if we sit for too long but I will. Ain't just a whole lot of men like you around. Thank you, again, for what you did. Ain't nobody been rude since then."

Corcoran gave her a big smile, ordered a beer and they took one of the small tables near the front of the saloon. "Ever see Henry Storm or any of his gang in here?"

"That filthy bastard comes in sometimes. Horrible man," Mindy said. "You just here for information? I was hoping you came to see me." Mindy's smile had a lot of questions and even a few answers in it.

"I am here to see you, my dear lady, but also to get some information on that killer. Stay off the streets in the morning, Mindy. It might get dangerous."

"I'll just stay close to you and be safe," she said. The little chuckle, blinking eyes, and devastating smile almost crippled Corcoran. "Bartender's gonna yell at me shortly, I think. We could go upstairs to my room. Then nothing would be said. You took fine care of me, maybe it's time I took care of you."

It was considerably later that Corcoran made his way downstairs and into the saloon proper. "Hold it up there, Corcoran. We need to have a chat." Iron Jaw Ransom was standing at the end of the bar. "Name's Ransom and I own this fine establishment. You might carry a badge but that don't give you cause to beat up my customers."

"If you're talking about Sam Brown, you're wrong, Mr. Ransom. My wearing a badge had nothing to do with our little dance. No man has the right to hit a woman and, if I'm around, I'll see to it that they understand that."

Corcoran tipped his hat and started for the door. "Don't push the issue, Corcoran. These women get a little mouthy sometimes, need to learn their position. Everyone needs to know their place."

The threat was subtle but real. Corcoran could see the challenge in Ransom's eyes, could see the man stiffen up some. "So, from saloon owner to educator, eh, Iron Jaw? Well, sir, I'm at your convenience. You're right to a business license is already in jeopardy. Are you sure you want to put me in my place?"

"What do you mean by that?" Ransom was stunned by the comment, stepped back half a step and glared at Corcoran. "My license? In jeopardy?"

"That's right. Allowing known criminals, killers, to have their own special drinking area, being an associate of known outlaws, allowing outlaws to feel safe, maybe even under your protection is justification to pull your business license, Iron Jaw." Corcoran was standing, facing the saloon keeper, his feet spread apart, his hands hanging loose at his side. He was staring at the squat man, daring him to make a move.

Instead, Ransom turned and left the bar area, walked across the floor toward the gambling tables and took the stairs to the second floor. He never said a word, never looked back and Corcoran chuckled, making his way to the heavy doors. "School is adjourned," he murmured.

Corcoran found the banker and his wife just finishing their supper and took a seat. "I'll be quick," he said. "Sorry for interrupting your supper but I'm pretty sure Henry Storm will attack your bank in the morning. He has two extra men now and they have experience in robbing banks."

"Been expecting this, Corcoran. What are your plans?" Poindexter had a grim look on his face.

"There's considerable loss involved here."

Corcoran wanted to simply say, 'Stopping them,' but knew, also, that he did not want to discuss his plans. "I think we have a good handle on it, sir. I want to be inside the bank with your guards when you open. What is your exact opening procedure?"

Poindexter looked around quickly before answering. "I'm usually there about nine each morning. As you've noticed, I'm sure, Mary-Anne and I have breakfast here at the hotel before going to the bank. Mary-Anne and my clerk get the vault open and cash drawers filled and all the paperwork completed. At ten sharp, my guard opens the doors and I step out on good days to welcome whoever might be waiting."

Corcoran wasn't aware that Mrs. Poindexter was a part of the operation. He gave her a long look. "Any way to change part of that? Is it necessary for your wife to be there? It's liable to be dangerous as all get out."

"I maintain those opening and closing books, Mr. Corcoran. Yes, I must be there." Mary-Anne Poindexter's eyes sparkled and Corcoran wondered if it was because of the possible danger or something else. "Mr. Poindexter and I have been doing this for many years. I'm always there when the bank opens and when it closes."

"If Henry Storm and his gang do hit those doors, Mrs. Poindexter, you find someplace to hide." Corcoran turned to the banker. "I'll have breakfast with you two in the morning, my men will already be in position, and I'll walk with you to the bank. I'll need your help convincing your guards how important it is to fire on the outlaws as soon as they are seen. Just remember what happened at the Ward Stock Exchange."

"It was horrible," Mary-Anne said. "They just blew poor Mister Shapiro into pieces."

"He recognized Storm but didn't respond immediately, Mrs. Poindexter. That's what I mean about firing at these men on sight."

"I understand, Corcoran. We'll see you in the morning." Poindexter said. Something about such a curt ending to the meeting surprised Terrence Corcoran but he didn't say anything. He stood, bowed slightly to Mary-Anne and started to leave.

"I understand you refused the offer of being White Pine County Sheriff," Poindexter said.

So, he was in on it. I wonder what the connection is between his bank and Commissioner Kleindorfer? "I don't always get along that well with Avery Johnson, Mr. Poindexter, but he is the elected sheriff. Mr. Kleindorfer can't simply appoint someone. I'm a deputy sheriff from Eureka County here to help out, not get engaged in White Pine County politics."

"There will be changes, Corcoran. Men have died because of Johnson's lack of action. Give it some thought, because according to Doc Bones, Sheriff Johnson may have to give up the job. Those wounds are not healing."

"Regardless, Mr. Poindexter, I have a fine job and I'm not looking for another. Enjoy your politics but leave me out of the picture. I'll see you in the morning." He bowed slightly to the couple and walked out of the restaurant and up the stairs to his room. When he got to the door, he turned and walked back down, watched the banking couple leave the hotel, and headed into the saloon.

"One cold beer with another to follow and two shots of your best whiskey, Frank. It's been one long day."

"Comin' up, Corcoran. You boys did a good job saving that payroll shipment. Think that's the end of the Henry Storm gang?"

Corcoran had to smile at the old man. "Not by a long mile, Frank. But when his end comes, it will be time to dance in the street."

"I'll play the fiddle."

CHAPTER EIGHTEEN

"Get that fire going, Louie. Time to make some money." Henry Storm was fighting to get his boots on, fighting an icy cold morning, and thinking mostly of the Ward Bank. "There's a lot of gold in that vault, boys. More than enough to make each of us rich. The big question right now is how best to get away."

"Me and Jack Mason are going to have to depend on you for that," Elmer Kelly said. "I've never been in this country."

"We may have to do some dodging but it's best to get back here. We can defend this place and both Louie and I know how to get out of here, also." Henry Storm splashed some whiskey into his tin cup and filled it with hot coffee. "Corcoran will have men with horses scattered around, so I want you, Kelly, and you, Mason, to be our outside men."

"Louie and I will kill whoever is inside the bank, you two kill anyone who tries to break up the party. Then we ride with the wind back here."

"We're forgetting something, Henry," Louie Hernandez said. "We've been all excited about having Kelly and Mason along but that bank is filled with gold. We will need a wagon and strong team or teams to haul it off."

The only sound that could be heard was that of the wood popping in the wood stove and coffee boiling in the pot. "Damn." Henry Storm was on his feet, pacing around the small cabin. "Where can we get one fast? We need a good farm wagon and if I remember, Jason Weed, and that foul mouthed wife of his, have just what we want. We ride to Weed's place first, take the wagon and team, and ride for Ward."

"We need to leave out right now, then," Louie said. "To make this work we have to at that bank when Poindexter opens those doors. Getting that wagon will take a bit of time."

"It will," Storm said. "We'd best take the time to kill Weed and his wife, too. Don't need more witnesses."

"That's good, Henry," Louie Hernandez said.

"When we get to town, if you hold the horses, Jack, Kelly can use that rifle of his to perfection." Hernandez looked at Henry and then around at the others. "The bank's at Third and Main, Henry, just one block north of the Stock Exchange. We can come in from the south just like we did when we hit the Exchange."

"And race west on Third, leaving town," Henry Storm said. "Any questions? If not, let's check our weapons, saddle up and ride hard, gentlemen. The Weed ranch is about two miles north, right on our way to town."

Skeets McDougall had a Winchester rifle, Colt pistol, Stevens shotgun, and enough ammunition to take a stand against the entire Western Shoshone Nation as he made his way to the Grand Hotel. "Need some help there, soldier?"

Jack Crawford was the day barman and was just coming on duty when Skeets made his way into the hotel. "That's quite a load you're carrying. Just saw Corcoran having breakfast with Mr. Poindexter. Something going on?"

"Help me get the doors open to the roof, Jack and I'll tell you all about it," Skeets said. They made their way to the third floor and up the last flight of stairs to the roof entrance. "Hard climb for these old legs, Jack. Thanks for your help."

They moved across the broad roof, around some brick and rock chimneys to the front of the building. "Corcoran is pretty sure that Henry Storm is gonna rob the bank this morning, Jack. If that outlaw and his gang shows up, I'm gonna sure as all hell blow at least one of them into the far reaches of hades." Skeets McDougall's eyes were dancing as he started to make up his camp behind the false front of the hotel.

"You got enough guns to whup an army, Skeets. I gotta get back to work. Good luck. I know I'll hear all the noise if they do show up."

"You don't want to stay and help me kill the Henry Storm gang?"

"No, Skeets, that's your job. Me? I'll buy you a drink if you do." Jack Crawford headed back toward the stairs and Skeets thought he knew now what Corcoran had been talking about. "Yup," he muttered. "they'll want the job done, just won't help much. Hope I get that telegraph job when this is over."

"It don't matter none to us whether you want us here or not, Mr. Whalen. We're setting up shop on your front porch. Will you still be arguing when the bullets start flying?" Marty Rosso was glaring at the man on a cold late fall morning. "As far as your windows are concerned, that's your responsibility. Mine is stopping a gang of killers."

Dean Miller had a little kid's grin on his face as he tied the horses off. *You tell him, Marty. Wish Corcoran could hear this ass whining.* Miller used a quick release knot so they could mount fast if the bandits made a run. *Hate to use this knot with this old gelding of mine. He's better at untying it than I am.* "Might want to put some boards across those windows, Mr. Whalen."

Whalen did some fine almost under-his-breath cussing as he headed back inside. "The county will be getting a bill if they're busted out." The Wells Fargo complex was on the corner of Fourth and Main and Miller had the horses tied to corral fencing on the south side of the building.

"Let's fort up right on the porch, Marty. We can move some of these boxes around to get behind and still see the street and the front of the bank."

"Think they'll just come riding right down the street? I think I would already have my men in town and ride in from several different directions."

"That's why you're not an outlaw, Marty. You're a thinker. They ain't." Miller had to laugh watching the huge man tuck himself behind a box full of harness and other tack. "I do think they'll come right down Main Street and from the south. It worked once, Henry Storm is sure it will again."

"A good meal before a big fight is always good," Corcoran said. He eased back in his chair and lifted his coffee cup. "Here's to the end of the Henry Storm outfit, Mr. Poindexter. I put him in Carson City Prison once. This time I'll put him in his grave. He's killed his last."

"I hope you're right. This may not be the right time to bring this up but I'd really like you to take a long look at our offer. You are the kind of man White Pine County needs for sheriff."

Corcoran didn't say a word, just rose from the table, offered to help Mary-Anne from hers, and grabbed his bullet-ridden buffalo robe coat. "I have the best job in Nevada, Poindexter. I've had many more than one county commissioner offer me the job as sheriff of Eureka County and I'll tell you what I told them. I like being Deputy Sheriff Terrence Corcoran. Now, let's get to work."

It was a short walk to the bank which sat kitty-corner from the Grand Hotel. They walked to the Third Street private entrance and were met by security guard Sydney White. "Got some bad news for you, Mr. Poindexter. Jerry won't be here today. He's got himself real sick and the missus says he's in bed with a high fever."

Jerry was Gerald Hand, the long-employed guard at the bank. "Oh, I'm sorry. He's not been well for some time," Mary-Anne said. "Did Mrs. Hand say anything else?"

Sydney shook his head and Corcoran almost had to push to get everyone inside the bank. "Come on, folks. Let's get this door closed. So, Mr. White, it's you and me when Henry Storm gets here. Let's have a little chat, shall we?"

"I need him to help me get the vault open and start moving money before Walt Gibbons gets here." Mary-Anne said.

"Not this morning, dear," Poindexter said. "I'll help you. Mr. White needs to be with Corcoran. Will Mr. Hand not being here interfere with your plans, Corcoran?"

"One gun short before the shooting starts? You bet, sir, but we'll manage, eh Mr. White?"

White wasn't the least bit sure. "I've never shot anyone," he stammered.

"Neither had I until the first one, Hand." Corcoran saw the man almost shaking and wondered how it was Poindexter even hired him. "Henry Storm is a killer and the men who ride with him are also killers. When you and I open those doors, at least two armed men are going to come at us hard. It's up to you and me to stop them. My men outside will stop the rest of the gang."

"How? Just open the doors and shoot? What if it's not Storm? It would be terrible to shoot someone who wasn't an outlaw."

Corcoran was not prepared for a bank guard who was afraid of guarding the bank, and walked to the doors, took a quick peek around a shade covering a front window, and sat down on a bench. "Mr. White, go help Mary-Anne and ask Mr. Poindexter to come out front, please."

"Corcoran?" Poindexter had a frown on his face. "It's quarter to ten, Corcoran."

"I know. White is not the man to take on Henry Storm, I'm afraid. You and your wife need to be well away from what might happen when I get those doors open. Tell me about Mr. Gibbons. I see he just arrived."

"He's been my customer clerk for five years. As you see, he's just a wisp of a man, about sixty I believe."

"I have a lot of defense set up outside, Poindexter.

Where we're short is right here, inside. One bank guard who is afraid of shooting somebody and me. I'm about to open those doors, sir, so you had best be well hidden and well-armed."

I wonder if good old Jerry is sick or just scared? Too late for those kinds of questions.

CHAPTER NINETEEN

"That's the farm," Henry Storm said. He was point-ing at a stand of cottonwood trees surrounding a small home. There was a barn off to the west along with a corral. On the east side of the barn stood a small grove of apple trees. The hog pen, separated from the house by a small garden, was filled and chickens could be seen scratching near the garden. Fredrick Weed, still limping from a recent acci-dent and his wife Betsy, often called Stormy, were walking toward the barn and turned when the four mounted men rode in.

Visitors to a farm showing up this close to sunrise was more than unusual. Threatening, frightening, and not a time for wondering who or why. "Run for the house, Stormy. Hurry," Weed said. She spun around and, despite being forty, made the run full out, almost splintering the door when it didn't immediately open. She raced for the shotgun and got both barrels loaded while hurrying to one of the kitchen windows.

Fred Weed had a heavy wooden bucket in his hand and was unarmed when Storm and his gang rode right up to him, shoving him back a step or two. "What do you want?"

"Need your wagon and team, Weed. Get out of the way." Henry Storm nudged his horse forward, pushing Weed aside. Weed swung the empty wooden bucket at Storm and took a bullet to the head for the effort from Louie Hernandez.

Stormy Weed screamed in horror and anger and came out the kitchen door with the shotgun at her shoulder. She let loose one barrel at Hernandez and the second at Elmer Kelly, but the distance was too much and there was little effect. Louie Hernandez was stung in the face, bleeding from several pellet punctures and Kelly took what few hit him in his heavy winter coat.

Henry Storm turned his horse toward the Weed woman, pulled his sidearm and shot her twice as she tried to reload. She fell to the ground, still trying to reload. Storm rode up to her and was about to put the kill shot to her when she rolled and let loose both barrels.

Stormy Weed didn't have the strength to get the barrels high enough and the double load of buckshot blew into his horse, killing it. The two fell to the ground together, with Storm trying to roll free of the falling horse. His ankle was twisted in the process but he was free. "Damn that woman," he said, shooting her twice from just feet away.

"Party's over," Louie hollered. "Find that wagon, get a team harnessed and let's be quick." He saw Henry trying to get to his feet and watched him limp to a fence for balance. "Looks like you're driving the wagon, Henry. Sure as hell can't rob a bank if you can't stand up."

"Shut your mouth, Hernandez. Get my rifle and saddlebags off my horse." Louie had the slightest grin as he did as he was told. *Gonna be some changes around here, Henry. Starting right now.* He got Storm's things, even helped the man into the barn where Kelly and Mason were harnessing a team.

"Timing has to be perfect, so let's get it on, boys," Henry said. The team was used almost every day so stood quietly as they were dressed and backed toward the wagon. "While they finish up, why don't you torch that shack Weed lived in. Might keep a few people from following us."

"Already done, Henry. Let's get you up in that seat and ride out." Louie was on his horse and it was up to Mason to get Storm onto the wagon. "That road out there becomes Main Street. Pull the wagon right up in front of that bank. Kelly, I want you to hold our horses, but Mason, it'll be you and me going inside the bank. Let's go."

Black smoke poured from the farm house as the gang moved onto the main road. At just two miles out, those in town could see it plainly. "Fire boys will be running soon," Louie called out. "We'll make a mess of things, create problems maybe get away with enough gold to make us all happy."

Louie was making plans as they rode, wondering just how fast Kelly was. *I can take Henry any day of the week, not sure about Mason and Kelly. Mason's a knife man, but Kelly might be fast. All that gold just for me.*

Kelly's thoughts were similar. *If the shooting starts, I'll see to it that Henry dies first, and then that pushy Mexican. Me and Mason can run hard for Elko.*

"Fire," Skeets muttered. "Looks like the Weed place." He had the best view in town from three floors up on the roof of the Grand Hotel. He saw a couple of men on the street below and hollered the news at them. They moved to the bell tower and started ringing the alarm. Men and boys raced for their respective equipment and the hose carts and hand engines began to move south.

"I'll bet my first paycheck from the telegraph office that Henry Storm is responsible for that smoke out there," Skeets muttered. He watched near collisions as fire equipment headed south, saw people starting to gather in front of shops and saloons, and knew this kind of chaos would be to the outlaw's benefit.

"They're gonna ride into streets filled with people and animals and our boys ain't gonna be able to just shoot 'em on sight." Skeets McDougall had his rifle at the ready and could see three riders coming into town accompanied by a wagon driven by one man. "I knew it," Skeets mumbled.

"Is that them?" Dean Miller was pointing at three horses and a wagon coming in from the south. Marty Rosso tried to see through all the dust made by the fire equipment racing south.

"Can't tell, Dean, but we better just assume it is. Shooting while this crowd is building ain't right. Gonna get innocent people killed, Dean."

Louie Hernandez and Elmer Kelly were riding

in front of the wagon and Jack Mason behind and kept as much to their left as they could as they moved slowly into town. They were just far enough into the middle of the roadway to hamper the fire equipment. The men and boys racing with hose wagons were in the most danger of serious injury or death if they fell.

Henry Storm was enjoying letting the team move over the center of the road, seeing men and boys pulling hose wagons wreck them, causing even more traffic hazards. Howls of pain were mixed with screams to get out of the way. The more chaos the less chance of a chase after the robbery.

"Enough fun, Louie," Storm howled. "Let's hit that bank." He snapped the buggy whip and the horses moved to a smart trot down Main Street. Hernandez and Kelly were humped low in the saddle, hoping to not be recognized.

"It's them," Miller hollered and pulled his rifle up just as six men pulling a hand engine came between the deputy and Louie Hernandez. "Damn it," Miller said. He stood up to get a better shot but Mason, on his horse behind the wagon, spotted him and fired a quick shot. Wood splintered in front of Dean Miller and he dove to the porch deck, unable to get a shot off.

Marty Rosso put a bullet into the wagon seat which caused Henry Storm to urge that heavy farm team into a faster trot. "Move it boys. To the bank, to the bank," he yelled. He pulled the team out onto more of the roadway, upsetting another hose wagon, and took pleasure in watching the men pulling the hose cart crashing into the dirt and rocks.

Kelly took the reins from Louie Hernandez and Jack Mason as they jumped from their horses. He tied the two horses to the back of the wagon so he would be free to use his guns. Henry Storm had the team halted in front of the bank, fully blocking Third Street, the side street. His rifle was at the ready and he smiled as Hernandez and Mason rushed for the bank doors just coming open. *Just like we planned it. Start shooting, Louie, don't wait. Shoot damn it.* He let a smile cross his face as several shots were heard from inside the building.

CHAPTER TWENTY

"Here they come," Corcoran yelled back toward the Poindexters, Gibbons, and White. The four were crouched behind desks and the cashier's cage. Corcoran tried to time it but the chaos on the street from on-lookers, fire boys and their equipment, and the outlaws ruined that. He unlocked the doors and pulled them open just as Louie Hernandez hit them hard.

Hernandez didn't know they were unlocked and ready to swing open and threw his full weight into the heavy oak doors with all their lovely brass. They swung open knocking Corcoran back and to the floor. His rifle skidded away but Corcoran had his Colt spitting fire and lead as fast as he could fan that hammer.

Louie Hernandez rolled across the marble floor of the bank crashing into the clerk's cage, his pistol hanging loose in his now dead hand. Jack Mason rushed past him and pushed into the cashier's cage where Mary-Anne Poindexter was crouched. Stephen Poindexter was horrified to see Mason grab her, turn and rush for the open bank doors.

All thoughts of carrying off a fancy bank robbery vanished when he saw Hernandez go down and now faced two armed guards in front of him and Corcoran's still smoking gun behind. The lure of a beautiful woman was never far from Mason's thoughts. This time, though, a beautiful woman would also bring a fine chest full of gold. *No time for the gold, woman. I'll take you and we'll get the gold if they want you back. In the meantime, you beautiful thing, you're mine.*

Gibbons and White were huddled at the side of the vault, both with holstered weapons, neither with a weapon in hand. Corcoran was back on his feet in time to see Mason and Mary-Anne rush through the doors. Mason flung the disheveled banker's wife into the back of the wagon, jumped in behind her, and yelled "Go, go," at the top of his lungs.

Corcoran came through the bank's doors, his rifle up and took a quick shot at Elmer Kelly, hitting him high on his shoulder. The team of horses bolted and started racing north on Main Street, Henry Storm desperately trying to get them under control. He stayed on the left side of the street and made the turn west at Second Street.

Skeets McDougall fired down on the outlaws, knocking Kelly off his horse with a killing shot. He couldn't get a good shot at Mason or Storm because of Mrs. Poindexter fighting like a wild woman with Mason. The outlaw finally bashed her in the head with his handgun. When Storm made the move west, Skeets did get a shot at Henry, putting a bullet through his hand, knocking the reins loose.

Mason jumped into the seat and was able to grab the reins and took control of the wagon. Henry Storm was busy trying to keep from bleeding to death. Second Street was one of the heavily used commercial streets and ran in almost a straight line toward the old charcoal ovens, several miles out.

"Horses," Dean Miller yelled and he and Rosso raced for the corral, pulled the ties loose and jumped on, spurring hard. They saw Mason throw something in the wagon from half a block away and were at full gallop when Henry Storm got the farm team moving.

"I'll chase," Marty Rosso yelled. "See if Corcoran needs help. They couldn't possibly have had time to get very much." He saw Kelly go down, was threading his way through the now panicked crowd, and followed Storm and Mason onto Second Street. He saw the saddle horses tied to the back of the wagon. "They'll make the change just as soon as they can," he muttered.

Miller jumped off his horse and ran to Corcoran. "You're bleeding bad," he said.

"Damn door knocked me a good one. What did you see?"

"Looked to me like they're running west on Second Street. Saw Mason throw something into the back of the wagon, but they didn't have time to get any of the gold."

"They didn't," Corcoran said. "They got Mary-Anne Poindexter. Get your horse. Mine's right around the corner, on Third." He was still woozy from being smashed by the doors but ran hard around the corner, found Dude, and mounted quickly. "Does Second Street go anywhere?"

"It's the main road west to the ovens and on into the Egans. This street will end in a couple of blocks."

"You lead, then, Miller. I don't want to think what Henry Storm will do with that woman." Miller led them west and into open desert. There was dust at least half a mile ahead of them and they turned north to connect with the main road. "That team they're using is a farm team, Corcoran. It won't last at this pace. It'll pull a plow for twelve hours straight but won't run for an hour. We gotta plan for a fight soon."

"Storm ain't got nothing to fight with," Corcoran said. "It's just him and Mason. Hernandez and Kelly are dead. Let's catch up with Rosso and chase 'em down."

The bank's doors were wide open, Louie Hernandez was lying in a pool of blood and Poindexter was in a rage, screaming at his two security guards. Many on the street took a moment or two to gape at the scene and listen to the banker.

"Neither one of you fired a single shot while those barbarians stole my wife," he thundered. "Get out. Get out of my bank." He picked up a shotgun that was on the floor near the open vault and Gibbons and White scrambled to their feet and rushed out the doors. Poindexter followed, shooing bystanders away and closed the big doors.

"Oh, my," he whimpered, trying to put what just happened into focus. He stumbled into his office and was slumped at his desk when Skeets McDougall rushed in. "What just happened, Skeets? It can't be. It can't. My god, they have Mary-Anne."

"I locked the doors, Poindexter. Corcoran, Miller, and Rosso are chasing them now. Louie Hernandez and Elmer Kelly are dead. What went wrong in here?"

"Everything," Poindexter whimpered. "The men I hired as guards never even drew their weapons. Oh, Mary-Anne, no, no, no." He simply laid his head on top of the desk and cried, saying no, over and over.

Skeets shook his head, somewhat in sympathy, and edged out. He left the bank by way of the employee door which locked behind him and walked slowly to the jail. "Go get 'em, Corcoran. Go get 'em, big man."

Skeets found Oliveira and Bono putting together kits for a long chase. "Might be gone for a while, I think. Need to get food and a mule, too," Bono said.

"We gotta dump this wagon, Henry. Got law racing down on us. Keep driving hard and I'll try to get on one of the horses. Keep this thing going as straight as you can." Mason was nearing fifty but, with the hard life of his, was in fair shape. Could he untie one horse, bring it alongside the wagon and get in the saddle? All the while the wagon is rolling fast down a dirt lane? Henry Storm doubted it but there was no better plan.

"Don't look back at me, Henry, just drive as straight a line as you can." Mason had one horse untied and was able to bring the horse around to the left side of the fast-moving wagon. He had a good grip on the lead line, brought the horse as far forward as he dared. If that rear wheel bumped the horse, it was all over. If the horse shied from the front wheel, it was all over.

Jack Mason tried to visualize what had to be done and almost decided not to go through with it. "Damn," he muttered. He was standing, eased the galloping horse in as close as the horse would come, reached out for the saddle horn, and leaped into the saddle. "Sumbitch," he said. Just the slightest smile crossed his face.

He was so intent on making the jump that he almost went all the way over the other side but caught himself in time. He reined the horse away from the wagon and dropped back to try to get the second horse untied. The two horses shied each time he moved in to loosen the tie-down. On the third try, he got lucky and the second horse was loose, but he didn't have hold of the leadrope.

It was a short chase through open prairie to catch the horse and trail it to the speeding wagon. "I can't make that kind of jump," Storm yelled out. "Only one hand working."

Jack Mason cussed at him, tried to get him angry enough to make the jump but Henry Storm would have none of it. Instead, the outlaw slowed the horses to a stop and leaped from the wagon. Mason took that opportunity to jump in the wagon, grab the still unconscious Mary-Anne Poindexter, and jump back on his horse. He had her laid out across the front of the saddle.

Mason didn't do anything but put spurs to the horse and raced on down the road, not seeing all the trouble Henry Storm was having. Didn't care if Henry Storm was having trouble because he had the gold. *This little bundle is mine until the banker pays for her. I gotta ride until I can't sit in the saddle, get away from whoever is following, and stay alive until I get my gold.*

When Storm tried to mount the frightened animal his bad hand failed to hold anything, mane or horn, and he dragged a spur across the horse's rump scaring the horse even more. He had one foot in a stirrup when the horse started bucking, twisting, raring, and generally doing what it could to get away from the man.

Henry Storm had the reins in his wounded hand, tried desperately to hold onto the saddle horn with the other and get his free leg all the way over the horse. The horse spun hard and slammed into side of the wagon, mashing his already twisted leg, the one Storm had in the stirrup into a wheel. Storm screamed in pain when the crazed horse again bumped into the wheel.

The crash spooked the two farm horses into a run through open sage-covered desert and Storm's horse ran with them. The running, instead of bucking, gave the outlaw a chance to get settled in the saddle.

The pain in his leg told him it was probably broken as he was unable to put any pressure in the stirrups. His bullet-wounded hand was bleeding freely and he was racing hell bent for leather across the open plain. He looked around, couldn't see Jack Mason anywhere but spotted three riders coming down on him hard.

"You ain't gettin' me, Corcoran." Storm almost screamed it out, urging his horse on. He was running hard in a northerly direction, far out distancing the farm team and wagon, but not on any kind of trail. He looked all around, spotted a jumble of rocks at least a half mile away and slightly to his west. He knew he would be there before the men chasing him and bent low in the saddle, yelling at

the horse. The two farm horses gave up and slowed
to a stop, gasping for breath.

He rode into the rocky hillside and fell hard into
the gravel when he jumped from the horse. "Leg,"
he howled in pain. He could see blood on his pant
leg, knew the break was a compound fracture, and
crawled as fast as he could for cover behind a rock
outcrop, crying out with every move. Through a rip
in his pant leg, Henry could see the end of a bone
and spurts of blood. His vision was blurred from loss
of blood and the effects of shock setting in, along
with his capacity to think straight.

"I ain't gonna die this way. You gotta kill me,
Corcoran before I kill you." He felt waves of nausea,
knew how weak he was, and pulled his Remmie to
check its load. "Come on, lawman, meet your end."

CHAPTER TWENTY-ONE

What the hell's going on?" Dean Miller was riding alongside Terrence Corcoran, pointing at what looked like a bucking horse at least a mile out in front of them.

"I don't know Dean. They're gonna give up the wagon it looks like. One rider is racing for the mountains and it looks like the other is about to have a big wreck." The three, Miller, Corcoran, and Rosso were riding hard to catch the outlaw gang. "Whatever he was doing, he's got it under control now. He's leading the wagon north, off the roadway. Mrs. Poindexter must still be in the wagon and that rider must be Henry Storm. Let's get him, boys."

The ride to the rise in the valley floor and jumble of rocks was furious and the three lawmen reined up quickly when Henry Storm fired two shots at them. They were well out of range and Storm gave his position away foolishly. "He's forted up, boys but that wagon is still moving off. I don't see anyone at the reins. Rosso, you stay with me and Miller, ride back out and get that wagon. Mrs. Poindexter must be frightened to death."

Corcoran was bent as low as he could get and raced for a large rock. Storm took a shot but wasn't close. *The Henry Storm I know is a far better gunman than that. He's wounded, hurt, and he's mine now. He must have injured his shooting hand for him, to miss by that much.*

Corcoran motioned to Rosso to move forward and fired three quick shots into the rocks. Rosso moved quickly and fired as well, giving Corcoran a chance to move. Corcoran let Rosso know that he was going to circle around and try to come in from the side. Marty Rosso brought his rifle with him when he jumped from his horse and laid down a barrage. Corcoran, as low as he could get, scampered out to his left and using as much rocky cover as he could find moved well off to Henry Storm's side.

Storm had a good position to fire on Rosso but was not able see Corcoran at all. Marty Rosso fired a shot into the rocks, hoping to get return fire. He

hadn't seen Storm once and wasn't sure of his position. The shot worked and Henry answered with
two quick shots. The white smoke gave his position
away as if he had stood up and waved a flag.

"Gotcha, buster," Rosso muttered. He crawled
across an open space and into a slight depression,
moved quickly forward more than fifteen yards, and
got behind a ledge of broken rock. He eased around,
rifle ready, and caught a glimpse of the outlaw.
"What the hell is he doing?"

Storm's gun hand was bleeding hard, his broken
leg was more painful than anything he had ever felt,
and he couldn't hold his pistol to get it reloaded.
His pain brought rage and his busted-up hand kept
him from being able to reload. If he held the gun
in his good hand he couldn't get the bullets in the
cylinder. If he tried to balance the gun and load it,
his good leg had to put pressure on the broken one,
and the gun fell away.

Corcoran had snaked, his way through sage and
rocks, and stood behind the killer, his Colt cocked.
He watched for a few seconds and almost chuckled
at the scene. "Give it up, Storm. It just ain't your
day," Corcoran said. He stepped forward when
Storm whirled around and slammed the man across
the side of the head with his pistol. Storm slumped

onto the rocks, unconscious and now, bleeding from his head, too.

Corcoran called to Marty Rosso to come on in and kneeled down to take a good look at his prisoner. "You are one broken up outlaw, Mr. Storm. Good thing we have that wagon. Bet you even money you're gonna lose that leg and you won't be a shooter no more, either." Corcoran was carrying on a full but one-sided conversation with Henry who couldn't hear a word. "Won't be robbin' no more banks, Mr. Storm. Won't be carrying off banker's wives, neither."

Dean Miller drove the wagon up to where Rosso and Corcoran were. "He didn't have Mrs. Poindexter," Miller called out. "There's blood in wagon, too. That other fella must have her."

"Damn," Corcoran said. "Pow wow time boys. Sit down." The three men sat in the rocks while Corcoran lined out what had to be done. "One of us has to take the wagon with Henry Storm back to town and gather supplies for our chase. Better plan on being in the saddle for maybe as much as five days, too."

"That's a lot of supplies, Corcoran," Miller said. "Hope the county's credit is good."

Corcoran knew neither Miller nor Rosso wanted to make the ride to town but it had to be done.

"I'm sure that was Elmer Kelly who died in the street and we know Louie Hernandez died inside the bank. Storm is right there. Must be Jack Mason holding the woman and I doubt he knows this country, so maybe our chase will be a short one. Who's going to town?"

"As you said earlier, Corcoran, since I'm the resident deputy in Ward, it should be up to me to bring him in." Dean Miller had the look of a man making a decision he didn't want to make. "Do you think I should try to put together a posse of some kind?"

"No," Corcoran said. "Bring Geno Oliveira and Tomaso Bono, though. Get with Buford Waring at the stables, pack two mules for us. We'll leave a good trail for you to follow. Start your chase from this point. Poindexter will be in a rage and your best bet is to stay as far away from the sheriff as possible. I don't think I have to say hurry but I will," Corcoran chuckled.

Miller had his horse tied to the back of the wagon already, so all the men had to do was load Henry Storm. "Even with these wounds and injuries, this man is a threat, Dean. Don't take any guff from the man and shoot him if you have to. Hurry back, old man, coz we don't even have any coffee with us." Corcoran laughed, slapped one of the farm horses, and watched Miller drive off.

"We'll leave a good trail, Mr. Rosso. Let's move." Corcoran and Marty Rosso mounted and rode off in the direction Mason took. "He was on the main road the last time we saw him. Let's start there."

"If he has Mrs. Poindexter, that horse will run out of steam fast in this high country we're headed to," Rosso said.

The only thing on Jack Mason's mind was distance. *Gotta get far away from those people. Find a cabin or shack in the mountains or run off a farm family.* He kept his horse at a strong trot and had constant trouble keeping Mary-Anne Poindexter from falling off. She was laid across the front of the saddle forcing Mason to sit far back, putting lots of pressure on the horse's kidneys. When she regained consciousness, she fought hard to get free of the man.

She twisted around and scratched at his face, bit his hand when he grabbed her wrist. She screamed loud but, of course, that was wasted energy. "It's just us lady, so scream it out. Bite me again and you'll lose teeth." He hit her on the side of her head, hard, and she passed out again. "This is gonna be fun," he almost moaned, pushing his horse to stay in a hard trot.

Visions of what he had planned for this pot of gold he was carrying brought ugly grins to his whiskered face and he had to put them aside. *Have to think about escape. The pleasures will come after we're off safe somewhere. Such pleasures, lady. Such pleasures.*

The nearby mountains were bare, no trees at all and this didn't make much sense to the man. He rode around a series of five bee-hive charcoal ovens, no longer being worked, and made his way into a narrow and steep trail that led into the high mountains. "Must have burned every tree around in those ovens. Ain't gonna be easy finding a hole for us to hide in, woman."

The narrow pass opened up after a couple of miles of steep climbing and Mason spotted a thin column of smoke about five miles ahead. "Meat hunters." He muttered and turned toward the smoke. Mason found the Egan Range steep and rough with razor-back ridges, vast fields of rock, and what trees were left, young and scrawny.

The higher the road led, the more trees he found until they were riding once again in a high mountain forest. In order to reach the area where the smoke was, he had to leave the main road and ride through the forest. It took some time to reach the cabin.

Trail manners would have Mason call out before

riding in but the outlaw didn't. Instead, he rode right up to the door of the cabin, jumped from his horse and dragged the woman off, throwing her over his shoulder. He barged right into the cabin waking a man sleeping on the single cot.

"What the hell?" The man, dressed in wool pants and shirt, but no sidearm jumped to his feet.

"Need help." Mason growled it out as he walked to the cot and flopped Mary-Anne down. "You alone?"

"Yes. Moving out in the morning. Got two deer hanging. What happened to Mrs. Poindexter?"

"You know her?" Mason looked around the tiny line shack and saw a sack of coffee, some flour and sugar, and best of all, a bottle, half full of whiskey. "Got hurt. Where you got these deer?"

The man nodded that they were around back of the cabin. "Let's see," Mason said. "I like fresh venison." The hunter led out the door, took one quick look back at Mary-Anne but didn't say anything. The big pistol in Mason's hand told him to be quiet. The deer were cleaned and skinned, hanging from the cabin's overhanging rafters.

"Nice," Mason said. He leveled his sidearm and shot the hunter twice. "Appreciate your help, mister." Along with the deer and supplies in the cabin, Mason also found a saddle horse, pack mule, a sidearm, and rifle. "All the comforts of home."

The horse and mule were in a corral and he brought his horse around, pulled the tack and put him in with them. "Get to know each other, boys. Gonna be moving soon." Back inside he stoked the fire, got a pot of coffee boiling and turned his attention to his prize, Mary-Anne Poindexter, who was coming around from her rough treatment.

Are things finally changing? Down to nothing when Kelly sent for me, and look at this. An extra rifle, fresh meat, and a woman. She's worth as much gold as we would have got in that robbery. Things have changed, indeed.

"Welcome to your new home, woman. If your head hurts just remember why. Give me any trouble and it will hurt more. What's your name?"

"I'm Mrs. Stephen Poindexter. My husband will chase you down and kill you. My husband owns most of Ward and will bring lots of men with him. You're going to die hard."

"My, my." Jack Mason chuckled. "He's a rich sumbitch, eh? Good. You and me are gonna be close friends, dear woman, and he's gonna pay me lots of gold to get you back. If you're a good girl, you'll go back to him in fair shape. If not, well, you'll still be worth gold. Now, here are the simple rules. You do as I say. Got it?"

"I will not." Mary-Anne stood up, woozy from the blows to her head, and glared at the outlaw. "I'll do no such thing."

The fist, came out of nowhere, knocking her back onto the cot. He moved onto her quickly but she fought like a wildcat, scratching at his face, biting his cheek, and for good measure, kicking him in the groin.

He fell off the cot, rolled up with his knees in his throat, groaning in pain. Mary-Anne jumped at him, kicking him in the head before reaching down and grabbing his pistol. She knew enough about sidearms to know she had to cock the piece before she could shoot him but had a hard time pulling the hammer back.

Mason was slowly unwinding, got up to one knee before she had the hammer all the way back. He made a lunge, she pulled the trigger, and Mason was thrown back across the dirt floor of the cabin. He was moaning, writhing around in the dirt, and she moved to the table, laying the pistol down.

"You've killed me," he moaned, holding his hands to his middle, moaning loudly from the touch. Mary-Anne was terrified at what she had done, looked at the dying outlaw, the fire in the stove, the boiling coffee, and sat down, holding her head in her hands. Jack Mason watched all of it, moaning, and slowly coiling for the strike. Would the gambit work? The bullet ripped out a chunk of shoulder but Mason wasn't going to give it up that easy. *Come on, little lady, feel sorry for old Jack Mason. Come on, now.*

He continued to pretend the shot was to his middle, allowing him to be able to lurch out if he could get her close. *This woman is a tiger and she's mine. She'll learn the hard way to do as she's told. Gotta get that pistol back and then teach her things that banker's never even heard of.* He was poised to strike when Mary-Anne stood up and walked to the door. "Don't leave me to die alone, woman. Look what a terrible thing you've done."

Mary-Anne had the pistol in her hand and turned back to him. He could see tears running down her cheeks as she cocked the heavy revolver and walked slowly toward him. "No," he cried out softly. The cry was followed by a simpering moan and she stopped, just a few feet from him.

Come on woman. One more step and you're mine. Come on, damn it. He moaned, pitifully, turned his head to look at her. She held the pistol with both hands and aimed it at his head. "No," he cried out and straightened his body out as fast as he could, both his feet kicking Mary-Anne in the knees.

The gun exploded but Mary-Anne's aim was way off as she crashed to the floor, the heavy outlaw on top of her and twisting the gun from her hands. He slammed the gun across her head again, knocking her out. He threw her onto the bed, saw massive amounts of blood pouring from her head. "Told you." He snarled and eased himself down at the table to tend his wounds.

The pain in his shoulder told him the wound was serious, blood from scratches on his face and bites to his hands were just bothersome. There was a continuing ache in his groin that needed tending soon.

"Oh, woman, what have you done?" He poured a cup of coffee, took what was left of his shirt off and tried to see the shoulder wound. The hot chunk of lead had gone right through the big muscle at the shoulder joint, he saw, and ripped meat away on its way out. "Needs stitches and I can't do it," he murmured. Anger and frustration boiled over and he flung the tin cup of coffee at Mary-Anne.

He picked up the pistol, reloaded it, and gave serious thought to shooting her dead. "Kill that beautiful woman before I get my share? No, not this time, Jacko," he chuckled. "Throw away that pot of gold? No, not this time." He calmed himself with thoughts of the woman as he heated water on the stove, poured another cup of coffee, well laced with whiskey, and prepared to work on his shoulder.

"My husband will be here soon, mister," Mary-Anne said. Her words were slurred but the anger wasn't. Her vision was impaired and she knew she would fall if she tried to stand. "He'll kill you. He'll bring twenty men, screaming and howling for your blood, mister. You better run while you can. It's getting dark, mister, and my husband is already on his way."

She didn't let up, just kept saying, over and over, that her husband was coming, that Jack Mason would die. He tried to ignore her, tried to work on his wounded shoulder, but he felt the rage coming on, knew he had to kill her, knew she was right, that he had to kill her and run. "My husband's a big man, mister, and he's bringing angry men to kill you. You better run, mister."

He scrambled to his feet and took the two steps to the bed, pushing Mary-Anne back. "I'm going to have you first, woman, then I'll run. I'll run but you're coming with me, woman. You're my woman now. If your husband shows up, I'll sell you back to him, but he ain't killing me and he ain't getting you back until I get my gold."

He had his way with her, viciously, letting all his desires come to pass and easing his rage. After, he tied her hands to the head of the bed and her feet to the foot end. "Sleep, woman and we'll do all of this again come morning. Then we'll run."

Mary-Anne was whimpering, suffering the pain and humiliation of the wild and anger-filled attack, and hatred boiled furiously, fighting with her as she tried to get some sleep. *I'm going to need my strength and it won't be Stephen Poindexter who kills this fiend, it will be me. No man has the right to do this and live. I won't miss next time I get my hands on his gun.*

CHAPTER TWENTY-TWO

"He's staying on the main road, Corcoran. Something I wouldn't do." Marty Rosso said. "I'd hightail it into one of the many canyons in these mountains and make up a fort somewhere."

"What it tells me is what I thought in the first place." Corcoran said. "The man's never been in this country before. He's hoping the road will take him somewhere safe. It's going to be dark and cold soon, Marty. Time for us to look for a place to spend the night. We won't see Mister Miller and the boys until sometime late tomorrow."

"This road winds through a long and steep valley or canyon to a narrow divide well above the tree line."

"I hope there are trees," Corcoran said. "Those boys at the charcoal ovens must have stripped these mountains. Were you around when they were fired up?"

"Sure. Just been a year or two that they've been down. Hell of an operation then and a good place to have a party now," Rosso chuckled. "Many a young couple has learned the lessons of life there." Rosso's face clouded over as he continued. "What's going to happen to Mrs. Poindexter?"

"It won't be good, Marty. Jack Mason will become even more desperate as we close in on him. He'll use her in every way you can imagine, I'm afraid. I hope she's half as tough as she is pretty. Let's set up camp under those cottonwoods," Corcoran said, pointing. "Probably water close by. I have some jerky in my saddlebags, so we'll have something to eat, anyway."

"Softened in hot water instead of coffee? Except we got nothing to get the water hot in," Rosso said. Both men were laughing as they unsaddled their horses under the cottonwood tree.

"You find that beast, Miller. I want my wife back and I want to see that man hang. I'm putting up a five hundred dollar bounty on his head right this minute. Bring him to me."

Dean Miller had two mules strung out behind him as he readied to ride out of Ward that early morning. "We'll bring her back, sir." Miller looked

over to Geno Oliveira and Tomaso Bono. "You sure
you can make this ride, Tomaso? It might get rough
as anything."

"I'm riding," is all the man said. His jaw muscles
ached from the pressure he was putting on them.
The bullet wound to his upper leg, on the inside of
the leg, wasn't fully healed, and sitting in the saddle
was going to be as painful as the shot itself.

"Skeets. You keep a close eye on Henry Storm.
Even without a leg that man is dangerous. Give the
sheriff a look-see, too, if you feel brave. I wouldn't do
it today, though. Let's go boys. Geno, ride out ahead
and find Corcoran. Let him know we're coming. Got
coffee? That'll be their first concern."

Miller looked back at Poindexter. *Why isn't he
coming with us? If I was married to that woman I'd
have two guns in each hand demanding that every man
in town ride with me to save her. This is wrong.*

Oliveira knew the country better than any of
them and rode off at a good lope. "I'll leave sign," he
called out.

Miller led the others out at a walk. *What's going
through Poindexter's mind is more than I could want.
His wife, more beautiful than any woman I've ever
seen, in the hands of a brute, a killer, and he's not in on
the chase. Why isn't he on the chase? Why aren't any*

of the town's other leaders on the chase?

He let the thoughts slip away and simply rode for the next several hours plainly seeing Oliveira's hoof prints in the roadway. It was when they left the road and moved into a grove of cottonwood trees that Miller started to focus again. "What have we got?"

"Looks like Corcoran and Rosso camped here last night. Geno's tracks head on back to the roadway. He left plenty of sign for us."

"Won't know how far Corcoran chased them today, then. We'll stay on Geno's trail. Wish I knew more about Jack Mason. Is he trail wise or just a town gambler and drunk? You ever heard anything about him?"

Tomaso shook his head. "Never heard the name before a day or two ago," he chuckled. "Corcoran seemed to know the whole gang. Said he put Henry Storm in prison once." *I should be up front, riding with Corcoran not feeling sorry because I got shot. I should lead this chase to save Mary-Anne.*

"What are you looking at?" Marty Rosso pulled up short when Corcoran took a quick move off the main trail. They had been riding at a solid trot up the steep trail for a couple of hours, able to follow Mason's tracks with ease. There had been no other travelers since Mason passed by.

"He left the trail here, Marty." Corcoran was standing in the stirrups, looking far off into the narrow canyon. "Is that smoke up there?"

Rosso rode up next to Corcoran, saw a wisp of wood smoke and nodded. "Must be a cabin or line shack up there. God help anyone who might have been there if Mason rode in with the Poindexter woman. God help the woman, too."

Corcoran put the spurs to Dude and the two rode the few miles up to the cabin at a solid fast lope. "Let's not get too close, Marty. Mason's got a rifle and he's good with it." They pulled up at a stand of pine and fir and tied off. "Nice and slow now. I'll move toward the front door. See if you can circle around and come up from the back. Let's not shoot each other."

Marty Rosso moved out through the trees while Corcoran worked his way toward the front of the cabin, moving between large rocks and trees. There was considerable open ground from a stand of fir to the cabin and Corcoran decided to move to his right in order to come in at an angle.

Didn't see that corral tucked in back there. He stayed low and crept as close as possible to the cabin. *This must be some rancher's line camp. Interesting.*

Smoke coming from the chimney but no horses in the corral. We're late, I'm afraid. Corcoran called out to Rosso as he walked toward the front of the cabin. "Missed 'em, Marty. I'll check out the cabin. Take a good look at the corral."

Corcoran slammed the door open, not expecting any response, but you never know. He found lots of blood on the floor, on the bed, even at the single table. There were two platters, one filled with an un-eaten venison chop, the other with the remains of a chop. Two coffee cups and an empty whiskey bottle.

"Got a body, Corcoran," Rosso yelled out. "You gotta see this."

"Be right there." Corcoran gave the cabin and the table another quick look and walked out. *There was a lot of violence inside that cabin. Too much blood from just one person. Both Mary-Anne and Mason are wounded.*

"They can't be too far in front of us, Marty. That fire is still hot and I'm afraid that both of them are wounded bad. Lots of blood in there. What've you got?"

"This is Pete Gustafson's body. Gustafson does some venison hunting for his market. Shot dead, but look at this," and he pointed at the two bucks hanging. "Mason must have just ripped that shoulder from the one buck. Doesn't look like his knife is very sharp."

"Or he only has the use of one hand, Marty. Gustafson must have had animals with him. Wonder where they are? Wonder why Mason didn't take at least one of these deer? Why just a shoulder?"

"You're right, Gustafson has his saddle horses but always goes into the mountains with mules to bring meat back." Marty walked up the hillside behind the corral and came back down a few minutes later, leading two mules. "These are Pete's animals. I knew they wouldn't be too far away. He treats them like puppy dogs. Mason must have his horse, though. He's only thinking of getting away, not staying alive."

"You're right. He didn't take the coffee cups but did take the pot. Let's go over that cabin and then find their trail out of here. Where does that main road go that we were on?"

"High, Corcoran. If he's on that road he'll be coming back this way soon. These mountains top off well over ten thousand feet and that road goes to the top. There will be five or more feet of snow up there already."

"Makes it even more important we find his trail out of here." Corcoran and Rosso walked down to the cabin and searched it for anything that might tell them something. "Gustafson is a longtime meat hunter, Corcoran. He had to have supplies here and I don't see any. Coffee, sugar, flour, canned fruit. Mason must have it all with him."

"He has his horse and Mary-Anne must be on Gustafson's. Plenty of room for those supplies and the shoulder of venison in their saddlebags. They're in better shape than we are, Marty." They had to laugh at the comment but both knew they hadn't had anything to eat for two days. "Let's cut away some of that meat and fry it up, cut some for our saddlebags, and find their trail. I fear for that woman. Can't believe the amount of blood in this cabin." Corcoran walked out followed by Rosso.

"Those boys are moving fast." Geno Oliveira muttered, riding hard up the steep canyon. "They had a fire in camp this morning but no food last night or this morning. A man with a growling stomach is a mean man in a fight," he snickered. "Better find them before they find Mason."

The main road was steep as it neared a ridgeline and Oliveira spotted smoke several miles out when he topped out. "Hope that's them." He stayed on the main trail until he came to where Corcoran and Miller jumped off for the ride to the cabin. He jumped from the saddle and left clear sign in the trail for Dean Miller to follow. "Hope I'm not too late for a good fight. That woman is in trouble."

Just as Corcoran and Rosso had, Oliveira pulled up short of the cabin and made a slow approach. *Corral is empty, but smoke coming from the chimney.* He kicked the door open and slammed his way inside. There was a note with his name on it pinned to the table. Rosso had to chuckle reading the note and did as it said.

I like this Corcoran fellow. Keep the fire going for the ones behind you, he says. You'll find a well-used game trail a hundred feet or so south of the cabin. We'll be on it, he says. Come join the party he says. You'll find fresh meat behind the corral, he says.

Geno Oliveira stoked the fire left the note on the table and headed for the corral where he cut away a large section of shoulder meat. "Bastard took the back strap, I see," he muttered, easing the fresh meat into a flour sack and tying it behind his saddle. Geno was mounted and on the now well-used game trail in minutes.

Oliveira knew the game trails usually moved from one bedding area to another with good feed in between. "We're heading more south than west, and more downhill than up. If we're chasing Jack Mason and the Poindexter woman, we're not running away, we're going to be running back soon." He noted they were still on the eastern flanks of the range and the intersecting game trails, while moving along the flanks, all went slightly uphill or downhill. *Mason has food, there's plenty of water, but does he really know where he's going? At this rate, we'll be back down in the valley soon.*

CHAPTER TWENTY-THREE

For a hunter or trapper, or for a buckaroo moving cattle in the high mountains, a trail like what they were on would not be difficult. For a town gambler and bank robber, it was more than difficult. Steep places, some going up, some going down, coupled with creek crossings, downed timber, and thick groves of trees a deer or elk could get through but two people on horses couldn't, were more than a test for Mason.

"You're lost mister and my husband and a lot of angry men are coming to kill you. You don't know where you are, do you?" Mary-Anne kept it up, hour after hour, until Mason finally let his anger overpower good sense. He turned in the saddle and smashed her between the eyes with his fist. She toppled from the saddle into a pile of rocks.

He was leading her horse and pulled up to a halt, dismounted and tied them off. *She's just worth too much gold to shoot her, but damn me if I don't want to. I gotta get out of these trees, be able to see that valley, and find Henry Storm's hideout. Send a note to her husband to bring gold.* He was smiling as he laid Mary-Anne across the saddle and tied her tight.

The next couple of hours were the most quiet he could remember since grabbing the woman and as he followed the various connecting game trails downhill, he finally caught sight of the wide valley, far below. He wasn't a woodsman, wasn't well traveled off main roads, and of course, didn't have a map with him. He was in a small copse of trees near a rock overhang and walked the horses to the rocks.

"We'll camp here, woman. I have more plans for you and I know you're looking forward to that." Mary-Anne Poindexter was still mostly unconscious and moaned when he got the ropes off and jerked her off the saddle. Mason simply let her flop to the ground. He tied the horses in some grass and made up a rough camp. "Where's the pot? I told you to pack that pot woman." He stormed to where she was spread out in the dirt and rocks and kicked at her. "You didn't pack any of the kitchen did you? Did you?"

"My husband will kill you mister. He's on his way with mean and angry men to kill you, mister." She snickered remembering how she left all the kitchen stuff behind the fence near the corral. "Your hours are numbered, mister."

He kicked her in the back again. "Get up and get a fire started, woman." He searched through the saddlebags from Gustafson's saddle and came up with a flint fire starter. "Here," he said, throwing it to her. "Fire, woman."

Mary-Anne Poindexter had been living the good life for several years, wife of the town's leading man, banker, mine owner, and had never been treated this way. Life in Ireland had been hard but she learned quickly, as a youngster, how to make life work. Start a fire? That fast, even in wet peat. Cook foul meat over that fire? Easy. Get men to do things for her? Absolutely.

It's just that she hadn't done it for years and was amazed how everything came back. *No more hits to the head. He'll kill me that way. Want that gun and the only way I can get it is to let him think I want him near me. He's hurt and I can help just enough to get that gun.* She spent time trying to figure out where they were as she got a fire started and gathered wood.

That's our valley, I know. So where are we? South

of Ward, but how far? If I kill him can I get down there? The more she thought about killing Jack Mason and riding down out of the mountains the more her head hurt. She had the wounds covered in dirty cloth ripped from her dress so the bleeding was under control but not the pain. *I need a good night's sleep. Get my strength back, and in the morning, I'll get that gun.*

Mason had a ragged slab of venison shoulder meat on a rock and was fighting to slice chops off it. "Damn it," he roared, not being able to hold it in place because of his wounded shoulder. "Cut this meat woman," he snarled. He laid his knife down next to the rock and moved back a step or two. He pulled his revolver and sat in the dirt. "One little wrong move with that knife will be your last."

She smiled slightly knowing that he was afraid of her. "I'll cut the meat, mister, and with every slice I'll think it's your heart I'm cutting. My husband will be here soon, mister, and he'll kill you. You'll die a long hard death, mister, when he gets here."

"Shut up!" He screamed at her, got up to smash her again, but caught himself. "Just cut the meat," he said. He sat back down, still holding the pistol, cussing under his breath. *I don't know how far it is to Henry's cabin. Can we be there tomorrow? Is she right? Is there a posse coming down on us? We got to leave out of here as soon as it's light enough to see.* The other urge returned and he told her the venison could wait.

He rushed her to where he had bedrolls laid out and threw her to the ground. Was this her opportunity? She watched as he unbuckled his gun belt and dropped it to the ground. Mary-Anne made a mad grab for it but he saw it coming and gave her a mighty kick in the ribs, knocking her back from the gun. "I like a woman what don't give up. You're mine." He rolled her unconscious body over and loosened his pants.

"Is he following some kind of plan, Corcoran? He's definitely working his way down but still going somewhat south."

"He's been to Henry Storm's hideout, Marty. Probably trying to find it." Corcoran remembered chasing Storm's gang across the open prairie. Remembered how, even when they attacked from the arroyos, they seemed to be heading in a specific direction. "That canyon," he said. "We couldn't chase Storm's gang into that canyon. That's where he's going, sure as I'm sitting here."

"I remember," Rosso said. "We're a full day's ride,

maybe more from it. As high as we are, we'd crest a ridge and drop down, but there are at least two, maybe three ridges between here and there."

"Mason wouldn't know that. I'm sure Mrs. Poindexter wouldn't either. He's planning to drop all the way to the valley floor in order to recognize the landmarks. If we ride hard tomorrow, we'll have that bastard. In fact, let's ride until very dark before making up camp,"

"Dean Miller and the others should be catching up, Corcoran. We've made damn good time today, though."

"Can't for the life of me figure out why we're heading back down toward the valley," Geno murmured. "Prints are fresh as all get out. Am I coming on Corcoran or Mason?" Geno Oliveira slowed down a bit, not wanting to ride up on the outlaw or endanger the Poindexter woman any more than she was.

"Gonna be dark soon, horse. We gotta set up a camp. Maybe another half mile." They were on a well-used game trail through sparse timber, all the time going downhill. "Smell that, horse? Smoke or I'm a goose." He had the horse at a slow walk and followed the trail toward a thick copse of pine.

"And there's a little fire, right there." Geno slipped down from the saddle, had his rifle in hand and moved forward another twenty-five feet or so before tying his horse off. He took the time to see as much of the area as he could before slowly moving toward the fire. He was as low as he could get, moved cautiously from tree to tree, expecting to take a round at every step.

Two men holding chunks of meat on sticks over the fire. That ain't Mason but I'm not sure it's Corcoran, either. "Hello the camp. I'm coming in peace. Name's Oliveira."

Corcoran smiled at Rosso. "Told you it was him. And you wanted to shoot him." He chuckled and yelled out to Oliveira. "Come on in, Geno. Been listening to you for ten minutes or more."

"Damn him," Oliveira laughed. "I wasn't that noisy was I? Glad to see you two. We can't be far behind Mason and the Poindexter woman. Your horse dung is still steaming."

"Figure we'll have him tomorrow. Bring food did you? Coffee pot? We were gonna eat this meat raw." Corcoran put another log on the fire and made room for Geno.

"Think she's still alive?" Oliveira asked. "Lot of blood in that cabin."

"He'll die a long hard death if she isn't," Corcoran snarled. The anger was white hot and still building. No woman was to be treated this way, according to the laws Corcoran lived by. A woman will be treated as a lady until she changes the rules and God help any man who disobeys.

Hours in the saddle following still warm tracks, plotting how to kill Jack Mason, how to make Jack Mason hurt more than any man had ever hurt and the tired and hungry Corcoran's fuse was short and burning. *She ain't my kind of woman. I don't mess around with married women, even if they want me to, but no woman deserves what Jack Mason is doing right now. He'll never have another opportunity.*

"Believe he's trying to get to Henry Storm's hide-out in that big canyon. That woman is his safety net. He'll trade her for some gold and a safe way out. He might get the gold from Poindexter but he ain't getting away. He's gonna pay hard for every bruise on that woman. For every tear that has fallen, for every ache in every muscle."

"Any chance that Dean Miller and Bono will catch up?" Marty Rosso offered a slice of venison to Geno.

"Bono's riding fine, at least he ain't complaining none. Dean's got the two pack mules, so they ain't moving faster than a walk. You boys were moving fast today."

"We'll be moving a lot faster tomorrow, Geno. We know where we're going, Mason don't know. Dean will catch up after we catch that murdering fool." Corcoran said. "Get that coffee pot boiling, Mr. Oliveira. We ain't had coffee for two days now."

CHAPTER TWENTY-FOUR

Morning in the fall, crisp clean air, high in the mountains of eastern Nevada should be a time of pure joy, but not today, not for Mary-Anne Poindexter. She was sure she had at least one broken rib, her head was throbbing and infection had set in, in the open head wounds. *I'm not going to die like this. I won't.* She did her best to stay away from Mason as she got a fire going.

She ripped more of her skirt away to tie off her ribs but every move, twist, or turn reminded her of the injury. She felt like she was going to fall, dizzy from her head wounds, but kept her mind on killing Mason, getting that gun and killing Mason.

"No coffee because of you." He took two steps toward her and she danced away, despite the pain it caused. She realized immediately that she was far faster than he. Her dress was already ripped to pieces and would not get in the way of a full-out sprint. "Heat some of that meat on the rocks, woman while I saddle up."

Yes, you bastard, I'll do that. I need the strength that hot meat will give me. Mary-Anne had sliced the meat the night before and laid a couple of thin chops on hot rocks. *Rocks. Maybe I don't need his gun. A rock to the head would do just as much damage as a bullet. I'm good with horses, I'm strong enough, I think.* She put a large rock, probably three pounds at least, into a pocket in her skirt, doing her best to keep it hidden while they ate the hot venison.

As usual, he just put a halter and leadrope on her horse instead of a bit. She rode saddled and Mason held on to the leadrope. He kicked the fire out, growled for her to get in the saddle, and they rode out. It was a cold morning high up as they were, and Mason sat slumped in his saddle. Mary-Anne nudged her horse closer to Mason's, pulled that heavy rock out, and slammed it into the back of the outlaw's head.

Jack Mason fell to the ground, unconscious. Mary-Anne hadn't planned past knocking the man out. She just sat in the saddle for a minute, wondering about what she should do. It came to her fast

and she climbed down from her horse and mounted
Mason's, still holding the leadrope from her horse.

Free, she almost screamed it out. *I've got to get to
the valley floor. Got to get back to Ward. Can't panic.
Don't run. Ride fast, but don't panic.* She spent the
next hour moving downhill, using game trails when
they were available, otherwise, going cross country,
evading trees, rock falls, and great ledges. It was
hard riding and during one particularly hard part,
she let go of the leadrope to the trailing horse.

"No," she moaned, watching the horse move off
on its own. "Can't take the time to catch it. Have to
keep moving." As she got lower down the mountain,
she noticed, there were fewer and fewer trees allowing her to make better time.

"I'll be in the valley late this afternoon," she figured. Riding with just her own horse made it much
easier. The view out across the valley was much
better with the lack of trees. She stopped just once,
at a small stream, and took the time to wash her
head wounds, fill the canteen, and give the horse
time for a good drink.

She couldn't help herself. She kept looking behind.
*Is he coming? Is that a shadow or is it him? Don't slow
down, girl. Ride, ride.* She was well down the side of
the mountain when she noticed that Jack Mason had

a rifle strapped to the saddle. *So busy working my way down, worried about him attacking, and I never saw this. Thank you, Stephen Poindexter, for teaching me how to shoot a rifle.*

Jack Mason slowly regained his senses and was in a rage, screaming vile obscenities, kicking rocks, even drawing his weapon, almost firing off a shot. When he calmed down, he realized he was afoot and the rage came back like a clap of thunder. He wore himself out with his cussing and foolish antics and sat down in the dirt. "Gotta think, Jack." He said, almost in a hushed voice. "Follow her, kill her dead, and get my horse back. Get the hell out of this country."

Seeing her trail was the easy part. Following on foot where the horses walked was difficult, and Mason tried too hard to catch Mary-Anne wearing himself out inside of an hour. "Gotta use my head. Slow down, think, Jack," he said, over and over. "She's at a walk, not trotting or loping. Just stay on the trail. Follow her and kill her."

His mindset had changed. No longer was he going to capture her and trade her for gold. Now, it was kill her. Be rid of this woman who was responsible for everything that was wounded and bleeding including his vanity. She stole his horses. Beat him unconscious. Left him for dead.

He was trying to get around a large grove of Cottonwood trees on a steep rocky slope. *Must be a spring in there. She's got my canteen and all the meat. Damn her to hell.* He moved into where the trees seemed the greenest this late in the season. "Will you look at that," he murmured. The haltered horse, saddled, stood in the mud of the spring. Mason wanted to rush the animal and had to catch himself. "Easy, Jack. Take it easy."

The horse wasn't going anywhere. When the horse had moved into the springs, the leadrope had wrapped around a downed limb and had the animal quite secure, standing in the mud. Mason moved slow, talking softly to the skittish animal, and got a hold of the leadrope. "Got yourself tied off, eh, big boy? Don't like riding without a bit but I've done it before." He tied the loose end of the leadrope to the other side of the halter and flipped the loop over the horse's head.

Mason was mounted and rode out of the grove of trees, back on Mary-Anne's trail. He came to the stream, took a quick drink and kept going. Didn't even see the dirty bandages that were left. "It should be easy following this trail," he muttered. "I'll have her back soon."

"What happened here, Corcoran? Mixed trails." Geno Oliveira and Marty Rosso were looking at horse prints going one way, and boot prints seemingly wandering around. Corcoran chuckled as he pointed out a boot print over the top of a horse print.

"She got away, boys. With both horses."

"Look at this," Rosso said. He held a large rock with bloodstains. "There's a lot of blood on this rock. That lady's got some fight in her. At least the second time she's had a fight with him."

"He's chasing her on foot, gentlemen, and that means we will be riding up on him long before we catch up to the lady. He will have the advantage of being able to hear us coming and hit us from ambush. Time to be quiet now." Corcoran led off from the little campsite. "Easy trail to follow."

Looks like all she wants is to get down out of these mountains, only using a game trail for short periods. "Ease up, boys." Corcoran stepped down and looked at the ground. "she's lost that second horse. I don't think Mason even saw this. The loose horse moved out and up the hill some."

Corcoran stayed on foot for the next several hundred yards. "Interesting here," he pointed out. It looks like Mrs. Poindexter rode right around that stand of cottonwood trees but Mason walked into the grove. Let's find out why."

Corcoran jumped back in the saddle and they made their way into the grove of trees, finding the spring and the prints where Mason found the horse. "He's a lucky sumbitch," Marty Rosso said. "I wonder if the horse called him by name. Walked right up to it, he did."

"Yes, and now we have to put some speed on, boys. He's mounted again and on the chase. That woman isn't safe yet." Corcoran rode out of the grove, cut Mary-Anne's trail and put Dude in a fast walk. "Still going downhill."

It was just another hour and they found the stream and bloody bandages. "Hers or his?" Corcoran held one up. "Her dress, so I would think her bandage. She's making better time than Mason."

They were about to ride out when they heard a loud whistle coming from the hillside behind them. Dean Miller and Tomaso Bono rode over a ridge and down to the stream, leading the two pack mules. "Wondered if we were ever gonna catch up," Miller said. You've left us plenty of sign but moved too fast for us to catch you."

"Wish we had time to build a pot of coffee but we don't." Corcoran looked over to Bono. "You feeling good?"

"I'm fine, Corcoran. Leg's getting a good workout. How far behind are we?"

"They're separated, Tomaso. Let's ride, boys. I'll bring you up to date as we ride. Can't let Mason find her. He'd kill her on sight, I'm sure. Marty, why don't you ride out a little faster and see what you can find. He's more than dangerous and don't forget it."

Corcoran spent the next few minutes bringing everyone up to date on the chase, urging as much speed as he could get from the mules. "The thing is, she's wounded, he's wounded, and if he gets there first, she's dead." They were riding across rolling hills now mostly devoid of trees but still well into the mountains.

"She's making for the valley floor," Corcoran said again. "When she gets there, how far from Ward will she be? Would she feel safe?"

"Won't be safe," Oliveira said. "If she keeps riding in this direction, she's going to come out just above the charcoal ovens, putting her several miles from the safety of town. It could turn out to be a horse race into town and Mason knows he has to kill her. He's already got a rope around his neck as far as I'm concerned."

"Only after trial, Geno. We are wearing badges,"

Corcoran said. "Is there some way we could get to where she might be any faster?"

"Not that I can see," Oliveira said. "All she knows is to get to the valley floor and she's simply following the terrain to get there. She could change direction on a whim and we'd be miles off."

"You're right, of course," Corcoran said. "And, Marty is out there, too. Can't leave him hanging, either. Let's just stay on the trail, then."

CHAPTER TWENTY-FIVE

Mary-Anne stopped on the crest of ridge to catch her breath, take a drink of water, and look behind her, again. *That's a rider. No, no. mustn't panic, girl. Just ride harder.* She looked quickly again and couldn't see the rider. *Behind a hill. At least a full mile behind me. Did he see me?*

She moved out at a fast trot, working through sage and other brush, but no trees. *I've got to find a place to hide. He's going to catch me out on the plain like this. Rifle. I have a rifle. He must have extra ammunition. Got to find a place to hide and shoot him as soon as he gets close.*

She was riding fast, threading her way through the brush, rock outcrops, and rolling folds of the mountain. Less than half an hour later she spotted the five bee-hive domes of the charcoal ovens, standing starkly in the late afternoon sun. *Can I hide there? Just too many miles to try to make a race into town. Maybe there will be someone there to help.*

She raced to the line of ovens, pulling up at the most western one of the group and jumped from the horse. She grabbed the rifle and led the horse up between two of the large structures and tied him off to some brush. She quickly pulled the saddle and got down on her knees to empty the saddlebags. *Meat, good. Coffee and no pot.* She almost chuckled remembering how angry Mason was to find out she left all the kitchen back at the cabin. *Bullets. Bigger ones must be for the rifle.*

She scrambled up on the ridge at the south edge of the line of ovens and tried to find a place to hide and still be able to shoot Jack Mason as soon as she could see him. *He has to be close and that man will never touch me again. Never.* She was nestled behind a large rock, had a good view of the trail south, and made sure the rifle was fully loaded, cocked, and ready.

"There she is." Mason said right out as he topped a ridge. "Looking back to see if I'm coming. I'm coming, woman. You better believe it. I'm coming to kill you." He kicked the horse into a strong trot across the ridge and watched as she did the same to her horse. "You'll be dead before the sun goes down."

Mason lost sight of her as she rode through the many folds, ridges, and ravines, but could see the hoof prints from her horse plainly. It was late in the afternoon and he would not catch her before the sun went down. "Damn that woman. I ain't giving her up." Mason's attitude changed when he thought he might be able to catch her, since he was horseback, not stumbling along on sore feet. "She's worth her weight in gold. I'm gonna get my gold."

Panic was starting to set in, he was thinking that when the sun went down he would lose her. *Will she keep going when it gets dark? No, I don't think so. She has the food. Damn. She has my rifle.* Jack Mason realized that last part could change all his plans. *She almost killed me with my pistol. Can she shoot a rifle? Damn.*

He continued to ride until the sun slipped behind the high peaks of the Egan Range and he knew he had to find a place to camp. Riding through open country in the pitch dark of night was too dangerous, he knew, but also, he didn't want to lose her. He rode until he simply had to stop. "Can't even see my hand," he grumbled, stepping down from the saddle. "Right here is good enough."

The cold was seeping deep into the outlaw when he realized he didn't even have the fire starter flint. A north wind was blowing and the stars were brilliant in icy cold air. The bullet wound to his side was infected and bleeding, it smelled bad and the back of his head ached. It would be a long night with little sleep for Jack Mason.

"Hello the camp. It's Marty riding in." The hail was answered and Rosso rode in slow and stepped down from his horse near the fire. "Mason is about five miles in front of us. Glad you lit a fire or I wouldn't have found you. There's no moon tonight, at all."

"Were you able to see Mrs. Poindexter? Could you tell where she might be going?" Corcoran poured a tin cup full of coffee for the man. "Is he close?"

"Never saw her but I think he may have." Marty Rosso said. "At one point he started moving much faster, as if he knew where he was going, not just following some prints in the dirt. I'm almost sure she's at the charcoal ovens. Plenty of places to hide, to attack. I wonder if old man Poindexter has any idea of how much woman he's married to?"

Tomaso Bono smiled, sitting in front of the fire, nursing some hot coffee. "No, Marty, he doesn't. He has no idea of who Mary-Anne might be or what she's capable of. She had a hard life in Ireland but learned how to take care of herself, how to survive."

Rosso didn't say anything back but wondered how it was that Bono would know these things. The same thoughts flowed through Corcoran's mind as well. *My mother survived being a poor woman in Ireland. If Mary-Anne is half as strong-willed as my mother, she's more woman than Poindexter could handle.*

"It was interesting watching them work together at the bank. He might just have an idea of how strong a woman she is. What I don't understand is why he isn't with us on this chase." Corcoran sat down near the fire. "If I spent every night with that woman, I'll guarantee I'd be leading this chase."

"I know I would." Tomaso laughed and limped to the fire. "Poindexter is like most of the rich people I've ever met. He tells people what to do, never does anything himself. Only person I've ever run into who is not like that is old man White at the mine. He insists on doing it himself."

"Poindexter was born rich, White had to fight his way to that status," Corcoran said. "I think our best bet is to ride straight for the charcoal ovens come sunrise. Tomaso, you lead the mules, Rosso, you ride with me, and Geno, you ride with Dean Miller. I'll ride in from the southwest, and Dean, you two come in from the southeast. Remember, the woman knows how to shoot and she doesn't know we might be the good guys."

It came as a shock to Geno that Mary-Anne Poindexter doesn't even know that they are on the chase. "My God, Corcoran. She doesn't, does she? She could just as quick shoot us as she would Jack Mason."

There were a few chuckles but most of the men took note of what was said and slept with the thought that they could be shot dead by the person they were trying to save. Morning came as a clear and cold day and a fire was rekindled quickly.

"Ah, coffee," Corcoran said. "Good whiskey is the nectar of the angels but coffee is what gives them the strength to make good whiskey." Groans and chuckles were equally mixed as the men crawled out of their bedrolls.

"Only a misplaced Irisher who thinks he's a poet would say something like that before sunrise," Bono said.

"I like laughter around a morning fire, Corcoran," Miller said. He called Rosso over and they cleared stones and debris from a plot of dirt near the fire. "Here's a good ideas of how best to get to those ovens." The group gathered around and Marty took over.

"Here is where we are," and he put a fingertip in the dirt. "This is about where Mason is. Remember, this is five miles," he said, making another mark. "My best guess is, the ovens are right about here. There are five of them and they're large."

"Large enough for someone to hide behind?" Corcoran asked.

Rosso and Miller laughed. "You might say so, Corcoran. They stand damn near thirty feet tall. Gotta be twenty-five, maybe thirty feet across. Those things burned more than thirty cords of wood at a time. That's why there aren't any trees around here." Marty laughed. "She could fort up and be relatively safe from Mason if she's thinking, not in a panic."

"From what I've seen, this woman doesn't panic. All right, then, let's move out like we talked about last night. Save the woman at all costs. Capture Mason if possible." He snickered. "If you can't capture the fool, kill him."

Mason had to go without a fire when he woke up. No food, no coffee. Everything in his body hurt but the only thing on his mind was the capture of that damned woman. *I'll exchange her for gold, and race for freedom.* His thoughts were jumbled as he saddled the horse. *How could he just ride into town and demand money?*

"They won't just give me the money," he mumbled. "They'll try to trap me, get the woman back, and get their money back." Would he kill her if he had the chance? Would he ride in with her alive and demand money? Jack Mason couldn't think or get his thoughts going in the same direction.

He was mounted quickly, cut Mary-Anne's track and moved out. Frost covered every bush and blade of grass, the sun offered brilliant rainbows in the crystals, but beauty wasn't to be seen this morning. He rode up and over a broad ridge and spotted the large ovens first, and then the small tendril of campfire smoke.

"Gotcha, woman." He rode down the slope on the other side of the rise so she wouldn't spot his silhouette and tried to work out in his mind how best to make his attack. "I'm at least half a mile out so can't just ride in hard. She'd have too much time to grab that rifle."

Instead, he tried to use the terrain and followed along the folds and bends of the hillsides, slowly getting closer to the bee-hive ovens. "Got to surprise that woman and not give her a chance. She's worth too much to kill, but I will."

He was behind a small hump of rolling ground when he dismounted and found a small sagebrush and tied the horse. He climbed the rise and got down on hands and knees as he neared the crest. It was a razorback ridge, almost spiky rocks covered the top and he crawled behind some to look down on the ovens, just fifty yards or so away.

He spotted the smoke, tried to figure out how to work his way through or around a couple of the ovens to get near enough to shoot the woman. "I gotta shoot her but not kill her. She's too dangerous to just try to capture." The ovens were in a straight line and the smoke seemed to come from behind the westernmost structure.

"Go around and come in from the west? Go between these two? Damn. What's on the other side? Ain't gonna just walk in. Gotta be on my horse." He scrambled back down to where the horse was tied and decided the best bet would be to ride in from the west. "I'll come around from behind that last big oven and ride her down."

Mary-Anne Poindexter stayed in her bedroll as long as she dared, wrapped in the filthy blankets that had been tied off behind the saddle. Sunrise was a long and slow thing of beauty, she thought, offering all the colors of the rainbow in the sparkling frost that seemed to cover everything. *I'm not safe yet. He'll be here this morning and I have to be ready.* She looked out to the east, and just a few miles away she could see morning stove smoke from homes and businesses of Ward. *So close and I would never make it. He'd ride me down, kill me before Stephen could do anything. Where is Stephen? He should be coming for me.*

She had used the fact that her husband was coming to kill Jack Mason, taunted the outlaw at every chance, but she also harbored the terrible thought that Stephen Poindexter wasn't coming. He was a strange man, so different from most she had known. *If I was back home in Ireland, and had a man, he would lead his brothers and cousins to save me. Out here in this primitive little village, I have the leading man and he might not come.*

She stood straight up at the thought. Yes, she thought, he might not. *The bank, his investments, his property, all far more important to Stephen than I would ever be. Tomaso, though, he's different. He'll come. And this huge fellow, son of Erin? Yes, Corcoran will come, but as a lawman, not because he loves me.*

She tried to let the thoughts go, had her coffee, and grabbed the rifle. "He'll be here soon," she murmured. Mary-Anne, often the poet, spent several minutes taking in the scene. *Couldn't see most of this last night. I've been here but it was for a picnic, not a killing.* She felt the shivers of fear dance down her spine and continued looking around. *If I go where I was last night, maybe I'll see him coming.*

She walked between the two westernmost ovens and laid out behind the small ridge that separated the ovens from the open prairie. She saw dust but it was behind a rise fifty yards of so out from her. She was amazed, watching the dust rise, almost in a line, along the ridge until its meaning flared across her thoughts.

"That's a man riding a horse on the other side of the ridge. That's the man I'm going to kill." She knew he'd come around that last large oven, probably fast, and raced to the north base of the oven she was behind. She fell to her stomach, rifle out in front of her, and waited for the attack. She could hear hoof beats as Mason moved from a walk to a trot, and came around from behind that westernmost oven.

He was bent low in the saddle and when he saw the campsite was empty, reined his horse to a stop. The crack of the rifle echoed for minutes in the surrounding mountains, but the thud of Mason falling to the ground didn't. The 45-70 bullet tore through his right shoulder, wrenching him right out of the saddle.

He scrambled hard for sagebrush north of where he fell and watched his horse run off as another rifle shot went off. The bullet kicked dirt in Mason's face and he crawled hard for that brush, fighting the pain of his wound. He was flat out in the dirt but couldn't get his sidearm. Couldn't make that arm and hand work.

Another rifle shot and Mason screamed out when the bullet tore through his boot, destroying his left ankle on the way. He cried out for mercy. "Please. Help me. Please. I'm dying."

Mary-Anne had heard that before. "That's right, mister. You are dying. Right here. Right now, mister. Throw your guns out here where I can see them and maybe I'll let you live." She didn't move from behind the edge of the adobe brick structure and kept the rifle aimed at the man. "I can see your head, mister. That's my next shot."

Mason tied to roll over, get even further into the desert dirt. "I can't get my gun. You shot my arm and I can't get it." He used his left hand and eased the weapon from its holster and cocked it. *Ain't shot left handed in a long time but I'll kill her as soon as I see her.* "I can't get at it. Please, help me," he was almost crying.

"Only help you'll get from me is a quick shot to

the head. Put you down like the filthy dog you are," she said. How many times did she see women fight off men when she was a child, so many years ago? So many miles ago. "Crawl out of there, mister. Crawl now." She put another round into the sand just in front of his face.

"Can't," he cried. "It hurts. I'm dying," he said. "Please help."

"Not going to, mister." She laughed. "Tell you what, mister. I'll just wait until you bleed out." She took that time to reload the rifle. *He's a snake. He tried to make me believe all this back at that cabin and I fell for it. Not this time mister. Time is on my side this time.*

CHAPTER TWENTY-SIX

"Hear that, Corcoran?" Marty Rosso and Corcoran were less than a mile from the charcoal ovens, could see them plainly off to their northeast. "Sounded like a rifle shot."

"Surely was, Marty. Let's pick it up. Can you see Dean and Geno? I can't but they had to have heard it too."

"I see their dust," he laughed. "Another shot, there. She's in trouble." They had their animals at a fast run and bore down on the westernmost oven, fast. "Somebody's doing a lot of shooting, Corcoran."

They rounded the oven, Corcoran spotted Mary-Anne's small camp, empty, saw two horses munching grass, but no people. The bullet put another hole in Corcoran's buffalo robe coat and he dove for the ground. "See where that came from?" He yelled at

Marty Rosso who was clawing his way to the safety of the edge of an oven.

"The other side of where I am," Rosso yelled back.

Corcoran had Dude laid out and was behind the horse, an old trick he learned from some cavalrymen he knew. He heard moaning off to his left but couldn't see anyone. The bullet came from his right. *This is a nice mess. Somebody over there is hurt and somebody over that way wants to kill me. Which one is Mary-Anne?*

"Mary-Anne Poindexter," Corcoran yelled out. "This is Corcoran, Terrence Corcoran. I have men with me, come to get you out of this mess. Can you hear me?"

There was a long silence and finally he got his answer. "I'm over here, Mr. Corcoran. Oh, my. Did I hurt you? I shot the man who abducted me, but he isn't dead yet. He's a liar. Will tell you he needs help and then hurt you."

He'll never hurt you again, dear lady. Corcoran had to laugh. "I'm fine but my coat isn't," he called out. Corcoran knew where the moans came from and eased around to give the area a good look. Heavy rabbitbrush and sagebrush, mostly. No trees.

"Cover me Marty," he called out, rolled away from Dude and sprinted to a heavy clump of sage, diving in. Rosso put three rounds into where he thought he heard Mason moaning in pain.

Dean Miller led Geno Oliveira in from the east and held up when Rosso fired. The two of them watched Corcoran worm crawl his way through the brush toward Mason. "We got you covered, Corcoran," Miller said.

Tomaso Bono, following the group with the mules, rode along the south line of ovens and stopped the animals as he came to the last structure on the west. Mary-Anne heard him, swung around with the rifle and recognized him just in time. "Tomaso. I knew you'd be here. I knew it."

Geno Oliveira rode his horse toward a stand of brush, rifle at the ready, and when Jack Mason took aim with his pistol, he shot him dead. "It's over," he called out. "Mason's dead."

Corcoran was on his feet and running for Mary-Anne who just sat in the dirt, crying, her rifle across her legs. Bono climbed down from his saddle and Corcoran slumped down next to Mary-Anne and gently put his arms around her, holding her tight. "It's over, Mary-Anne. It's over." They sat in the dirt, rocking back and forth for several minutes, not speaking.

Geno pulled Mason's bloody body out from the

brush and went through his pockets while Dean Miller got the fire re-started and a pot of coffee boiling. It was just a few minutes later that Tomaso Bono brought the mules up to the campsite.

"Anybody hurt in all that shootin'?"

"Only Jack Mason," Geno said. He pointed down the long road to a group or riders coming. "Looks like they heard all the noise in town, too. Better get ready for them just in case they ain't the good guys comin' to rescue us."

Corcoran had Mary-Anne on her feet and walked her to her little camp. "I'll get you some coffee. A wee bit of whiskey?" He asked.

"Aye, Terrence, a wee bit and a wee bit more too," she chuckled. "Is he dead? I shot him twice but he was still talking."

"He isn't talking any now, dear lady. Looks like we have company coming, boys. Make sure we know who they are before you let them in."

Skeets McDougall was at the blacksmith's talking with Buford Waring about replacing the window bars in the jail when he heard the first shots. "Somebody's got their deer," he said. "Long way out there" More shots were fired. "Either they can't hit a barn close up or there's a whole herd of dead deer out there."

"Those shots are a long way off, Skeets. I think somebody's in trouble."

"Well, if that's the case, and since I'm the only law left in this town, I better ride out there. You're on the town council, Mr. Waring and I think you need to be deputized so you can ride out with me."

They chuckled and made fun of what they were doing but were ready to ride out when mine owner White rode up. "Looking for you, Skeets. Hear all that shooting west of us? Must have been near the old ovens."

"That's where we're going, Mr. White. Care to join us?"

The three men made good time on a well-used road and came into Mary-Anne's camp at a trot. "I'll be damned," Skeets said. Along with the posse was a body. "Corcoran, is that you?"

"Good timing, Skeets. Good morning Mr. White, Mr. Waring. Coffee's hot and so's the fire. Set a spell. The dead one is Jack Mason, the last of the Henry Storm gang, and the lady covered in a buffalo robe is Mary-Anne Poindexter. Didn't bring the banker with you?"

"Didn't know it was you." Skeets looked over at Mary-Anne and shook his head. "Poindexter's in Hamilton, working to get a new sheriff in office. Avery Johnson died the afternoon of the bank robbery. Bones said it was blood poisoning."

"Hamilton?" Mary-Anne looked around at the newcomers. "Not trying to save me?"

"Bastard," White said. "He talked several men out of helping in the rescue, Mr. Miller. Did you know that? More interested in working with that criminal Kleindorfer than saving his wife."

Corcoran sat down in the dirt next to Mary-Anne. It was rare that Corcoran didn't have something to say and this was one of them. He simply put his arm around the woman, could feel her sobbing, and wondered what kind of man would ride off like that. "You seem to be aware of Kleindorfer's activities, Mr. White. Tell me what you know."

"He didn't get rich from the cattle he runs, Corcoran. He has his fingers in most of White Pine County's business interests. Kleindorfer is behind the movement to relocate the county seat to what they are calling Ely. Big copper strike there and Kleindorfer has his fingers in that, too."

"I was led to believe that Kleindorfer was more outlaw than rancher. You haven't mentioned any crimes. Where does Poindexter fit in all this?"

"He's loaned a lot of money to Kleindorfer," Mary-Anne said. She almost whispered the com-

ment. "Most of Kleinddorfer's business is partner-
ships with others. He worms his way in, and that
includes the businesses he has with Stephen. Most
have a criminal element that his partners don't want
known, including Stephen's."

There was a long silent moment as the men
around the fire let what she said soak in. Ward's
leading man, banker, land owner, developer, was in
criminal cohorts with Clive Kleindorfer. Buford
Waring stood up and walked around the campsite,
scuffed his boots at pebbles, and cussed softly for
a full minute.

"He's invited me and other members of the town
council to take part in some of these investments
of his, even to the point of lending us the money
at almost no interest. Kleindorfer's name is always
mentioned as one of the partners. There are mining
corporations selling shares in non-existent mines,
corporations selling stock for railroads that can't
possibly travel across ten-thousand foot mountain
ranges, organizations working to build massive irri-
gation dams to hold precious rains that never would
be enough to fill them."

"Falsified assays, shares in fake mines, and land
schemes that would rival the railroad barons," Corcoran said. "We've been worrying about a bank robbery,

not a banker robber. Mr. Henry Storm's activities may have opened some interesting doors for us."

It was a sad blacksmith that sat back down at the fire. He looked each person, one at a time, in the eye. "Why haven't I said something before? Embarrassed, I guess. And afraid of what the consequences would be. Stephen Poindexter has a lot of economic power in this little mining camp of ours." Buford sat, hang-dog-like, staring into the fire.

"Well, Skeets, I've got a job for you and those flashy fingers you always talk about," Corcoran said. "It's time we get Mary-Anne home." Corcoran hugged her tight and could tell she was still crying. "Bones will make you well, darlin'. We have a fine man in Carson City sitting in the Attorney General's office who will be glad to receive the wires I'll be sending."

These will be difficult times for Mary-Anne Poindexter, I'm afraid. Corcoran filled his coffee cup again and sat back down next to her. *I'm going to have to get all that information, names, dates, amounts of money, from her and send it to Jeremiah. A simple bank robbery gone wrong, a beautiful woman abducted, and how many White Pine County leaders will be on their way to prison when it's over?* The irony of his thoughts almost brought a chuckle but the reality of having his arm around Mary-Anne stifled that.

"You heading to Hamilton, Corcoran?" White asked. "Not sure it would be safe."

"No, I'll let the state handle that mess. Jeremiah Odom was a federal marshal before he ran for attorney general. He'll tear that criminal organization to shreds. Let's get packed up and get this lady home."

"I have a house to live in," Mary-Anne said. "Can't call it a home. If Stephen goes to jail because of all this, I'll lose that too." *What's going to happen with the bank? All those people who trusted us might lose their money and property. And they'll blame me as much as Stephen.* It was hours later that she remembered that she and Poindexter also owned The Grand Hotel.

It was quite a parade coming into the old mining town as businesses were opening and people were moving about. A cold mid-morning parade for the local folk. Men, women, and children stopped to watch, pointing to Mary-Anne, commenting on the body laid out across a horse, and smiling or laughing at the grubby men who had made the successful chase.

"Meeting at the sheriff's office about three this afternoon," Corcoran said. "We have a couple of days' worth of paperwork in front of us." Buford Waring said he'd take care of getting Jack Mason's body to the undertaker, Skeets headed for the telegraph office to see if it was still working and Tomaso and Dean Miller headed for the Grand Hotel Saloon.

Corcoran delivered Mary-Anne to Bones. "It won't be easy, Mrs. Poindexter, but I'm going to have to ask you for all the names and dealings your husband has had with Kleindorfer and others in White Pine County. Do you have any close friends here in Ward who can help you through all this?"

"I'm a strong daughter of the Emerald Isles, Terrence. You should know that." It was almost a pained smile she offered. "I'll be fine. I have all the information you're thinking of in my books. I've been keeping the bank's books for at least three years and have every loan, investment, and deal that Stephan has made during that time in the ledgers."

Corcoran stood next to the bed and took her hand. "It will be painful but I'll try to make it as easy as possible." He gave her a big smile and turned to the doctor. "She's all yours, Bones. Take good care of this lady. She's far tougher than her husband ever was."

CHAPTER TWENTY-SEVEN

Corcoran stepped from the large metal tub, dried off, and dressed after a long hot bath and shave. His massive auburn mustache glowed in the late afternoon sunlight that poured through the hotel window. Mindy Shepherd folded the towels and watched the big man dress.

"That must have been terrible for Mrs. Poindexter. Can a woman own a bank?"

"Your friend owns a millinery shop, doesn't she?" Corcoran asked with a smile and a wink. "Well? Doesn't she?"

"I guess there isn't a difference. Such a terrible thing, though."

"You're right," he said. "What a nasty turn this has taken. That lady left town as a very rich abductee and comes home destitute, married to a man who thinks money is more important than family. What he's done to her is just as obscene as what Mason did."

"Destitute? You said she would own the bank and hotel."

"Would, Mindy. Not until all the court appearances, not until Poindexter is found guilty, not until a court declares it. In the meantime, she has nothing unless she has tucked some aside somewhere."

"Doesn't seem right," Mindy said.

Corcoran found himself fighting two battles, both of which he was good at. Battle number one, ruin the man who hurt the woman. Mason of course paid the ultimate price but Poindexter's actions demanded that Corcoran intercede on Mary-Anne's behalf. Poindexter must pay for that.

Battle number two was a little easier to deal with. Poindexter, Corcoran believed, committed crimes that must be paid for. He spent an hour putting together several wires he wanted Skeets to send. The one to Attorney General Odom was the most difficult to word. *That banker is as much an outlaw as Henry Storm and his gang.* After more than an hour, he gathered his papers and headed for the office. He stopped in the restaurant on the way out of the hotel. Mindy was already at a table.

"Mindy, my love, I'll be back in a few hours and it would be the perfect ending to a long day if you would set a huge steak in front of me and then sit with me while I attack it. I'd want a flagon or two of whiskey to get it settled properly and some warmth, later on, to give me strength for tomorrow."

"I would like that, too, Terrence Corcoran. You've been gone too long, big boy."

"Yes, we have," he said. He gave her bottom a pat or two and walked out, headed for the office. He had more than little Mindy on his mind. More than Mindy Shepherd at the Silver Springs saloon.

Do I want to leave? My job is done. Henry Storm is no more. Do I really have to leave? Sure as hell Odom will ask for my help and I could stay. And that would put my sheriff in Eureka in a fine bind. Oh, Terrence, lead with your left, not your heart just once, old man. He had come to enjoy his time in Ward, had made a number of acquaintances. Was it time to leave?

Thoughts of his cabin in Eureka, the people he called friends, the town he had sworn to protect carried him all the way up the street to the sheriff's office.

"Henry Storm has done this county a huge favor by robbing that bank of Poindexter's," Corcoran said. *I've got quite an army lined up for this fight.*

Tomaso, Geno, Marty, Skeets, and Dean. Poindexter and Kleindorfer don't stand a chance. Poindexter must have someone here in Ward, though. Can't imagine who.

"What did you find out at the telegraph office, Skeets?"

"First off, Terrence, I have to turn in my badge. They want me to start immediately since no traffic has moved after we put Fingers in jail. So, sending wires for you will be no trouble. It seems the sheriff's office has an account with the company."

"So does Eureka County," Corcoran said. "We're going to miss you around here, Skeets, but this is good for you." Corcoran gave each man a good look before he began. "We're about to put a lot of people in White Pine County government in jail. These wires I'm sending should be billed to Eureka County. I'm authorized to do that but will send a wire, which I'll pay for, to my sheriff to make sure. Don't want anyone in Hamilton to find out what we're about to start."

He poured some coffee and laid out the wires he wanted to send and the plans he hoped they would follow. "Everything we do from now on cannot leave this office. Agreed?" He got nods from everyone. "Mary-Anne has been keeping the books at the bank and we have records of every deal Poindexter made so those illegal mine deals and other activities Mr. White talked about are real. I want you to send these wires off right now, Skeets. After you send them, you get these notes back here. Don't leave them sitting around your new office."

Corcoran quickly wrote out another wire, put a cartwheel on top of it and handed it to Skeets. "This one too. Sheriff Connors should respond. Whatever responses you get from Connors or Odom, get to me quick and no notes left at your office."

"You make it sound like Poindexter might have someone here in town that is involved in the illegal dealings." Dean Miller sat back in his chair behind the desk with notepaper in front of him. "Someone special that we might know?"

"That's just it, Dean. If there is someone, we don't know who it or they might be. You better make sure that leg is working good, Tomaso. These next few weeks might get exciting. Until word comes down from Hamilton, you're still the resident deputy around here. With Johnson dead, Poindexter will push hard for someone to replace him and when it gets out what we're doing, you're sure to be fired."

"Thanks for all that, Corcoran." Tomaso and the others laughed and toasted Corcoran with their tin cups. "What happens if I am? Probably all of us."

"Probably," Corcoran chuckled. "Jeremiah Odom is sure to deputize me and I'm sure to deputize each of you. We'll be working for the Nevada Attorney General and we might have to arrest White Pine County Sheriff Deputies come to confiscate evidence. It could get rough."

"Hell, we're already bruised and bloody, Terrence. What's a little more?"

"Mr. Kennedy, will you come in here, please?" Jeremiah Odom, forty years old, wiry and long of limb, was pacing his large office in Carson City. "When did this wire arrive?"

"Less than an hour ago, General. Something wrong?"

"No, not here, but there sure as hell is in Hamilton. Call a meeting for an hour from now. All the investigators who are in town. Be prepared for a little journey."

"Yes, Sir," Kennedy said. "Where to?"

"To start, Ward, then Hamilton."

Along with Odom and his assistant Jake Kennedy, the three A.G. investigators were Hoyt Fair, Cameron Fitzgerald, and Orion Olsen. "Mr. Fair, you've been leading the investigation into corruption in White Pine County. How's that coming?"

"We know there's corruption, Jeremiah, but can't bring anything to court. Stumbling block seems to come from a money source we can't locate. Every scam needs seed money and some of these mining scams are well funded." Fair was a bull of a man, two hundred pounds tucked into a five-eight frame, square head, no neck, and hands big enough to crush another man's head.

"Politicians are all involved in the mine schemes. Money is rolling in from the east. Those people in New York and Boston will believe anything they hear about gold mines in the west." Fair chuckled. "Kleindorfer comes up with a new mine every other month or so, I think."

Odom sat back in his chair and lit a cigar. "Leave on the evening express for Elko, Hoyt, and ride south to Hamilton. Anyone there know what you look like? Like you to be unknown for at least a while."

"Never been there, General. You know something, don't you?" Fair's smile would hurt any other face but fit him well.

"Mr. Fitzgerald and Mr. Olsen, I want you to

pack up for a long ride to Ward. No trains going that way, I'm afraid. Leave immediately and I'll be a day behind you."

Fitzgerald was hired out of the Pinkerton assemblage and Olsen came by way of the federal marshal service, as did Odom. "Here's what we have, boys," Odom said. He settled back in his big leather chair and outlined what Corcoran had sent in his long wire. "I'm sending Corcoran a wire when we break up here. He'll be lead investigator in Ward until I arrive. Hoyt, you're lead in Hamilton."

"Corcoran?" Olsen sat up straight at the mention of the man. "God help us. I've worked with him more than once. Love the guy and he gets the job done. He does tend to bend the rules some. How is it you know him?"

"Helped him a couple of times. Looking forward to this," Odom said.

"So, you're coming into the open field, are you?" Fair again smiled that awful smile.

"Need the fresh air, Hoyt. Offices are not where men should do their best work. Go pack Hoyt. Fitzgerald and Olsen, arrange for two mules, food for several days, and good footed horses. You'll be making fifty to sixty miles a day. This Poindexter/ Kleindorfer group is going out of business."

"How do I keep in contact, General?" Fair asked. "Telegraph isn't very safe, most of the time. I'm not supposed to be known, so what do I do?"

"Anything you need to know, I'll send in such a manner as not to be understood by the telegraph operator. Don't send anything to me. When we bring it together, it will be quick, just remember that."

CHAPTER TWENTY-EIGHT

"Wire for you, Corcoran," Skeets said. Corcoran and Mindy were having brandy after their supper at the Grand. "Got the bees buzzin', you do."

"I've got to get to work. Come by later," Mindy said, letting Corcoran and Skeets have their meeting. Corcoran held her chair and watched hurry off.

"We wouldn't be able to pull this off if Fingers was still the key operator." Corcoran chuckled. "I like this from Odom. He says 'raise your right hand. Good, now you're my deputy.' Man has a fine sense of humor. I've got to get down to the office."

Corcoran walked with Skeets out of the hotel and turned for the office. "Important for you to be on your toes, Skeets. Poindexter has one or more people here in Ward working for him and they are sure to try to get information from you. Play dumb but get me their names and what they were after. It'll take Odom three days of hard riding to get here."

Corcoran found Tomaso Bono and Dean Miller in the office. "Wish Geno and Marty were here. Well, gentlemen you two are now working for the attorney general as deputy investigators. For the time being, I'm lead investigator. General Odom will be here sometime in the next few days and, in the meantime, we need to find out who Poindexter's man is here in Ward. There may be more than one."

"Would Mary-Anne know? As you said, she was pretty close to that bank's operations." Dean Miller said. "He hired me as a combination bar man and saloon security but I never saw him with anyone other than employees at the hotel."

"Do you have any idea where Geno and Marty might be?" Corcoran asked. He poured some coffee and wondered if maybe he was wrong. That Poindexter acted alone, didn't have men helping in his schemes.

"Probably at the Silver Springs Saloon. Most of the mining crowd calls that home." Tomaso said. "Without the criminal Henry Storm element, it's just a rowdy saloon again."

"Keep your ears working," Corcoran said heading for the door and the walk to the Silver Springs.

As he passed the gun shop, he caught the reflection of movement in one of the windows. *That was quick. Been an AG investigator for less than an hour and I'm being followed. Let's see if we can figure out who this shadow is.*

Corcoran slipped between the gun shop building and Morris's General Merchandise and stood in the dark alley with his back to the gun shop. *Footsteps on the boardwalk, but oh so quiet. Come on buster, meet Corcoran, the worst part of your day.* Corcoran caught the movement before he heard a sound. The knife pinned his buffalo robe coat to one of the wooden planks of the gun shop building.

Then he heard running feet. Corcoran ripped the knife free and jumped out from between the buildings. *Not a soul on the street. Means our friend is either in the Grand or across Third in the Silver Springs.* He got under one of the few street lights to examine the knife. "This is one fine piece of work. Quality work, elk antler handle. Someone just threw it away?" He was muttering all the way to the Grand's long oak bar.

"Brandy, my man," he said. Corcoran looked up and down the bar, at the gambling tables, even at the few men enjoying a dance with a 'hostess'. He couldn't determine if any of them had just rushed in and wasn't about to ask the barman since the hotel was owned by Poindexter. Anybody could be a Poindexter man. As he, most of the men were dressed for the cold so he drank his brandy and headed for the Silver Springs Saloon.

"Marty, glad to find you here," Corcoran said. "Anyone come in fast in the last few minutes?"

"One feller came in, almost at a run. Didn't recognize him but when he saw me and Geno standing here, he lit out the back door. Geno followed him and hasn't come back yet."

"Maybe Poindexter's man. Threw this at me. Damn fine work on this knife."

"That's a real gem, Corcoran. Buford makes these knives and sells them for high prices. I think each one is just a little different. Buford is proud of his work and probably knows who he made it for. Here's Geno."

Oliveira walked up to the bar, still panting from his run in the cold. "So, Corcoran. Buford sold you one of these, eh? Wish I had one. Word is they rarely lose their edge." He nodded at the barman who set him up a cold beer and shoved a bottle of whiskey his way. "Man I was chasing is fast. He lost me inside of a block. Went into one of those building on Alpine, north of here. Too dark and he was too far in front of me to tell which one. Anybody know why I was chasing him?"

"Yup," Corcoran said and showed where the knife penetrated his fine buffalo-robe coat. "Never said a word. Snuck up behind me and threw the knife. Seems like we have woken up the bad men. You boys are now working for me and I'm the lead investigator for the AG. All right with that?"

Geno and Marty smiled and nodded while Corcoran poured some whiskey around. "Dean Miller and the barman at the Grand can't remember Poindexter having meetings or socializing with anyone in particular. Because of the knife, we have to believe he has at least one person looking out for him. Either of you think of anyone?"

Both men shook their heads. "Something else that's peculiar," Corcoran said. "Poindexter was working hard to get me named acting White Pine County Sheriff. At the time, I was flattered but turned him down cold. With what we know now, why would he want me as sheriff? My background is far from the criminal world."

Geno chuckled and took a quick drink. "That is the truth. It would be easier to track you if you were looking into his business. As it is now, he's operating blind."

"No, no, Geno. Somehow, he already knows we're on him, otherwise there's no answer for the knife. He's a conniving bastard, Geno. What if he did this? It would look really good to get me named acting sheriff and then have me knocked off. Then he could put one of his or Kleindorfer's men in the office?"

"Whoa," Marty Rosso said. "That's nasty, Corcoran, but it makes sense. Especially when we're looking at that knife sitting on the bar."

The barman came down to see if the three needed anything. "Mr. Poindexter ever come in here?" Corcoran asked. This same man was friend-ly on his first visit and acted like he'd never seen him before on his second. What kind of response would he get this time?

"He'd come in late in the afternoon, before the bank's closing, for a shot or two. Liked to play a few hands of five-card, too, but that was late at night."

"How late at night?" *With Mary-Anne waiting in his bed he would come in here for a game of stud pok-er? That man is more of a fool than I thought.*

"Late. Midnight or so, I guess. He and Lem Stewart would play for an hour, have a few drinks, and head out." The bar keep filled their glasses and moved on down the bar.

"Stewart?" Rosso's hand, lifting a drink, stopped

at the comment. "Lem Stewart is lead man in White's assay office. Never known the man to take a drink, more or less play stud poker."

"I wonder if some of White's assays have made their way into some of the bogus mine offerings Kleindorfer and associates are involved in." Corcoran had a crooked smile on his face. "Using a legitimate assay for a stock offering in a non-existent mine would sure look good," Corcoran said.

Geno and Marty quickly looked at each other. "Hal Antone," Geno said. "One of the best assayers at the mine wins the Ward Founders' Day races every year. Fastest man I've ever seen." Oliveira chuckled. "I like drinking with you, Corcoran. Do you solve a lot of mysteries this way?"

"It ain't solved, yet. I think the bunch of us need to pay a visit to Mr. White first thing in the morning. I'm sure we will also need a new office to meet. Skeets is sure to get a wire in the morning telling us we no longer work for White Pine County. Good night, gentlemen." Corcoran picked up the knife and walked out into the cold night air.

It was a short walk across third Street to the Grand Hotel but Corcoran walked west on Third to Alpine and turned north. The west side of the street was filled with rooming houses and Corcoran stayed on the east side as he slowly walked along in the dark. Many of the windows shone with candle or oil lamplight.

"What did I think, that the man would be standing in the window? Wouldn't know him if he was." Corcoran murmured as he walked. He cussed quietly, turned and walked back to the Grand Hotel. *Poindexter must be one of those making decisions in Kleindorfer's scams. Probably his idea to sell stock in mines that don't exist. How deep, then, would Lem Stewart be? Selling assay reports isn't necessarily a crime. Using them to sell stock in mines that don't exist is.*

"So where does Hal Antone come in?" He said it right out, walking across Main Street for the Grand. *Maybe Stewart is just making some money on the side, but Antone is in deep. Attempted murder of a law enforcement officer can get a man hung. Need some background on Mr. Antone. Hope White can help.*

CHAPTER TWENTY-NINE

"Good morning Buford," Corcoran called out. "Got us a cold one this morning."

"Coffee's hot, Corcoran. Come on in. Hope you're coming with something good to talk about. These past few days haven't held much good news." Buford Waring swung the big doors to the stables and blacksmith shop wide open. Corcoran got as close as he dared to the smitty's forge and took the tin cup that was offered.

"Maybe some good. Found something last night that people tell me you made." He pulled the knife from his heavy coat. "Recognize this?" He handed Buford the knife with the gleaming blade. "This is some kind of fine work, my friend."

"Sure," Buford said. "I make a few of these a year. Good money in good knives." He moved it around in the light taking careful look at the tang. "Made this for Hal Antone, well not really, made it for the winner of Great Ward Races during Founders' Day. Hal won it last year. How is it you have it? Didn't gamble it away did he?"

"You might say that, Mr. Waring. Yes, you might say he took a big gamble." He walked over to saddle Dude when Oliveira and Rosso came in. "Gonna be a cold ride out to the mine, I think, boys. How do the men get to work? Surely they don't ride horses out."

"No, White has a long wagon they ride in, out and back. There's also limited housing for the lead men at the mine site." Marty Rosso said. "Anything from Buford about the knife?"

"It's Antone's. Won it at the races just like Geno thought. Think about this, Marty. Poindexter is involved in selling stock in non-existent mines and buys assay reports from Lem Stewart to use as bait. County Commissioner Clive Kleindorfer is his business partner. Where does Mr. Antone fit in? People who run fast are rarely big and heavy. People who aren't big and heavy are rarely hired as body guards."

Rosso chuckled and pulled his saddle up tight. "A good knife man doesn't have to be big and heavy, Terrence. How long before the Carson City boys get here?"

"Three days at least. Maybe Mr. White can add some information to our little mystery. Let's ride. I've just get too many questions roaming around this old head of mine."

"Your man good enough for this kind of job, Poindexter? Corcoran needs to die but it has to look like a simple murder-robbery, not the killing of an investigator. Pockets ripped open and contents taken."

"Yes, yes, Clive. He's good and won't get caught. Who is it that has turned on us? How did the state's attorney general get wind of our operation? You said your man in Carson City is sure the state is sending investigators? How? This is a money making machine, Clive. One more year of this and all of us will be set for life. We need to kill whoever has turned on us."

"Our broker in New York would never give up the kind of money he's making off of us, our man in San Francisco is selling stock in our mines faster than the mines in Virginia City. No, Stephen, I don't think it's one of our people. Somebody in Ward is working against us, working with Corcoran, and now the attorney general is involved."

Poindexter stood up and paced about Kleindorfer's rather elegant office, rubbing his hands as if they were cold. "Lem Stewart is well paid for those phony assay reports, Clive, and except for the man I hired to kill Corcoran, no one in Ward has the slightest idea about our operation. No one," he repeated. Poindexter continued his pacing, stopped at Kleindorfer's desk and poured some brandy.

Except for one person, he thought. The alarm on his face was caught by Kleindorfer. "Oh, my God," Poindexter said. "Mary-Anne knows about some of it. Some of the loans, some of the payments. She's kept the bank books and the bank is involved to a degree."

"We need to get word to your man to kill that woman," Kleindorfer said. His anger flared like a kerosene torch when he said it.

"No, she would never tell anyone. Besides, she can't possibly have told. She was kidnapped, remember? She's probably already dead." Poindexter poured another brandy and drank it fast. "I've got to get back to Ward. I've got to put an end to this. If there's someone here in Hamilton talking too much, take care of it, Clive. If it's someone in Ward, I'll handle it."

"Investigators from the attorney general's office will be coming, Stephen. They are on the way. We have three thriving mines, according to our brokers, and the money is pouring in. This isn't the time to get stupid. We've made an excellent deal to move the county seat to Ely, which just happens to be the site of one of our credible mines. Bought that land cheap and tripled our money when we sold it to the county." He took a drink of brandy and scowled.

"Is that slimy telegraph operator still working with us?"

"He was working with Henry Storm as well, Clive and may be in jail. That damn robbery has changed everything we had going for us. Storm's gang has my wife, the bank is closed, and now the attorney general is involved. I'm riding out in an hour. I'll try to keep you informed from my end. Please do the same from yours."

He had a mule packed and was on the road in less than an hour. For a wagon, the trip would be two long days. For a man and mule, a day and a half, and Poindexter was going to push for making it in a day.

Is Mary-Anne safe? Did they catch the bandits and save her only to have her give all the bank's records to Corcoran? No. She wouldn't do that. The thought wouldn't go away and hammered at him well into the night. The idea that he rode off instead of mounting a rescue of the lady never entered the banker's mind. The fact that something like that might anger the woman didn't, either.

A late camp and early morning found him on the trail, riding south. *I should never have allowed her to work at the bank. So good with numbers, so good at keeping the files in order. Damn but I was stupid. If she got away from those outlaws and gave that information to Corcoran, they both have to die. Oh, Mary-Anne. So lovely. So charming in her own Irish way.*

Hamilton's mines were running out of ore fast, some mines had already closed, and the population was moving quickly to the new town called Ely, where vast fields of copper were said to just lay about. Hoyt Fair found a room at the Hamilton House and unpacked. It was more of a boarding house than hotel but there was a saloon next door. One thing Fair knew for an absolute fact was if you want to know what's going on in a small town, ask the barman.

"Just ride in, stranger? Lot of dust on that hat. What'll you have?"

Hoyt Fair chuckled and called for a cold beer. "Looks like half your town is closed up."

"The action's in Ely now. Copper is the king up that way. There are rumors of some exciting gold strikes, too."

"Gold, eh? Always have liked the sound of that

word. It has a melody of its own. I represent a stock exchange group looking into new properties. Who would I most likely get good information from on those gold interests in Ely?"

"Couldn't do better than talking to Clive Kleindorfer. I believe he's one of the locators. He's a county commissioner so, if he's in town, you'd probably find him at the courthouse or the Old Globe Saloon next door. Don't want to throw cold water on your thoughts but Kleindorfer can be, let's say, oily, slippery in his dealings."

"I appreciate the warning, my friend. Better give me a shot of your good whiskey before I go looking for the varmint." He was chuckling as he said it but his thoughts weren't. *Just as Odom said. Kleindorfer's gang is at the heart of all this. I wonder who sold the land to White Pine County to build the town of Ely?*

Hoyt Fair stood at the county clerk's counter, smiling at the man behind the polished oak. "The land was purchased from a partnership of Stephen Poindexter and Clive Kleindorfer. The county offices will be moving just as soon as the courthouse is finished. Anything else I can do for you?"

"Just one thing. Where would I find the sheriff? I have some wanted posters to distribute."

"None with my picture," the clerk joshed. "We

don't have a sheriff at the moment. The chief deputy, Holt, Jimmy Holt, is holding the office down until the commissioners call for an election. Sheriff Johnson died after being shot breaking up a gold shipment robbery."

"That's terrible," Hoyt said. "Thanks for your help. See you again," he said and headed out the door. *The Old Globe Saloon it is, and let's see how many lies Mr. Kleindorfer can tell over a shot or two of whiskey.*

"Morning Mr. White. Got something interesting to discuss. Can we help ruin your morning?" Corcoran, Rosso, and Oliveira made the ride from Ward in good time and caught the mine owner as he arrived at the office.

"Someone got ahead of you, Corcoran. My lead assayer didn't show up this morning. Didn't even bother to call off. Don't suppose you're an accomplished assayer, are you, Corcoran?"

"Afraid not, but that is the subject of our calling on you. Which one, Stewart or Antone?"

"I think we need to sit down in my office." He looked over to the man at the counter. "Bring us some coffee, will you Gypo. Lots of coffee."

The lawmen settled in leather chairs and the

mine owner slumped behind his desk. "How is it you know my assayers, Corcoran?" He opened a box of cigars and offered them around before taking one for himself. "Hal Antone, one of the best in the business but undependable to his roots. Didn't come in this morning and no one's seen him since yesterday afternoon."

"That might not be true, Mr. White," Corcoran said. "I think I caught a glimpse of him just before he tried to kill me." White's eyebrows shot straight up and Corcoran continued. "How about Stewart. Did he show up?"

"He has his place here at the mine. I provide housing for my department heads. Yes, he's in the shop. What's going on? What do you mean Antone tried to kill you?"

"Poindexter is at the heart of your question. He and Clive Kleindorfer. I believe that Poindexter and the commissioner are peddling stock in mines that don't exist and I believe that Lem Stewart is selling or providing fake assays showing those mines as being incredibly rich. I believe he's using your assays but on different paperwork."

"Bastard better not be selling my assays," White said.

"They probably are yours but they look like they

are the fake mines' reports. Near as I can figure out, Mr. White, your men, Stewart and Antone both work for Poindexter. We'd like to talk with Mr. Stewart and it would be fine if you were in on the meeting."

"Fine," White said. "You talk to him and then I'll shoot him."

"Best if you don't." Corcoran chuckled. "We might need him." Corcoran knocked the ash off his cigar as Gypo brought coffee and cups in. "Where does Antone live?"

"Betsy's Beds," Gypo said. "He's right across the hall from me. Heard him making noise last night but didn't try to find out what he was doing."

"Probably packing," Marty Rosso said. "Bastard is gone, I'll bet."

"Go get Stewart, Gypo. Don't say anything about Antone or about these gentlemen being here. Or that I'm going to kill him."

Gypo was almost running from the office. "I'm going to make a fast ride to Betsy's Beds," Marty said. "Might get lucky." Corcoran nodded his approval and took a drink of coffee.

"You stay here with me, Geno. Go ahead Marty. Too early for Bono to be in, so you'll be on your own." Corcoran said.

White stormed around the office, his cigar looking more like a freight train engine, waiting for Lem Stewart to arrive. "Might be best if I ask the questions, Mr. White." Corcoran said. "This is a criminal investigation. People have died, people have been attacked."

"Humph," White responded but his pacing slowed some. "My best assayer attacked you, Corcoran? My lead assayer is selling copies of my assays? And I have to be quiet?"

"Only for a short time. You'll have your turn," Corcoran chuckled.

"Ain't funny," White said. He took two more steps and started laughing in that big deep voice of his. "Damn you, Corcoran," and the laughter continued until Lem Stewart stuck his head in the office.

"You want something, Mr. White?" He said.

CHAPTER THIRTY

"Hello Mrs. Rooney. Mr. Antone sleep in this morning?"

"No, Mr. Rosso. I think you'll find him at the stables. He's leaving town, I believe. Said something about new digs at Ely. Do you know what that means?"

"Afraid I do," Marty said. "Thank you." He hurried out of Betsy Rooney's boarding house for the short ride to Buford Waring's stables. "Come on, critter, we might get lucky and catch that fool before he runs." He put the spurs to an already tired horse.

"Antone still in there?" Marty Rosso yelled it out. Buford was standing in the street outside his stables and blacksmith works.

"Just missed him, Marty," Buford said. "Headed north on Main Street. Just has his horse, no pack animal, not even a heavy saddle pack. He'll be riding fast, Marty."

"Thanks." Marty spun his horse and put him in a hard run. "Come on, boy, we got a murdering fool to catch." Rosso didn't see anyone as he raced along Main Street in Ward. The street became the main highway north and the well-used road made for easy riding. At a hard gallop, Rosso felt the miles melt away. Problem was, he couldn't see the man he was chasing.

He doesn't have that much lead time on me. I should at least see some dust. Coming up to that narrow pass. Does he know he's being chased? Is he waiting to shoot me dead? Rosso's mind was racing as fast as his horse was and he pulled up to a trot as he neared where the gold shipment had been attacked.

"Those have to be his prints I'm following. Nobody else out here this early." He eased the horse to a walk and looked around quickly. "Where would he be? Those rocks to my left? To my right?" He wasn't mumbling, he was talking right out loud. The bullet ripped through the left sleeve of his heavy coat and Rosso jumped from the saddle, scrambled behind an outcrop, and had his sidearm in hand.

"Left it was," he almost chuckled. He felt his arm, discovered the hot lead blew a goodly hole in his coat but not his arm and put his attention on the man looking to kill him. "You, Mr. Antone, are a dead man."

The outcrop fell off to his right and dropped into a gully. *If I can roll into that gully I can move north fast. He's on the west side of the pass and I will be almost across the road from him.* Not another shot had been fired since the one and Rosso took a deep breath, coiled, and leaped and rolled twice, dropping into the gully. No shot was fired.

Did he take the one shot and run? No, that's not his style. On the other hand, it is his style. Throw the knife and run. Shoot good old Marty and run. Marty ran hard along the bottom of the gully, keeping his head down as much as he could, and dove in behind a rock near the entrance to the narrow pass.

He eased up enough to see Hal Antone at his horse, about to mount up. "Stop!" Rosso yelled it out, jumping to his feet. "Stop. You're under arrest, Antone. Let go of your horse, ease your weapon out and drop it on the ground. Do it or die."

Rosso's pistol was aimed at Antone's head as he slowly walked across the roadway. Antone's back was to the deputy and Rosso saw the outlaw let go of the reins, spin, and try to pull his gun. Rosso fired twice, knocking the small man to the ground. Antone was still trying to get his gun free of leather when the third round pierced his heart.

"Didn't have to die, Hal. Damn fool." Rosso gathered the animals and had the body across the saddle and was tying it in place when Tomaso Bono rode up.

"Waring came to the jail to tell me you were chasing Antone. Thought I might help. Sorry I'm late. You hurt?"

"Not a scratch, Bono, not a scratch. Thanks for coming." He stepped into the saddle and they rode back toward Ward. "Sure didn't want to kill him," Marty said. "Can't get no answers from a dead man. Hope Corcoran is doing better."

"It'll be late in the day when I get back to town," Poindexter mumbled. He trailed a pack mule and was making good time on the road to Ward. His mind had been busy on the ride. Should he go home? What if Mary-Anne had been saved and was there? Should he go to the bank? Maybe he should go the Grand and take a room. So many questions. Was Mary-Anne still missing? Dead? Saved? Each answer had so many sides.

I'll do as I would returning from any trip. Go straight home. I'll find out the answers to all those

questions in their own time. It was early evening
when he rode through town, and the banker nodded to the few who were out and about. He turned
east on Third Street and rode to his home which
sat on a rise less than half a mile from the center
of town. He was surprised to see light from many
first-floor windows.

He sat still and thought about it for several minutes. *Those lights mean Mary-Anne is home. Is she
angry that I wasn't trying to help rescue her? Is she
responsible for the attorney general coming? What has
she told Corcoran?*

He couldn't slow his mind down, couldn't stop
worrying that he would ride up and find Corcoran
standing on the porch with a rifle in his hands.
"Damn." He spat it out. "My beautiful wife must
die," he whimpered. "I can't kill Mary-Anne. I can't
kill my beautiful wife." He wanted to scream. Instead, he whimpered.

He turned back toward town at a slow walk.
"Have to find Antone. He'd kill his own mother if
the price was right." He rode to Buford Waring's stables and found the man getting ready to close shop
for the evening. "Will you take care of these until
morning, Buford?"

He just rode into town and wants me to take care

of his animals before even asking about his wife? That isn't right. He rode out instead of mounting a rescue, and now? Buford Waring glared at the dust-covered man and nodded. "Not until after supper but I'll take care of 'em, Poindexter. Just tie 'em off and I'll get to them. By the way, your wife is fine."

"Thank you," is all Poindexter said. Buford took the leadropes and tied the animals off. Poindexter simply walked back toward Main Street as if in a dream. Knowing she was alive settled it in his mind. Mary-Anne must die and so must Corcoran. So much money at stake, so much more to make. *Where would Antone be this time of the evening? I'll have a drink at the Silver Springs Saloon and let the word out that I need to see the man.*

A long ride, worries piling on worries, and it was a haggard Stephen Poindexter who walked through the heavy doors of the saloon. Several miners, just off the day shift at White's mine were caught by surprise when the banker walked right up to the bar and asked about Antone.

"Best bet to find him right now is at the under-takers, Mr. Poindexter." The barman was enjoying his laugh and those standing close were, too. "He died from lead poisoning earlier today, I'm afraid."

Poindexter did a poor job of not showing his

surprise, gripped the bar with both hands and asked for a brandy. It was obvious the news about Antone had an effect on the man as those close by watched his shaking hands try to get the brandy glass to his mouth. This was quite the show for many, the town's leading man, married to the beautiful and flirtatious Mary-Anne, now reduced to a nervous wreck at the news of a death.

My God. Antone dead? Mary-Anne alive? Investigators from the state on their way? I've got to get back to Hamilton. No, I need money and a place to hide. Money and then ride out for Hamilton.

He nodded to the barman, turned and walked out of the saloon, hunched, looking quickly from side to side as a wounded animal might. He made his way across Main Street to the bank and used his keys at the employees' entrance. There was no one in the building and no lamps were lit either. Poindexter didn't need the lamps and moved to his office where he kept a small safe with several thousand dollars.

He found the top of his desk covered with the bank's private records, books of deals and loans dating back to the opening. "My God. They know everything. She told them everything." He filled a large canvas bank bag with the cash from the safe and poured lamp oil over everything in the office.

Papers, books, upholstered furniture, even throw rugs were drenched in the volatile liquid.

"They won't have these records," he snickered, lit a match, and tossed it across the floor. He raced for the unlocked employee door and made for Waring's stables at as fast a walk as he dared. He said it over and over, "Don't catch anyone's attention." Poindexter was in the saddle and riding north out of town before the fire bells started their clamor. "Have to be back in Hamilton and get rid of those records, too." Questions of who shot Antone, how Mary-Anne was safely home, who spread all the bank's records across his desk would not be answered tonight. He didn't make camp until he found himself so tired he almost fell from the saddle. It was a long cold night filled with unanswered questions.

Corcoran, Bono, Rosso, Oliveira, and Skeets were enjoying a roasted elk dinner at the Grand, talking about the day's activities. "So, we've been fired from White Pine County," Corcoran chuckled, "and told to leave the county jail, eh Skeets? Well, under the powers entrusted in me as lead investigator for the attorney general, I claim this table as our new office. Supper, my fellow investigators, is on the state, tonight. I hope."

"I find it interesting," Tomaso Bono said, "That we're eating supper at Poindexter's hotel while holding state warrants for his arrest. Other than what Marty has told me about his fight with Antone, we haven't heard about the rest of the day. Did White shoot Lem Stewart?"

"I got ahead of myself, there, Tomaso." Corcoran smiled, took a drink of wine, and continued. "The AG sent a wire to Hamilton telling them that he has taken possession of the Ward jail, so we will have a place to work and somewhere to tuck our prisoners in."

Corcoran got serious quickly. "As to today, Tomaso? Mr. Stewart wasn't as stupid as Antone. He simply sat down and confessed to everything. Poindexter paid him well if he would doctor White's assays onto letterheads from their phony mines. The only crime is selling after stealing the private property of mine owner White. He's in jail now and willing to testify."

He started to continue when Buford Waring interrupted. "Poindexter's back, Corcoran. Looks like hell. He dropped his horse and mule off at the stables and headed this way. Apparently you haven't seen him."

"No, we haven't. Mary-Anne's alone at the house. I better get up there. He's sure to blame her for the investigation. Sorry to ruin supper, gentlemen, but you boys need to scatter and find the banker-man."

They were interrupted when Mary-Anne Poindexter burst into the dining room. "I think I saw him," Mary-Anne said. She was breathing hard. "I'm sure I saw Stephen in our driveway. I got here just as fast as I could." She was trying to talk fast, breathe hard, and not collapse all at the same time.

Did you run all the way here?" Buford Waring stood shaking his head.

Corcoran helped her into a chair. "He must have ridden to the house, got frightened because of the lights, and left his horse with you, Buford. Means the man is in town. But where?"

"The bank," Mary-Anne all but whispered.

The group was halfway across the dining room when the fire alarm bells started their clamorous ringing. "Evidence," Corcoran said. "He's burning all the evidence."

"No he's not," Skeets said. "I did what you asked, Corcoran. The largest part of it is tucked away in the telegraph office safe. I got all the really important papers that you and Mary-Anne pointed out but didn't get everything that was there. If he lit that fire, he isn't burning the important stuff."

"Mr. Bono, take care of Mrs. Poindexter. Skeets,

a wire to Carson City that we are in pursuit of Poindexter. Rosso and Oliveira, you're with me. Are the big doors unlocked, Buford? We gotta get our horses."

"Not open, but never locked, Corcoran. Poindexter's horse and mule were tied off at the front rack just outside the doors."

It was a three-block foot race to the stables and they found Poindexter's mule still tied off but no horse. "The only smart thing that man has done in a long time," Corcoran said. "He has to be riding hard for Hamilton, boys. Let's get it on. Grab that mule, Geno. It's got food and stay on our trail."

"He wouldn't dare try to cross the Egan Range at night, Corcoran." Marty Rosso yelled. "He'll be heading north, toward the new Ely digs. Good road all the way."

Corcoran and Marty rode off on the road north. They were at a trot with Geno Oliveira walking along behind. Keen ears could hear Geno's cussing. "Sure, Corcoran," he said over and over, "I'll bring the mule."

"If it was a straight line we'd be there in a long day, Corcoran, but we've got to skirt the Egan range and then challenge that mountain Hamilton sits on. That town's gotta be eight thousand feet up."

"Yup," Corcoran said. "Right now we have to ride until it gets so dark we'd hurt ourselves. Poindexter will have to quit, too, but let's get as close to him as we can."

"Couple of creeks north of the narrow pass we should be able to make," Rosso said. "Got more than one elk there."

CHAPTER THIRTY-ONE

"If I can still read a map, I'll be in Ward some-time in the morning. Need to break away from that desk more often than I've been doing. I'm one tired old man right now." Jeremiah Odom, not quite forty years old and serving his first term as Nevada's Attorney General was in better condition than most men his age, despite his own words. He spent years as a Deputy U.S. Marshal before adventuring into politics.

He had left Carson City accompanied by two of his deputies, Cameron Fitzgerald and Orion Olsen, but changed his plans and sent them on to Hamilton. He had Corcoran and his deputies in Ward but Hoyt Fair was alone in Hamilton and would need help.

"How many mountain ranges have we crossed or worked our way around, old boy?" Neither the horse nor the mule bothered to answer. "Gonna be dark soon and that bunch of cottonwoods will be home tonight." He got the animals undressed, watered, and settled for the night in a good bed of grass.

Good grass for the boys and cold water for us. Love these cottonwood trees. They don't cut nice but you can break them up for a good fire. Gonna be a billion stars up there tonight if this wind doesn't cover them in clouds.

Rocks for a fire pit, wood busted up for a fire, bedroll laid out near-by, and Odom turned his attention to supper. "Fried sidemeat and coffee soaked biscuits again, I guess. Hope there's a fine restaurant in Ward. Just a few years ago and I lived on sidemeat and biscuits. Gettin' mighty soft old man."

Night, and the cold that comes with it, came on fast along the western edge of the large plain and Odom threw more wood on the fire. He lay back in his bedroll, could see clouds move in front of the blanket of stars, and shivered in the wind that was kicking up. "Oh, good. Be riding in a storm tomorrow."

It was an hour later he was awakened by his horse snorting. Years of marshal service duty kicked in and Odom was out of the blankets, Winchester in one hand, Colt in the other, eyes wide open. *Make a move, whoever you are and let me see you.* Was there someone there or was it just the horse coughing? Maybe a coyote sneaking around?

Movement to his right and he ducked down low, took two quick steps behind a cottonwood trunk, and tried to make out what the movement was. A figure. A man? It moved, one slow step at a time, toward the fire. Odom let the man get close enough for the coals to shed light on his features.

I'll be damned. That's Stephen Poindexter or I'm not Jeremiah Odom. He watched the figure pick up a broken limb and smash it down on the bedroll. "Get him, did you?" Odom stepped out from the shadows, revolver in hand.

Poindexter heaved the chunk of wood at the man with the gun, turned and raced for his horse. Odom had to duck out of the way of the limb that weighed at least ten pounds but was able to get one shot off before the banker was lost in the darkness. Odom listened in frustration as the sound of horse's hooves drifted off.

Odom's shot nicked Poindexter's side, just enough to cause some bleeding and a bit of pain, and the banker spurred the horse hard, racing through trees, brush, and rocks. It was a full ten minutes of hard riding before the banker pulled up to a walk. He was back on the highway but heading back south.

Who was that? Can't go north, can't go south. Need to get to Hamilton. Can't cross the Egan Range this time of year. Poindexter was in a trap. "I needed that man's food. I've been riding since sunrise, haven't eaten," he whimpered. He knew then that unless he started thinking straight, he would be a dead man soon.

He knew Corcoran would be coming from Ward, knew attorney general investigators would be coming from the north, and knew he couldn't cross the mountains, already covered in feet of snow. "They're not just gonna ride up and take me. They're gonna regret trying."

Stephen Poindexter wasn't a strong man to begin with, had spent most of his life at a desk, had others split wood for him, and was whimpering as he directed the horse off the main road. *I'll circle out close to the mountains and move north. Find someplace to hide until morning. Got to get back to Hamilton.*

A trapped and desperate man is the most dangerous animal a lawman has to face and Poindexter was already planning how to ambush the forces gathering to end his career as an outlaw. He didn't give a thought to hiding his tracks, simply lit out cross country with the hope of finding a stand of rocks, a deep ravine, even a stand of cottonwood trees where he would have good vision.

Fatigue and hunger made the decision on where to hide and the first stand of rocks Poindexter came to became his home for the night. He didn't bother with a fire, was too tired to break up one of the hard biscuits he had in his saddlebags, just curled up in his bedroll and slept fitfully, dreams of men chasing and shooting him ruining his sleep. Missing from those dreams was the warmth and love of Mary-Anne, replaced by anger and hatred knowing she gave records of his criminal behavior to Corcoran. What else did she give him?

The fact she had been kidnapped and held by killers wasn't considered, nor was the truth that he didn't form a rescue posse or join in her search. Poindexter's thoughts were on protecting the vast sums he held and the life he enjoyed. He awakened often during the night and went back to sleep with the thought of riding hard for Hamilton at first light. *How to get there? Can't cross the Egan's, have to ride around them. Need food.*

Odom was up at first light and had fried sidemeat with biscuits getting soft in hot coffee. It was a cold, blustery morning, heavy black clouds cascading down from the top of the Egan Range. "First things first, General," he mumbled. "Break out the weather gear, then find those tracks from last night. What was Poindexter doing out here? He tried to kill me without knowing who I was. He's running but which way?" The one-way conversation continued but did not reach any conclusions other than finding the tracks the man left.

Odom circled out from the cottonwoods looking to cut the tracks and found them with no problem. *That horse is at a full-out run. Turning toward the main road.* He followed until Poindexter turned off the road toward the mountains to the west. *Surely, he isn't that stupid. Nobody's crossing that range.* Peaks, already covered in snow, were well over eight thousand feet above sea level and what few passes existed, were snarled in several feet of early snow.

Fighting his way over that range would kill him. He must know that. If he's heading for Hamilton, he'll have to go north and cut around the north end of the range. Why is he off in the brush like this?

Ambush. The thought came almost at the instant the bullet killed his horse. Odom fell to the ground, clear of the thrashing horse, and scrambled into some brush. He was able to grab his rifle on the way down. *Has to be in those trees up there. Well, Mr. Poindexter, you're mine.* The trees were a good fifty yards away and rolling ground gave Odom his chance. Odom's mule was still tied snugly to the saddle horn of the dead horse.

Odom rolled into a slight depression, didn't draw a shot, and moved to his right along the depression until he came to a small outcrop of rock, tucked in behind it and tried to pick Poindexter out. It was a few minutes before he caught some movement and watched Poindexter work to saddle his horse.

He thinks I'm dead. Not yet, bucko. Odom moved quickly from the rocks to another outcrop and ducked down into a small ravine to be able to move even closer. He raised his rifle and was about to take his shot when Poindexter's horse threw a fit, trying to rear, kicking out, knocking the saddle out of Poindexter's hands.

Odom took a quick sight and pulled the trigger just as Poindexter was knocked to the ground by the riled horse. The bullet tore some cloth from the banker's coat and nothing else. "Damn that horse," Odom said. Poindexter crawled behind one of the large trees, still holding his rifle.

"That was a rifle shot, Marty," Corcoran said. "In front of us, but several miles out, I'm afraid. If it was Poindexter, we're closer than I would have thought.

Let's pick it up." They put their horses in a good lope and moved fast through the early morning cold. "Think he was shooting his breakfast?"

Marty had to chuckle. "Blew a sage hen apart with his Winchester? No, Corcoran, it's my guess that someone's in trouble."

Corcoran spotted the two sets of tracks coming south and moving west off the main road. "Somebody's chasing somebody. Leave a sign for Geno to follow us. Glad he caught up with us last night. Easier to catch an outlaw on a full stomach."

Corcoran led them into the brush, following the tracks. "We have two sets of prints here, Marty. Overlapping, so someone is following the first set. Looks like they're heading toward that stand of cottonwoods."

"That's a fortress designed for ambush," Rosso said. "Don't want to ride right in."

They slowed to a walk as they neared the copse fully anticipating an ambush. "That's a dead horse over there." Marty pointed toward Odom's horse and saw the mule standing near-by. "Saddle scabbard's empty, too." He was about to say something else when a rifle shot to his right front went off.

"What are you looking at, Corcoran?" Marty was off his horse, flat on the ground, rifle in hand.

"The shot was aimed into those trees. A horse was dancing around in there, just before the shot. I thought I saw somebody falling down. Let's move slow as cold honey toward those trees, Marty. Either the man who owns the dead horse or the man who owns the spooked horse is an outlaw and we don't know which."

"Love the way you talk, Corcoran," Rosso said. They crawled from sagebrush to piñon pine to rock pile and were within twenty-five yards of the still riled horse when Corcoran spotted Poindexter behind a cottonwood, aiming his rifle at something off to Corcoran's right. Corcoran brought the sights down on Poindexter and squeezed the trigger.

"You got him good," Marty said. "What was he about to shoot at?"

"Don't know. Tried to just wound him, Marty. Get up there and make sure he's out of the game." Corcoran rolled onto his side and yelled out. "Hello out there. This is Corcoran, Terrence Corcoran, deputy sheriff."

"About time you got here," Odom yelled back. "Are you always late?"

The two men walked toward each other and turned to join Marty Rosso at Poindexter's camp. "Glad to see you, Jeremiah. Who were you chasing?

I'm chasing Stephen Poindexter."

"Yup, one and the same. Tried to kill me last night. Hope you didn't kill him. We need his testimony and, if I know bankers, he'll do what he can to save his skin. I need to get a wire off to Hoyt Fair in Hamilton to make as many arrests as he wants."

Rosso stood over the wounded Poindexter, nudging him with his boot. "You ain't hurt that bad, Mr. Poindexter. Sit up now." Corcoran's shot hit the tree and the exploding bark knocked the banker down, spilling a limited amount of blood. Shards of bark penetrated open skin.

"I'm going to die, you fool. Don't kick me, help me."

"I'm gonna give you just as much help as you gave your wife," Rosso snarled. He kicked him hard, in the ribs. "Get up or I'll kill you like a dirty dog."

Poindexter's horse was still trying to come loose from being tied, kicking and raring. Odom reached out during one slightly calm moment and ripped the saddle blanket from its back. The horse calmed immediately. "Sharp twig stuck to the blanket will do that every time," he said. He chuckled, throwing it at Poindexter.

"That's why we always check our tack before using it, right, Mr. Corcoran?"

"Surely is, General Odom. Yes, sir, it is indeed. Would you like to do the honors?"

"Ah, what a pleasure." Odom got Poindexter on his feet so he could look him in the eye. "You, sir, are under arrest." Odom looked at Corcoran and got a nod. He looked at Marty Rosso who didn't know what to do, so shrugged, and Odom hit Poindexter between the eyes with a fist that started at his shoulder. "You should be ashamed," he said as the man fell into the dirt.

"We need to get back to Ward pronto," Corcoran said. "We're short one animal. I guess Mr. Poindexter will have to ride with the packs on a mule. Let's get put together and head back."

They were less than half an hour on the trail when they met up with Geno Oliveira. "I don't much care for being on another of your posses, Corcoran."

Corcoran laughed and took that moment to question Poindexter. "Were you hoping to destroy all the evidence against you when you torched your bank, Poindexter?" Corcoran asked. "I'm under the impression that your lovely wife— oh, by the way, she's safe and sound, thanks for asking. I do believe she has the bulk of the evidence in a large file at the sheriff's office. She's really good at filing and keeping records. Did you know that?"

Corcoran didn't let up for the entire ride back to Ward. Rosso took Odom to the telegraph office, Geno took all the animals and packs to Buford's stables, and Corcoran walked Poindexter into his jail cell with the new barred window and strong casing in place. "Welcome home, Mr. Poindexter. We'll begin our question sessions shortly. Enjoy your ride, did you?"

CHAPTER THIRTY-TWO

"This is good news, Skeets. Thank you." Jeremiah Odom had the old cane back chair leaned back against the wall, the wire in one hand and a cup of coffee in the other. "Corcoran, bring our banker friend out here, will you? He'll be most interested in this."

Poindexter's face was wrapped in various bandages covering the many scrapes and cuts from the flying tree bark and walked with pain from the kick in the ribs. "I demand to see a lawyer," he snapped at Odom. "I won't say another word to you until I see a lawyer."

"Good." Odom said. "Tired of listening to your whining anyway. Got a wire here you might be interested in, though." He waved it around. "Says County Commissioner Kleindorfer has resigned his office while awaiting trial for fraud. Claims he was just a messenger for the real fraudster, a banker in Ward, Nevada named Stephen Poindexter."

"Liar!" Poindexter shouted. "The mining claims were his idea to begin with." Poindexter realized what just happened and shut his eyes and his mouth. *Stupid, stupid, stupid. Can't let them lead me like that. Be smart.* Poindexter slowly opened his eyes and caught the smile on Odom's face.

"Thank you," the attorney general said. "We'll be sending you to Hamilton tomorrow and you and Kleindorfer can work out your stories. Mrs. Poindexter will be in shortly. She asked to see you so, when we're through here, we'll put you back in your cell. That's where she wants to see you."

Corcoran poured a cup of coffee, pulled a flask from the desk and added some flavor to it, and sat down. "According to these papers that were filed, you, Kleindorfer, and a few others claim ownership to several very active and producing mines in the county. Offering shares at slightly below current market prices seemed to be a lucrative way to do business. Anyone ever ask to actually see one of these operations, Mr. Poindexter?" Corcoran held some papers in his hand and smiled, looking up at the banker.

Poindexter didn't say a word. "What do you think, Mr. Rosso?"

"I'm familiar with the area where that one claims is a heavily producing gold and silver operation, Corcoran. A creek runs out of the Egan's and helps water more than one ranch. There is no mine within twenty miles, though."

"What are your plans, General Odom?" Corcoran couldn't hide the smile. It had been a whirlwind after getting back to town and the two hadn't discussed any kind of future plan. "Winter's coming on fast, I don't have any wood cut, larder's empty, and some of the young ladies in Eureka are going to waste away from lack of attention."

Odom blew coffee across the office floor, laughing and coughing. "I'll have to get with the U.S. Attorney. You'll be heading home soon enough, my friend. You've done a fine job here, Corcoran, blowing this enterprise wide open."

"Thank you, Jeremiah." Corcoran walked around the stove, sipping his coffee. "Came here to end the Henry Storm gang and stepped into this mire. If anyone can be held up high for praise, it should be Mary-Anne Poindexter. Without those detailed notes and record keeping, most of their operation wouldn't be known."

Odom nodded but pointed his finger at Corcoran. "No, my friend, she did us all a great favor, but it was you broke things open. Nevada mining law has been shattered by this operation and I'm sure that federal law has been soiled as well. These men will probably die in prison; it's just a question of whether it will be state prison or federal."

"I see Mary-Anne walking down the street," Corcoran said. "Better get this criminal back behind bars where he's safe." He hustled Poindexter into the rear of the building and into his cell. "I'll bring her right in, Poindexter," he said. The banker didn't say a word, just shuffled into his cell and slumped onto the cot.

Mary-Anne Poindexter wore an emerald green gown that highlighted her reddish hair, making her green eyes sparkle. "Good morning, Mr. Corcoran," she said. "And you other fine gentlemen." She stepped up to Tomaso Bono and took his hand, gazed for just a second into his eyes, and continued. "I just came from the bank and Buford Waring says he's sure he can save the building. There was considerable interior damage but little structural. My attorney, Jessup Clavin, says that I will be the legal owner when Stephan is found guilty and sent to prison."

"There will be a number of legal hoops to jump through, I'm afraid," Odom said. "Poindexter used the bank committing his fraudulent activities and the bank might be responsible for some losses by investors. There are federal laws and state laws involved."

"Yes, Mr. Clavin pointed a lot of that out." Mary-Anne's smile was devastating and filled the room with light. "I think it's time to visit with my husband, now."

"Yes," Odom said. "Mr. Bono, would you escort Mrs. Poindexter into the cell area, please? You'll want to stay with her."

Tomaso Bono led her into the cells and to Poindexter's. "Visitor for you, Poindexter."

She squeezed Bono's hand tight and held on. "Hello Stephen. Aren't you even going to ask if I'm well? You seem out of sorts. Is something bothering you?"

She felt Bono trying to hold in a chuckle and squeezed his hand harder. "Don't you think he looks a little pale, Mr. Bono?"

Bono laughed, patted her hand with his other hand. "Yes, I do believe he's been under some stress lately. I'm glad you're feeling well, though. We were all so worried." It was as if the two of them were alone, that Stephen Poindexter wasn't standing on the other side of the wall of iron bars. "So terrible for you," he said.

She turned to him and smiled. "I knew you would be among the posse, Tomaso. You've always been so kind. How's your leg? All healed?"

"Almost, yes."

"Did you come to see me or not?" Poindexter asked.

"Yes, Stephan, if you must know, I've come to see you behind bars. Tomaso is wearing a badge, so he might say it was his duty to come save me, but you, Mr. Poindexter are my husband. It was your duty to come save me. You are a vile man, sir. You have shamed yourself before what was our community, shamed our marriage, and are going to pay for it. I will own your precious bank, sir, and I will do it as Mary-Anne O'Toole, the waif from Cork. Good bye, Stephan and may your soul burn in hell."

She turned to Bono. "Would you escort me to lunch at the Grand, Mr Bono? We have a lot to talk about. Mr. Clavin is already getting my divorce papers in order but nothing will be done until that rat standing over there behind those steel bars is found guilty."

"I've waited a long time for this, Mary-Anne. Yes, lunch will be a good start for us." They walked back through the office and out the door, not even nodding to anyone.

"Seems as though that went well," Odom joshed. "You can pack up and be gone when your paperwork is cleared, Corcoran. You'll be called for your testimony, of course, and I might have need of a conference or two before trial." Odom found himself pacing around the office and stopped in front of the desk.

"Put something in the cup, Corcoran." He plunked the coffee cup down. "Lots of it if you please. I'm going to be sore and bruised for a long time, I think. When that horse fell, all I could see was a bed of rocks coming at me. Every one of them put a bruise on me somewhere."

"We'd probably find a full bottle behind the bar at the Silver Springs Saloon, old friend. That is, if you can walk that far. Need some help?"

"Off with your head, Corcoran. Get away from me," Odom laughed, shoving the big man back. "Sore, not out of the game."

They were at the Silver Springs just long enough to order a bottle of brandy when Skeets came rushing in. "Bono with you? Have a wire here from the county. He's the new White Pine County Sheriff. That is, if he accepts the offer."

"Dollar to a dime he don't," Corcoran said. "That

man has other plans. You'll find him at the Grand, Skeets. He's just weeks away from being the new owner, I think."

"Might take a little more time than that," Odom said, "but Mrs. Poindexter is sure to be named as overseer of all their properties until after the trial and she is sure to name Mr. Bono as property manager."

Mindy Shepherd slipped up to Corcoran and grabbed his hand. "I'm going to miss you, big fella. Not one jerk has tried to manhandle this girl since you started coming in here."

"You're a lovely lady, Mindy. No man has the right to hurt a woman. I'm not leaving until morning. Maybe we could dance a time or two this evening?"

"I think we could do a little more than that, sir," she said. The dancing eyes coupled with a devastating smile said so, also.

Odom guffawed, said something about charming ladies pining away in Eureka and caught a fist aimed for his chin. "Now, now, old friend. Have a good night. I won't be up early to see you off." He walked out of the saloon, laughing.

"There you are," Skeets said. He almost ran to the table where Tomaso and Mary-Anne were having lunch. "Got a wire here, Sheriff." He thrust the paper out.

"Ain't no sheriff sitting at this table, Skeets," Tomaso said. He read the missive and handed it to Mary-Anne. "Don't think that's gonna happen. Seems as though I already have a fine position, right here."

"Be nice in your refusal," she said. "Why nor suggest Dean Miller for the job. He'd have to live in that new town, Ely, but that shouldn't bother him any."

"Marty Rosso and Geno Oliveira could be resident deputies," Bono said. "Well, we've cleared that up nicely. I'll write it up for you, Skeets. Send it with care."

"Let's walk over to the bank and see just how much damage was done," Mary-Anne said. "I'd like to get it re-opened just as soon as possible. The people in Ward need their bank and it is theirs, you know. I just hope they'll accept me as their banker. You have to help with that, Tomaso."

I'm not wrong in what I'm doing. Mary-Anne had been worrying about the town's reaction to her claiming Tomaso Bono and being the banker. *I've felt strongly about that crazy Italian since the day he came to town, stronger than I ever felt for Stephen. He was cold even on our wedding night. All he saw was my beauty, never felt my soul, never knew real warmth. Everything related to the dollar. I can feel Mr. Bono's soul singing every time he holds me.*

"The whole town's talking about your escape from that killer and how you helped get the mine scams known."

"They're also talking about us, Tomaso. Will they turn on us?"

"Not by what I see at the front door," he said. They stood in the bank's burned-out lobby looking at a small crowd at the open doors.

"Gonna get her open, Mrs.?" One person asked.

"Just as soon as I can, Mr. Quiggly. Just as soon as I can." She looked at Tomaso, smiled, and nodded her head gently. "We'll be open soon. Very soon."

CHAPTER THIRTY-THREE

"Well, Buford, it's been an interesting few weeks. Your grain and good grass has put some pounds on old Dude here, thanks for letting me have my mule back, and for the fine packing job. I'll be off for home."

Mindy Shepherd had walked him to the stables from the Grand Hotel. She looked at Buford Waring and smiled. "I tried my best to talk him into staying, Mr. Waring. He ain't having it."

Waring smiled and shook his head. "Gonna miss you, Corcoran. Won't be missing all the excitements you brought with you but you sure did clean up this old mining camp. You found outlaws where nobody ever looked before. You'll be welcome at my stables any time. Have a safe journey."

The two big men shook hands and Mindy threw

her arms around Corcoran and wouldn't let go. "You do like we talked, pretty lady. Mary-Anne is going to need all the help she can get and it's a perfect opportunity for you to get out of the saloon. You're a seamstress, you read and write, and you know your numbers. You are what she needs right this minute." He pulled her loose, gave her a quick kiss and stepped into the saddle.

It was a long ride back to Eureka but Corcoran had a head full of good thoughts to keep him smiling. The mine fraud scheme was smashed and the men behind it were behind bars. Two unhappy women were going to be happy and several men found new careers behind a tin badge. "All right, Dude, it's just you and me again. Let's go home." He didn't need to touch the spurs Dude stepped right out in a strong trot that would eat miles before sunset. "Yahoo," Corcoran cried out and the horse responded with a full-out gallop.

"I can almost taste an elk steak, feel my own bed, drink out of my own cup. Ed Connors will be as glad to see me as I will be to see him." He had a busy mind for three days and rode into Eureka in the middle of a strong winter storm, with high winds, heavy snow, and icy cold.

"We're home, Dude."

A LOOK AT EZEKIEL'S JOURNEY
BY JOHNNY GUNN

His life is shattered, his wife, his children dead. A lesser man might just give it up; but Ezekiel Hawthorne isn't a quitter. While thousands head to the California gold fields in wagons, Ezekiel loads his mule and embarks on an amazing venture across the continent alone, bound for the good soils and abundant waters of Oregon. Savages, tornadoes, and a lack of knowledge don't slow the man down a bit. It's a beautiful half-Shoshone woman who has the biggest impact on Ezekiel's new life.

AVAILABLE NOW ON AMAZON

ABOUT THE AUTHOR

Reno, Nevada novelist, Johnny Gunn, is retired from a long career in journalism. He has worked in print, broadcast, and Internet, including a stint as publisher and editor of the Virginia City Legend. These days, Gunn spends most of his time writing novel length fiction, concentrating on the western genre. Or, you can find him down by the Truckee River with a fly rod in hand.

https://wolfpackpublishing.com/johnny-gunn/

Made in the USA
Las Vegas, NV
09 January 2022

40625208R00204